What the critics are saying...

"With sizzling sexual content, an action-packed plot and dynamic characters, this is a pleasurable fantasy that's not to be missed." ~ *Tanya Kacik, Romantic Times Booklover's Magazine.*

"*Ms. Summers* is a magnificent author who writes with much flair and draws a story with her words. This is a page-turner that will keep the reader enthralled and captivated from start to finish. WOW!! Is all this reviewer can say." ~ *Dawn for Love Romances*

"*Jordan Summers* has written a wonderful story that touches the heart and soul of a romance reader. From the first page to the last, you'll be drawn into a world full of passion, love, betrayal, and jealously. I recommend this book with total belief that you will not only be swept away by it, you'll be begging for more. I read this story twice just so I could feel the passion and love all over again." ~*Diane T. for the Romance Studio.*

"In this second novel of *Jordan Summers's* exciting *Atlantean's Quest* series, I was again struck by the talented way in which *Ms. Summers* combines suspense, humor, eroticism and romance. The passion is incredibly hot, as Ares as Jac simply cannot stay away from each other, but there was nothing gratuitous or excessive. *Exodus* is sexy and smart and just a fun, fun read." ~ *Astrid Kinn for Romance Reviews Today*

"*Ms. Summers* has created a well-written tale sure to delight readers and keep them glued to the screen from beginning to end." ~ *Nicole La Folle for Timeless Tales*

EXODUS
ATLANTEAN'S QUEST

JORDAN SUMMERS

ELLORA'S CAVE
ROMANTICA PUBLISHING

An Ellora's Cave Romantica Publication

www.ellorascave.com

Atlantean's Quest: Exodus

ISBN #1419953532
ALL RIGHTS RESERVED.
Atlantean's Quest: Exodus Copyright© 2003 Jordan Summers
Edited by: Briana St. James
Cover art by: Syneca

Electronic book Publication: June, 2003
Trade paperback Publication: December, 2005

Excerpt from *Atlantean's Quest: Redemption*
Copyright © Jordan Summers, 2003

Warning:

The following material contains graphic sexual content meant for mature readers. *Atlantean's Quest: Exodus* has been rated E-*rotic* by a minimum of three independent reviewers.

Ellora's Cave Publishing offers three levels of Romantica™ reading entertainment: S (S-ensuous), E (E-rotic), and X (X-treme).

S-*ensuous* love scenes are explicit and leave nothing to the imagination.

E-*rotic* love scenes are explicit, leave nothing to the imagination, and are high in volume per the overall word count. In addition, some E-rated titles might contain fantasy material that some readers find objectionable, such as bondage, submission, same sex encounters, forced seductions, etc. E-rated titles are the most graphic titles we carry; it is common, for instance, for an author to use words such as "fucking", "cock", "pussy", etc., within their work of literature.

X-*treme* titles differ from E-rated titles only in plot premise and storyline execution. Unlike E-rated titles, stories designated with the letter X tend to contain controversial subject matter not for the faint of heart.

Also by Jordan Summers:

Atlantean's Quest: Atlantean Heat (Quickie)
Atlantean's Quest 1: The Arrival
Atlantean's Quest 3: Redemption
Gothic Passions
Tears of Amun

Exodus

Atlantean's Quest

To Si:

I've waited a lifetime for you and would do so again in a heartbeat.

Acknowledgment:

Many thanks to mom and dad for their investment in my future, you're the best. Aunt Viney, I love you, but I still don't think you're 'old' enough to read my books. Thank you D. Miller for your unfailing encouragement when I needed it most.

Chapter One

After a hellish week away litigating, Jac entered her sleek apartment and tossed her mail on the entryway table. The Toronto business trip had been sheer torture, but she'd argued effectively enough to save her company millions. Those Toronto boys never knew what hit them, she was the best when it came to fighting and winning. And she always got what she wanted in the end. Just the same, sometimes being a top corporate attorney was a bitch. Jac dropped her suitcase and walked to the phone. The light on the answering machine blinked like the warning light on a bomb set to explode.

Damn, thirty un-played messages. I haven't been gone that long.

She pressed the button as she retrieved the mail. She was flipping through the envelopes when Rachel's voice came on the line.

"Hey, Jac," was all Jac registered of her friend's message. Jac smiled for the first time that day as she realized how much she missed Rachel. Hopefully her friend would let her know what date she'd be returning.

Then Rachel screamed and the line went dead.

The envelopes slipped from her fingers and Jac stood by the phone, frozen, unable to breathe. Her mind went blank as the room filled with the harsh sound of a dial tone. Did she just hear her best friend die?

The answering machine clicked on to the next message, as Jac sank to her knees the room swimming around her. She was dimly aware of Brigit's frantic voice informing her that Professor Donald Rumsinger had returned from the expedition — without

Rachel. Jac's jaw clenched, her stomach somersaulted, and something deep inside her spoke:

I knew it. I knew that low-down son-of-a-bitch was up to something.

Muscles at the base of her skull took that moment to tighten into the mother of all headaches. Jac shook as the overwhelming panic subsided, slowly being replaced by a fury the likes of which a volcano couldn't contain. She spent the next hour phoning the museum and then the local authorities down in the god-forsaken jungle, but to no avail. Apparently, one missing museum employee wasn't worth their time.

Jac knew exactly what she had to do.

* * * * *

Two days, twelve inoculations, and fifteen hours on four different charter flights later, Jac's plane circled the jungle runway. She had managed to get an expedition arranged by phone, but god only knew what she would find when she stepped off this tin can masquerading as an aircraft.

She was hot, sweaty, and pissed that the Professor had somehow managed to slip in and out of New York before she could get her hands on him. Rumsinger had a three- day head start on her. If he hurt Rachel, she'd make whatever country they were in expedite his happy ass back to New York so fast that his head would spin. Then Jac would personally castrate the bastard.

Hell, she'd cut his balls off here, if she could find him.

The plane landed with a thud, jarring her to the present, then skidded to a halt. There was nothing to see out of the tiny window other than miles and miles of trees. The pilot popped through the door and made his way down the aisle. His eyes wandered over Jac's nipples and then to her mouth, before meeting her gaze. He reached out at the last second to retrieve her bag.

"I've got it, thanks." Jac's gaze pinned him.

The man gave a curt nod and backed away.

Jac stood, grabbing her pack in one fluid motion, and then lugged it to the door. She jumped over the step that had been placed on the ground. The air was thick enough to slice with a blade. Jac patted the knife strapped to her calf. Mosquitoes swarmed around her in a tiny cloud. Her Tomb Raider outfit supplied little protection against the carnivores. She reached in her pack and grabbed her can of OFF.

"Take that, you greedy little bastards." She pressed down on the top and sprayed the killer mist over her arms and legs. "You're not getting my blood."

After the fumes cleared, Jac shaded her eyes and looked around. The guides she'd hired were a few hundred yards away and the tents were already set up. Jac lifted the backpack into place and began the short hike across the clearing. All the green made her miss her house plants back home. She sent a silent prayer to the heavens that Brigit remembered to water them. Considering how absentminded her friend was Jac didn't hold out much hope she'd return to anything living. Brigit had left the same day Jac had to attend Conlunar, a huge sci-fi convention in upstate New York.

She'd walked several yards when the hair at her nape stood on end. Jac swung around, dropping her pack, the OFF can held out in front of her like a weapon.

"Just try something, whoever you are. Go ahead, make my day," Jac growled in her best Dirty Harry voice, daring anyone or anything to come forward out of the jungle to face her. She felt antsy, anxious, as if the nerves in her body were firing all at once.

At this point, she could use a good fight to relieve some of the tension. She hadn't worked out all these years to get her Linda-Hamilton-in-Terminator-2 arms for nothing.

A breeze swayed the tops of the trees. The green canopy tilted from side to side, like the waves on an ocean, the slight swooshing noise the only sound she heard. Jac scanned the shadowed line.

Nothing.

She stood there, one hand planted on her narrow hip, straining to hear that one snap or crunch that would give her enemy's position away. "I didn't think so." Jac shrugged off the unease.

It was time to proceed on her mission to find Rachel, kick Donald Rumsinger's ass, and get them both back to New York before the weekend was up.

* * * * *

From the protection of the trees, Ares watched the tall blonde. Her hair was cropped close to her neck and those long legs were bare except for a scrap of material at the top, covering her woman's center. He'd never seen a woman in short pants. She was lithe and muscular, like a sleek jungle cat, and her breasts were compact and firm, as was his preference. Her composure was cool and aloof, daring anyone or anything to step into her territory.

Ares' lips twitched. He was willing to accept that dare and more.

Queen Rachel's memories had been true in every respect. She'd be angry with him if she had known he'd eavesdropped on them so easily. Ares hadn't been able to help it. The woman known as Jac had intrigued him from the beginning, and now she was here, not more than a hundred yards from him. Tempting, calling, provoking.

Ariel the seer had been right. His mate had arrived.

It was time to hunt.

* * * * *

Jac reached the tents without further incident. She dropped her pack and stretched her arms over her head. Her muscles were sore from being cramped in little seats for hours. She'd managed to dismiss the weird foreboding, but couldn't shake the sensation of eyes boring into her back and over her limbs. Her body was still hyper sensitive, which did nothing for her peace of mind.

A handsome young guide, looking no more than twenty-five, approached her. "My name is Xavier." He stuck out his hand. "You must be Ms. Ward."

She nodded, grasping his palm to shake it.

Jac's gaze ran the distance from his well-developed calves, up his long legs, to his wide muscular chest. Xavier's eyes were a soft cocoa and his skin the finest sienna. He had rich black hair shorn to a short made-for-the-weather crop. His lips were full and sensuous as they split into a dazzling white smile.

Jac's clit twitched—she hadn't gone native before. Her eyes flicked to the front of his shorts, taking in the slight bulge behind the seam. Jac gave him a telling smile. Maybe she wouldn't have to rough it in the backwoods after all.

Xavier raised an eyebrow, but said nothing as his eyes zeroed in on her tits. He guided Jac to her tent, pointing out the trail leading to a nearby stream.

"You have plenty of time to explore if you like before the meal will be served. I recommend the stream." His eyes traveled up and down Jac's legs, licking his lips, Xavier added. "Don't go too far—it will be dark within an hour."

"Thanks." Jac saluted, then turned and stepped into her tent. The space was small, but adequate. Lucky for her, she wasn't expecting the Ritz. Jac began to unpack. Pulling out the items she'd need for tonight, she glanced over her shoulder in time to see Xavier staring at her ass.

Jac smiled, then purposely dropped a pair of thong underwear onto the tent floor. Like an exotic dancer, she slowly bent at the waist, picked up the scrap of material, then slid it up the length of her long, long legs. She heard what sounded like choking, but by the time she turned Xavier was gone. Jac laughed. If she got bored later, she knew where to find him.

Two semi-automatic pistols were holstered and sitting on her cot. She picked them up and strapped them on against her thighs. Now she really did look like a blonde Lara Croft. She rifled through her pack and pulled out a baseball cap, shoving it on her head. Jac threw the opening of the tent back and inhaled.

The jungle had an odor of the untamed, even the flowery scent on the air smelled wild and savage. Her eyes took in the workers, each assigned to a specific task. They busied themselves with few glances coming her way. She couldn't see Xavier, but figured he hadn't gone far.

Jac trotted around the back of her tent to the trail Xavier had pointed out earlier. Despite the hour, the sun shone bright and unyielding, until she started down the path. Vines and roots grew in a mass tangle on the jungle floor, snaking their way up the various trees, clinging like parasites in search of elusive sunlight. Jac pushed giant ferns out of her way, taking care not to damage the plants. She'd always had a green thumb and prided herself on her ability to appreciate all things wild.

The sound of rushing water caught her attention and she picked up her pace. Just the thought of getting in a few laps before dinner had her salivating. The tri-athlete in her came out and she started to run, jumping over low vegetation, ducking around branches. In a few moments time she arrived at the edge of the stream, barely winded. A waterfall flowed twenty yards away churning up frothy bubbles before smoothing into a steady current. The spray was surprisingly cool and way too inviting to pass up. If she spotted an anaconda, she'd use it for target practice.

Jac drew one of her guns out of its holster, slipped the clip to check the ammo, before slamming it back inside, and then removed the safety. She wasn't about to be caught unprepared. She set the pistol down and started to undress. The air was palpable and hotter than Hades. How could anyone live down here?

Jac forced away a lump in her throat as she thought of poor Rachel. Somewhere in this god-forsaken place her friend was hurt, or even worse. She brushed her fingers through her hair, knocking her hat to the ground, and blew out a frustrated breath. Jac wouldn't allow herself to even go down that road.

The last of her clothes dropped to the jungle floor. She walked barefooted across a thick blanket of grass, before reaching the waters edge. Jac bent over, stretching her tired calves. It felt wonderful to be naked. A light spray from the falls coated her skin, making it glisten in the sunshine. She stood up to her full height of five foot eleven, her nipples puckering in the warm air.

She stuck her toe in the water and was about to step in when a tingle of warning lanced through her a second before a set of large hands came from behind, covering her eyes. Jac sucked in a surprised breath. She hadn't heard a thing, not a single step. A low growl near her ear told her the visitor was most definitely male, not that she'd had any doubt. Jac knew with a few select strikes she could drop this intruder, but she decided to see what kind of game he played first.

"Who's there?" she called out, her body quivering with excitement.

Another low rumble sounded by her other ear.

"Xavier is that you?"

He gave her a quick lick at the base of her neck.

Jac purred. "You want to play?"

He stuck his nose against the side of her head and inhaled, taking in her scent.

Jac shivered, her nipples tightened to marbles and her pussy grew wet.

He pulled one hand away. Jac heard him fumble with something at his side, then a soft piece of cloth replaced his hands, covering her eyes. Jac smiled. She didn't think native men would be so adventurous. Her heart kicked up a notch and she licked her lips in anticipation. Strong arms surrounded her, easing her to the ground, until she was flat on her back against the cool blades of grass. Feather soft, the grass caressed her bare skin, elevating her need with its tiny green fingers.

Jac loved games, especially sex games. They were always about trust and control. Although this was a first for her, Jac never allowed her lovers to have the upper hand, to be in control, especially when it came to sex. But for some reason, given the circumstances, she didn't mind being subservient this time, so she decided to go for it.

Ares crouched beside Jac, his eyes caressing her naked form. He couldn't believe she'd allow him to touch her like this without a struggle. His adrenaline surged, he'd been looking forward to the fight and eventual taming. Disappointed, but undeterred, Ares tried not to think about the fact that she thought he was someone called Xavier. Fiery rage burned inside, as Ares fought the urge to find the man and kill him.

His gaze flicked over the thin line of curls on her shaven mound. Ares couldn't wait to follow that strip with his tongue, to see what hidden paradise he could find. Soon there would be no one else for Jac, and only he would be able to satisfy the need within her taut body. But first she had to get used to his touch. Ares palmed Jac's small globes, squeezing the satiny flesh between his fingers. Her skin heated beneath his touch, flushing a pale shade of pink.

Ares wondered if her body turned a darker shade of that color when she came.

He licked his finger and swirled it around each nipple. Jac's breath caught and her lips parted, forming a silent 'O'. Scraping her smooth skin lightly with his fingernails, Ares ran his hands from her shoulders to her toes, leaving gooseflesh in his wake. Switching positions, Ares straddled her and began licking and nibbling her nipples as if she were covered in sweet cream. Her rosy buds protruded, springing beneath his seeking mouth, stabbing skyward, with each pass of his tongue.

She smelled of the ocean, her skin salty and almost translucent like breaking waves. Ares's breathing stuttered as he inched down toward the tawny strip of hair between her firm thighs, his hard body pressed, marking hers with his scent. He could already smell her rich, musky fragrance. Her woman's juices eased from her opening, calling for his cock to claim what was rightfully his. He gritted his teeth and closed his eyes, trying to fight the overwhelming urges coursing through his veins as he positioned himself on the ground between Jac's legs.

Ares spread her legs wide, then dipped his head, sticking out his six and a half inch tongue. Jac moaned as he followed the thin strip of hair to her hidden pearl, flicking his tongue along hidden nerve endings.

The second he stroked the tiny nub, the taste of her exploded in his mouth, sending Ares into a primitive, feral, and all around dangerous state. She was his. He swiped at her slit. Her honeyed essence ran over his tongue, into his body, through his mind. All his. No longer able to control his need, Ares stiffened his tongue, plunging inside her receptive core. He sent an energy burst out as he neared her womb.

Jac felt his huge, throbbing cock as he slid down her body, branding, teasing, torturing. She wanted to feel that shaft plunging inside her slit, pummeling her into mindless surrender. Just the thought of having him buried inside her moist walls was almost enough to send her over the edge. Her clit pulsed and Jac dug her nails into the thick grass. If they did end up having sex, she'd retrieve the emergency condom in her shorts pocket. Like traveler's checks, she never left home without it.

He continued his downward path, tempting her with kisses along the way, finally reaching the point of her building need. He pressed his lips to her clit a second before his tongue plunged inside of her, Jac screamed and her head thrashed from side to side, as one orgasm after another rippled through her body as though she was at the epicenter of an earthquake. Her legs shook and she couldn't seem to catch her breath. She was on fire. The native between her thighs didn't hesitate or stop, he kept on consuming her, until Jac thought she'd burst from the physical overload.

Never in all her years of experience had she ever run across a man as voracious as Xavier. He devoured her as if she were the only woman on the planet. Jac surrendered to the pleasure, her body balancing on the precipice of madness.

Ares continue to feed, his hunger insatiable, drunk on her desire. He couldn't seem to get his fill. Without looking he sensed the change in time, soon it would be dark. He had to let her up to ensure that she safely reached camp. Tomorrow when they entered the jungle, he would claim his woman and take care of the red-haired bastard threatening his people.

Reluctantly he rose from between her thighs, his chin dripping with her releases. He swiped his face with the back of his hand and then wiped her essence onto his loincloth. Her body lay twitching on the ground, racked with shudders, mewling noises coming from her throat. A rosy flush tinted her fair skin. Ares smiled, it was as he suspected, Jac did blush crimson when she came. Her pussy lips puffed up, pink and swollen from his overzealous ministrations.

Ares licked his lips. It was only the beginning.

He leaned in, taking in her ripe mouth, so red, full and luscious. Ares dipped down and captured her pout, running his tongue along her bottom lip. She moaned and he plunged in, ravishing, nipping and biting. He knew she could taste her own essence on his lips. Sparks flew, his skin heated. She was everything he had expected, wanted — needed.

And she was his…all his.

Ares tore himself away, then bounded into the thick brush without looking back. He feared that if he did, he'd discover the whole thing had been an illusion. His heart slammed in his chest and his cock ached beyond the point of pain. His breathing sounded choppy as he took to a liana and climbed to the treetops, his muscles straining with the effort. The vegetation grew so dense that he could not see Jac from this distance, but he could hear her. She started to stir. He sent out an energy burst, warding away nearby predators.

Jac rose from the ground, pulling the material from her eyes. She no longer had to worry about tension, because her body had the consistency of a bowl of wet noodles. She crawled to the water and slid in. The cool liquid surrounded her, leaving her buoyant and free. She didn't even have the strength to do a single lap. Instead she floated reliving the glorious sensations her body refused to forget.

Several minutes passed before Jac finally dragged herself from the water. The sun had set behind the treetops, time to get back to camp. She stood on wobbly legs and dressed. In the many years she'd been sexually active, Jac had never experienced being totally sated, until now. It exhilarated and frightened her all at once. She snatched up the blindfold from the ground, turning the thin material over and over in her hands. She'd never seen anything like it. The scarf seemed to change colors with the touch of her fingertips.

I'll have to ask Xavier where he got it, when I see him again. Jac licked her lips at the thought. Perhaps they'd have a go at round two in her tent.

Jac decided she owed Xavier a raise. A big one. Hell if he could do it again, maybe she'd try to find him a permanent position as house boy in her Manhattan two bedroom condo. Or perhaps he could become her pet. Jac imagined him with a collar and leash. She smiled, playing fetch would take on a whole new meaning. Xavier's hard cock had been impressive, even through his clothes as he slid down her body. If he was half as big as he seemed, she'd be in heaven.

Jac swallowed hard and squeezed her legs together to deter the familiar ache building inside. She was a red-blooded all American girl with a healthy sex drive and enjoyed flaunting the fact. It wasn't like she was a nymph or anything, but foreplay like this didn't come along every day, and Jac wasn't about to miss an opportunity.

She shoved the scarf into her pocket and scrambled back to camp. A fire had been built in the center of the encampment, a pig roasted on a spit over the flame. The smell of the meat made

Jac's mouth water. With her hair slicked back and the baseball cap shoved in her pocket, Jac dropped by her tent and slipped the holster off before joining the men.

Conversation quieted when she neared. Her gaze sought out and found Xavier. He sat with a couple of the older guides on a log opposite the tents. He grinned and raised a plate, but made no move to join her. Jac shrugged it off. It was better to play it cool in front of the men. She didn't need them finding out about their liaison on her first day in camp.

A table stood off to the side, holding vegetables and empty plates. Jac snagged herself a plate and strode to the fire. Another native sat with his knife speared into the coals. As she neared he picked it up and sliced off a hunk of the pig and placed it on her plate. Jac thanked him and walked back to the table to gather a few veggies.

Xavier strolled over a moment later for second helpings. Their eyes met, but there didn't seem to be any fire behind the gaze. Jac's brows furrowed. Wow, talk about hot and cold. There was no way a man could go from having so much enthusiasm while he ate her out, to nothing. He filled his plate and started to return to his seat, when Jac reached out and placed a hand on his arm, stopping him.

"Yes, Ms. Ward. Can I help you?"

Jac laughed, she couldn't help it. He sounded so formal, so professional, so different. He stood there with a queer expression upon his face, as if he thought he should laugh with her, but wasn't quite sure what was so funny.

Jac stifled her reaction, then leaned in so no one, but him could hear what she was about to say. "I enjoyed my time at the stream."

Xavier smiled. His head cocked slightly to the side. "I'm glad you did."

"Do you want to go for a repeat performance, later?" Jac's pussy flooded, thinking about it.

His eyes narrowed into a frown. "Performance?"

"You know." She nudged his elbow. "Don't play shy, no one can hear us."

"I don't know what you're talking about." A look of utter confusion painted his features.

Jac's heart did a little flip in her chest. She knew Xavier toyed with her, but for the life of her, she didn't know why. She put her plate on the table and planted her hands on her hips. He was cute, but he wasn't that cute. It was time to cut the crap. Jac remembered the scarf. She pulled it out of her pocket and waved it in the air.

"Does this jog your memory?" Jac held the material closer for his inspection. "Xavier, we're both consenting adults. There is nothing to be embarrassed about. If you don't want to do it again, just say so."

His face flushed as Xavier looked from Jac to the scarf and back again in bewilderment. She could see the color change even in the low light. The men's conversations had stopped. All eyes were upon them. And Jac didn't give two shits.

"Ms. Ward, I'm sorry. I think there has been some kind of misunderstanding."

Jac felt heat rise in her cheeks. She couldn't believe after what they'd shared he could stand there straight faced and pretend it didn't happen. Nothing pissed her off more than a liar. Her temper flared.

"The water, the blindfold, you ate me out, remember?" her voice rose with each word.

Xavier's face lost all color and his eyes practically bugged out of his head. "Ms. Ward." He swallowed convulsively, glancing around at the men nearby. "I haven't been anywhere near the stream today."

"Stop lying!"

"I swear to you," his hand flew to his heart. "If you don't believe me, ask my men." He pointed at the gaping faces around them. "They can vouch for me." Xavier stepped away, shaking his head. "Gringa loca."

Jac's head began to swim. She looked at all the faces around the fire, not an inkling of familiarity flashed in their eyes. Stumbling to a nearby log, Jac sat down, her body racked with shivers. Jac stared out at the blackened jungle, trance-like.

If Xavier hadn't been the one devouring her by the stream, then who had?

Chapter Two

Jac awoke the next morning to the sounds of men shouting. She turned over and peeked out the flaps on the tent door. Most of the camp had been torn down and packed up. All that remained was her tent. She groaned. It'd taken her forever to fall asleep after the fiasco around the campfire, then she'd slept like crap.

Not one to dwell on the negative, Jac swung her long legs over the side of the cot and got dressed. Jac folded her belongings in the pack, along with the scarf from the stream. She didn't know why she hung onto the silly thing. She should throw it away, but couldn't seem to bring herself to part with it.

Since when have I been into sexual souvenirs? Jac pulled the scarf back out with every intention of leaving it behind. Glaring at the offensive item, her fist clenched the jade colored material. With a groan, she wrapped it around her neck and then re-checked her equipment.

Armed and ready to go, ten minutes later Jac strode across the encampment to where Xavier stood. His eyes warily watched her approach. Jac saw the exact moment he noticed the scarf, because he cringed. She unflinchingly met his gaze and launched straight into the business of the day.

"Are you sure we'll be able to catch up with the professor in two days or less?" she asked, not giving him a chance to allow his discomfort to fester.

Surprise played on his features, but he readily accepted her lead. "I'm sure we can reach him, if we head down river."

"How long will it take to reach the water?"

Xavier shrugged. "About six hours. We'll be toting the inflatable canoes."

Jac looked at her watch, it was five-thirty. If all went well they'd be floating down the river by one at the latest. She wanted to reach Rumsinger before he slithered back under a rock.

Xavier stood in front of her as if wanting to say more.

She inclined her head. "Yes?"

"I'm sorry about last night," he stammered. His chocolate colored eyes held genuine regret, as he shoved his hands in his pockets. "If you like we can —"

"I don't think so." Jac interrupted, then shrugged. "The moment's past."

She wasn't about to get into a conversation about last night with Xavier. She didn't dwell on what might have been, only what was. If he wasn't down by the water, then he wasn't down by the water. None of the other men she'd seen in camp fit the physical impression she'd been left with. So that meant that they were not alone. She stared at the jungle, ignoring the chills racing down her spine.

Jac glanced at her holster, giving herself a quick once over. Knife, check. Pistols, check. Her hand patted the side of her neck. Scarf, check. She turned on her heel before Xavier could say anything more and headed to the table containing breakfast and coffee. Jac ate while the men dismantled her tent. She grabbed extra jerky, slipping it into a baggie for later. She bypassed the caffeinated coffee for water, as much as she was sweating from this humidity, she'd have to drink a couple of gallons to maintain her potassium levels or succumb to exhaustion.

Within twenty minutes everything was lifted on the guides' backs and ready to go. Jac walked to where her pack sat on the ground and shoved the jerky and a couple of extra water bottles inside, before slinging it over her shoulders. She'd taken one step when her nipples beaded beneath her white t-shirt. Jac's gaze shot up, she scanned the area to see who watched her. Xavier directed men into the jungle, his back turned to her. The men worked diligently, caught up in their tasks. No one seemed to notice Jac. Heat spread from her breasts, spiraling to her mound and over her clit.

Jac's breath caught in her throat, her gaze zeroed in on the tree line. It felt as if she was being physically caressed, her nipples stroked. Her panties grew damp as her pussy moistened. Her clit ached and began to vibrate as if an invisible finger plucked it. Need flowed through her body, like flowing lava. Jac squeezed her legs together, stifling a moan, her heart slamming in her chest.

This isn't possible. I'm imagining this.

But even as the thought tumbled from her head, she felt the familiar pleasure-pain begin to build. Breathing ragged, Jac clutched the pack as if the canvas bag could protect her from the unseen hands. Her knees wobbled, threatening to give out. The pressure increased, until Jac thought she couldn't take a minute more. As if sensing her impending release, the heated touch dissipated. Her body quaked.

Jac exhaled, her hands shaking, as relief mixed with a healthy dose of frustration, flooded her system. Whatever it was had stopped.

Suddenly as if reading her thoughts, a giant imaginary tongue licked her slit from end to end. Jac convulsed as the orgasm shattered her, knocking her legs out from under her and driving her to her knees.

She knelt on the ground, resting on all fours, desperately trying to catch her breath. Jac felt a brush of weight against her back, as if she were about to be savagely mounted. She knew no one was behind her, yet her muscles locked and she shuddered in anticipation. Her gaze bulleted to the jungle, Jac wasn't sure what in the hell was going on, but she'd damn sure find out...as soon as she could function again.

Moments later, Jac pulled herself up and brushed off her legs. She glared at the trees as if the look alone would send a message. She scooped her pack from the ground and got in line with the men, who were now staring at her as if she were truly insane. None of the bastards had even bothered checking on her to make sure she was okay.

It's comforting to know that I'm on my own...as always.

Monkeys scattered and screeched as she stepped into the rainforest. The air thickened in the shaded undergrowth. Red, green, and white parrots squawked and flapped their wings. Any other time she'd find their commotion irritating, but after what occurred in camp, Jac barely noticed. She focused on the trail in front of her, eyes peeled for any flash of movement.

She'd sent one of the guides ahead to search for signs of Rachel. He'd bring back information if he noticed anything out of the ordinary. Perspiration from the intense humidity dampened her shirt. Despite the heat, Jac rubbed her arms, in an attempt to ward away a chill. Something wasn't right, but she couldn't put her finger on what. She didn't believe in ghosts—at least she hadn't up until this moment—but she couldn't think of any other explanation for what had occurred.

I'm not imagining this.

Jac slid her hand to the pistol and removed the safety. The next time the phantom visited, she'd be ready.

They marched through the rest of the morning, reaching the river at two o'clock, an hour behind schedule. Fortunately for Jac, the jungle had remained relatively quiet with no more unusual happenings. Upon reaching the water, the men inflated the canoes and settled the equipment inside, tying it securely. The current was swift, churning up sediment from the bottom, making visibility close to nil. Before pushing off from shore, Xavier ordered another guide to run ahead through the jungle to search for signs of Rumsinger's party.

Jac was relegated to sharing a boat with Xavier. They paddled in silence for the first hour, the only sounds coming from the ripples the oars made when they sliced through the water and the occasional flap of wings overhead.

From the river, the jungle seemed different, somehow less threatening, as if viewing it from a distance kept the danger at bay. Jac relaxed for the first time since arriving and leaned back. She imagined having the flow of the water washing over her, cascading through her tired muscles and taking the tension from her body. Staring trance-like at the water, Jac watched as a pair of dark eyes surfaced about ten feet away. The black caiman watched them with the lazy appreciation of a predator sizing up a meal. Jac bolted upright and rowed hard. There couldn't be enough distance between her and that leftover dinosaur.

They'd been on the river for a few hours, when the guide on land shouted that a track had been discovered. Jac's heart raced, as thoughts of Rachel ran through her head. She wondered if the professor had fed her. Had she been tortured? Would they find her body tied to one of the trees?

No, no, no…in her mind Rachel was happy, healthy, and doing fine. She simply waited for Jac to find, rescue, and return her to her rightful place—New York.

The sun had set by the time the guide returned with news of Rumsinger's safari. He had pitched camp about five miles away as the crow flies. Jac's party couldn't reach him before nightfall, so they'd have to camp here for the evening.

Jac didn't like the idea of camping in the heart of the jungle, especially when the hair on the back of her neck had been standing on end for the past ten minutes, as if aware of a predator stalking the area. Her fight or flight response had kicked in and she couldn't seem to shake the feeling of impending doom.

Jaclyn Monroe Ward, knock this shit off.

She wasn't prone to normal female outbursts. Jac prided herself on the fact that she could, at any given moment, behave exactly like a man. She'd had to, to survive in the corporate world of law, but this was different—it felt different. For the first time in her life, Jac knew she was up against something formidable and she had no way of predicting the outcome. And that fact alone freaked her out…and excited her.

The tents were set up within an hour and a fire had been built after clearing away some of the vegetation. Jac thought to protest to the crew about disturbing the plants, but since there hadn't been an alternative she kept her mouth shut. After a dinner of fruits and dried meats, Jac headed straight to her tent, zipping the door closed behind her, desperate to escape the feeling of prying eyes upon her back. If she didn't think he already considered her a freak, Jac would've invited Xavier to stay with her. Not for the sex, but for the company.

She hated to admit it, but she was scared. The faceless stranger at the creek had brought out emotions in Jac that she'd managed to keep tamped down for years, hidden even from her own mind. Primitive thoughts of being possessed completely by a dominating male, letting go of her hard won control, relinquishing her power, and allowing herself to feel, protected, cherished — loved. She'd fantasized about the stranger's mouth, his spicy animalistic scent, and that incredible body ever since. Even though she hadn't caught a glimpse of him, it was as if Jac held his invisible brand somewhere on her skin.

Jac removed the scarf from her neck. The unusual material had managed to keep her neck cool all day, despite the sudden spike in the afternoon temperature. Clouds were building on the horizon and it had looked as if they were in for one heck of a storm. In her tent, the air practically crackled with electricity. Jac rubbed away the sudden gooseflesh rising on her arms, determined to get some sleep tonight, come hell or high water.

* * * * *

Several hours later, Jac tossed the sleeping bag off her legs and tried to get comfortable. It had been raining off and on for most of the night. She readjusted the mosquito netting, throwing her arm over her eyes, and fell back to sleep. The invisible touch she'd felt this morning haunted her thoughts all the way into her dreams.

The image was fuzzy at first, then she recognized Xavier. He stood between her thighs, getting ready to lower his head to her aching pussy. Jac shifted, spreading her legs in anticipation. Suddenly his image was wretched aside, by one much more powerful. She blinked, trying to focus once more.

Tall and muscled, a dark stranger stood on a precipice, looking over his shoulder, his jade gaze intense, fierce, holding wicked promises of things to come. His expression was solemn, save for a sinful glint in his eyes. Black hair, the color of night, hung like a blanket to his trim waist. A loincloth hugged his well-developed ass, exposing his thick thighs and long legs. His large hand extended out to Jac, but yet he made no move to reach her. His massive body moved fluidly with the grace of a cat, as he turned to her. A few scars marred his beautiful chest, as if he'd battled many enemies and won.

Jac gasped at the beauty of his face.

Like an erotic fantasy come to life, he waited for her reaction. Jac's eyes ran down the length of him, pausing at the bulge beneath his loincloth. Familiarity prickled at the back of her mind. She glanced up, her gaze locking with the stranger's, drawing her near despite her efforts to resist. His power was palpable. His need tangible. Jac fought the urge to throw herself at his feet and beg him to fuck her. Her nipples engorged, as if her body recognized his, yet she knew she'd never seen him before.

Just as Jac was about to ask his name, the man smiled and then stuck out his six and a half inch tongue, rolling it provocatively, taunting her—reminding. Jac's breathing seized, recognition slamming into her as if she'd been tackled from behind by a linebacker. Everything came back in a rush—the stream, the blindfold, endless orgasms, and that tongue. The stranger threw his head back and laughed. The deep rumbling sound sent delicious vibrations over her body, straight to her cunt.

Jac jackknifed up, her slender hands gripping the sides of the cot for support. Her breathing was labored and a thin sheen of sweat covered her skin. She blinked a couple of times as her mind scrambled to recall where she was. The green canvas walls of her tent came into focus. She could hear the steady patter of rain as it struck the canvas. Humidity embraced her like an old friend and animals stirred within the cover of the jungle.

She was alone. Always alone.

Her body continued to tingle from the vivid images. But that's all it was…a dream. Jac pulled the mosquito netting apart and stood up. The phantom stranger had shaken her to the core. Logically, she knew he didn't exist, but she couldn't seem to stop herself from imagining what if. Jac looked down at her body, her nipples were erect, and she could feel her clit pulsing. There was no way in hell she'd fall back to sleep this aroused.

Jac rummaged through her bag and found her jack rabbit vibrator. She could care less if the guides could hear the steady buzzing coming from inside her tent. She needed some relief — now. Jac slipped the vibrator in place and turned it on, allowing the delicate rabbit ears to stimulate her clit while the dildo made slow, sensual circles inside her channel. She lay back on the cot, spreading her legs wide for maximum enjoyment, picturing the dark stranger's amazing tongue.

It only took a few minutes of imagining the stranger's mouth feasting upon her clit, the weight of his body spreading her as he impaled her with his impressive tongue, his lips practically rimming her anus, as he drove inside her velvet channel harder and harder, before Jac's breathing deepened and she came hard.

Jac bit down on her lip to keep from crying out. Her skin heated from her release, blood rushed in her ears, pounding, muting the sounds around her. She inhaled deeply, enjoying the musky odor of sex wafting in the air.

She closed her eyes and once again saw the dark angel from her dream. This time his gaze held an unspoken promise. Jac shivered and got the distinct impression he was out there somewhere…waiting.

* * * * *

Ares had spent the night in a tree a hundred yards away. He'd awoken on occasion throughout the evening to reach out and touch Jac's thoughts, projecting his own back. When his mind received the carnal pictures floating through her during dream state, he'd almost fallen from his perch. His cock still ached. The fact that she'd imagined Xavier getting ready to stroke inside her only made matters worse.

Anger over her mistaking him for another man fired Ares's blood, so much so, he'd sent images of himself to taunt, tease, and remind her of what they'd shared yesterday. He'd expected shock, perhaps withdrawal, but hadn't anticipated her acceptance, the insatiable hunger that lingered just below her cool surface. It took every fiber of Ares's being to keep from going to her, but he wanted them deeper into the jungle, closer to the red devil he sought. Then when the moment was right, he'd claim her. In the meantime, he'd move to the other side of the river, where he'd be able to keep an eye on her canoe, and hopefully avoid temptation.

Ares made his way through the trees and across the water, before dawn. The foliage was less dense on the far side, so he'd have to be twice as vigilant to keep his presence hidden. He found a limb to wait on that allowed him clear access to Jac's tent, then made himself comfortable and slept.

* * * * *

The next morning after breakfast they broke camp. Xavier directed the men in boats into the water, then turned to face Jac. "We should catch up with the professor tonight, if we're lucky."

Jac searched Xavier's face, looking for any sign of deception. She really needed to find the bastard, rescue Rachel, and get the hell out of this jungle before her mind snapped completely.

"Luck has nothing to do with it. We'll find that asshole even if we have to push forward in the dark." She rolled her shoulders. "I'm not letting him get away."

Xavier nodded and waited for Jac to step into the canoe before shoving off.

* * * * *

They had been paddling for seven hours when the first gunshot exploded from the rainforest. The guide in the front canoe screamed as a bullet ripped through him, tearing a hole into his side.

Blood spurted out, spraying the men in the canoe beside him. The guides started shouting. Several hands flew up, pointing to the bank. All eyes turned to the trees. Several natives lined the shore, rifles raised in their direction, then utter chaos erupted as more shots were fired.

Nightmarish screams rang out. Painful cries for the dying blended with slaps as the paddles hit the water. Jac's anger erupted as she saw Rumsinger smile and slip into the undergrowth. She pulled her pistols out and opened fire, dropping two of the natives on the shore. The river rippled as guide after guide dove into the murky depths, seeking escape. The ones lucky enough to reach the shore fled into the jungle.

Xavier shouted instructions to his men to paddle to the opposite shore. Two more guides were felled. The current flowed eerily red as the blood blended with the water. Serpent-like heads broke the surface as the black caiman closed in, drawn by the powerful scent of blood and death. More men abandoned their canoes and started swimming for the shore, taking their chances with the second deadliest predator in the area.

Pop, pop, pop. Bullets whizzed by Jac's bowed head. She ducked low and fired back, giving Xavier the time he needed to paddle to shore. The buzz was horrendous as the groups exchanged gunfire. Crack. Pow. Pow. Metal ricocheted off equipment, zinging like giant mosquitoes, before striking one of the canoes. The craft exploded from the hail of gunfire, sending bits of yellow rubber soaring through the air, then raining down upon their heads. Jac watched in horror as canoe remnants disappeared below the surface, swallowed by the murky depths.

Frantic she scrambled forward on her belly to ask Xavier what they should do next. He was bent forward, muscles straining, paddling with all his might. She made it to the front of the canoe, as a bullet shattered Xavier's skull. Fragments of bone flew in all directions. Blood sprayed Jac, oozing down her face, drenching her clothes until the white of her t-shirt stained crimson.

In her mind she screamed, but no sound came out. Her instincts took over and she stood, diving into the swirling, muddy water.

Jac broke the surface several yards away, her pack full of water and weighing her down. Undeterred, she swam for the far shore. Jac could hear the screams of a few of her guides as the current or the caiman began to suck them under one by one. Jac closed herself off. If she was going to survive, she'd have to stay focused and keep moving. The current was strong, but Jac was stronger. Her muscles strained. Gradually by swimming kitty corner to the shore, she reached solid ground, and collapsed on the bank.

* * * * *

Ares's chest squeezed when he heard the first round of gunfire. He'd moved ahead in an attempt to out pace Jac's party. Now, he raced back through the trees, hoping he wasn't too late, his thoughts automatically reaching for Jac. Branches scratched at his skin, leaving red welts behind. Terror flooded his mind. Ares wasn't sure whether it was from her or himself.

His hand gripped liana after liana. Iguanas scurried down the bark of palms, tree frogs leapt for their lives, while macaws and blue heron took to flight. Ares sent out an energy pulse warning predators of his impending approach. Rage the likes of which he'd never felt, exploded inside. If the red devil took his mate away, there would be no safe place on the planet for the bastard to hide.

Ares arrived at the scene of the massacre, just as Jac staggered to shore and collapsed. His heart dropped to his knees. She lived. Her eyes bulged with fright as she coughed up lungs full of water. He watched as she forced herself to kneel, and then stand, her limbs trembling with exertion. His gaze scanned over every inch of her creamy skin, searching for any sign of injury. Her clothes clung to her, stained with watery blood. She turned and stared — transfixed, at the far shore.

Biting back a curse, Ares vowed again to get the red-haired demon.

* * * * *

Excited shouts from the other side of the river drew Jac's attention as she gasped and sputtered for breath, as the bastards celebrated the massacre. Anger boiled inside of her like a caldron, and Jac bit the inside of her mouth so hard it bled. She spit the coppery tasting substance onto the grass and ran her trembling hands through her short hair, slicking it back.

One of Jac's guides floated facedown in the water, his lifeless body now subject to the whim of the lapping waves. Jac swallowed, fighting the threat of rising bile in her throat.

Rumsinger wouldn't be allowed to get away with this. He'd gone from bastard to murderer in a matter of seconds, even though Jac hadn't seen him raise a weapon himself or fire a single shot. Coward. She knew beyond a doubt he'd ordered the attack. Her heart clenched as she thought of poor Rachel. If he was capable of this, what had he done to her defenseless friend?

Jac's resolve hardened into a black, seething ball of hate. If he wanted war, she'd damn well give it to him.

Chapter Three

Jac clenched her fists. Stormy black rage coursed through her body. She settled her backpack and glanced up at the sky. It would be dark soon. She'd have to seek shelter. Jac threw one last glance over her shoulder and then slipped into the jungle. Vines and shrubs crunched beneath her soggy boots. Luckily the air was muggy and she wouldn't freeze to death.

She didn't know if the professor would start looking for her or if he'd leave her for the jungle to take. Either way, she wasn't waiting around to find out. He'd truly fucked with the wrong woman.

Jac blew out a heavy breath. The air on this side of the shore seemed overly perfumed. Orchids grew wild, clinging to the sides of trees, snaking their way toward the sunlight. Huge harpy eagles sat perched high in the branches, watching, their size intimidating enough for Jac to recall the scene from the Wizard of Oz where the monkeys carried Dorothy away.

She trembled.

This was the jungle, not Oz. Jac continued hiking until the fading light made it impossible to see her next step. The hair on her arms raised and a shiver tingled over her spine. Jac glanced over her shoulder again. She'd had the distinct impression she was being followed, so she had kept moving long after she'd reached the point of exhaustion. She found a tree that was easy to scale because of its many branches, and proceeded to climb.

Finding the widest branch, Jac settled in for the night, her eyes peeled on the jungle floor. She dug through her pack for the bit of jerky buried at the bottom and greedily ate the dried salty meat, washing it down with bottled water. Tomorrow she'd search for tracks, maybe make her way back to base camp to regroup.

* * * * *

Ares watched Jac drift off to sleep from a nearby branch. He'd been following her since the horrible scene at the shore, ducking behind trees when she happened to glance over her shoulder. She'd been well aware of his presence and had done a good job of zigzagging her way through the underbrush, mixing her trail enough to confuse an inexperienced tracker. He smiled, his heart swelling with admiration.

There was no sense in capturing her tonight. She'd been through too much. One more stressful incident and she might snap...but he didn't think so. His mate was strong—a true warrior woman. She would not go down without a fight. His cock bucked under his loincloth as he thought about how much he would enjoy taming her.

Ares tuned into Jac's thoughts. Vengeance raged through her mind. His muscles tensed as he saw the vivid pictures of what she planned to do to the red-haired devil. A smile played at the corners of Ares's mouth. Jac truly was perfect for him. It was too bad he could not allow her to follow through with her plans. The risk of harm was too great. So much so, that he would be remiss as a mate if he allowed her to pursue that deadly path.

Eventually, she'd come to understand.

Ares pulled the bindings from the pouch attached to the side of his loincloth. The fabric looked flimsy at first glance, but the delicate green material was deceptively strong. Tomorrow he'd secure Jac and head back to the village. He ran the silky fabric through his fingertips. His skin heated as he imagined her wrists bound behind her back, the position shoving her small breasts out, exposing her nipples to his hungry gaze.

In his mind's eye, he could see the pink tips thrusting out, seeking the warmth of his mouth as he laved each one. She tasted of the sweetest honey, the tangiest fruit. Her intoxicating scent had driven him mad with desire, and her woman's center had nearly been the death of him. Ares imagined his tongue buried in her wet channel, her inner muscles gripping him as she experienced her release, the shimmering contractions sucking him deeper inside. At that moment they had become one. It had been all he could do to keep from coming within his loincloth.

Ares growled deep in his throat.

He longed to sample her again, touch the silk of her thighs, suckle from her berry-like nipples, caress her hidden nub, and consume the cream from her channel as she came hard in his mouth, over his tongue. Ares groaned as his cock lengthened. He shoved the fabric back into the pouch and fisted his hands in frustration. The object of his desire lay perched a few vine swings away. He loosened the ties around his hips, allowing his long, thick shaft to spring free. Taking himself in hand he began to stroke.

Ares pictured Jac's pink mouth wrapped around the crown of his cock. His breathing hitched as he visualized his length sliding deeper into her warm, soft, moist recesses. He could almost feel her lips close around his girth as she began to suckle him. With one hand encircling him, she'd reach down with the other and carefully cup his balls as she increased her speed.

He stroked faster, gritting his teeth against the spiraling sensations. Ares imagined gripping her short, blonde hair, guiding her movements, plunging his cock into the back of her throat. He imagined a deep purr escaping her mouth, caressing his length in feminine appreciation. Ares groaned, that was all it took to send him over the edge. He fisted his hand as the first of his seed spurt from his body. Muscles clenched in his abdomen as he sprayed the ground below. He had the strange urge to bellow, to make his presence known, but he couldn't and wouldn't. Not yet.

He continued to aggressively milk his staff. This would be the last time he'd waste his life giving fluids on the vegetation. The next time he came it would be buried deep inside of Jac, no blindfolds, no illusions, and no doubts about who claimed her.

Ares wiped his hands on the loincloth and fastened his ties. Tomorrow they had a long day ahead of them. He'd need all of his strength and mental acuity if he expected to face Jac and win. He rested his arms behind his head and leaned against the trunk of the tree. Jac was the last thing Ares saw as he closed his eyes.

* * * * *

Jac awoke late in the day to the sensation of something slithering over her calf. Her eyes opened in a flash. A huge brown python made its way to a higher branch, using her leg for leverage. Her mind froze. Jac's heart skipped a beat. She sat perfectly still praying the snake didn't decide to have her for a snack. Her left hand itched as she moved a fraction closer to the pistol on her hip, while her right palm dug painfully into the bark.

Stay calm.

There is a giant snake crawling over my leg.

Stay calm.

I'm going to be squeezed to death before I can fire off a round.

Stay calm.

Jac screamed, a blood curdling, fear of dying, grab you by the balls sound that was probably heard by every living being on the planet.

So much for staying calm.

She jumped up as the snake's tail left her body. The swift action, coupled with the weight of the backpack, threw her off balance, and over the edge of the limb. The next thing Jac knew, she was falling.

"Oh shi…i…t!"

Wind whistled around her ears. Branches whooshed by her head as the ground rushed up to meet her face. At the last second, Jac closed her eyes for impact, sticking her hands out to brace.

There was a loud whap and Jac jerked to a stop so forcefully that it knocked the air from her lungs and made the bone in her hip pop. Her eyes flew open. Her pack dangled, blocking her view of the tree. Even though Jac couldn't see, it felt as if something grasped her foot.

Jac gasped for air, trying to catch her breath. Her arms flailed as she tried to reach out and touch the earth. The ground smelled like greenery and dead leaves, musty and damp. She twisted trying to look at her leg, but all she could see was her own blonde hair, bark, and leaves. Blood rushed to her head. She bent at the waist, as if to sit up, when her foot slipped free. Jac dropped to the ground, landing on her butt and back with a thud.

She lay there for a few moments, willing air into her lungs before pushing herself to stand. Jac rubbed her bruised rear, her gaze automatically following the trunk of the tree up to the lower branches, scanning each one, until it locked onto a set of jade green eyes.

The phantom.

Jac forgot how to breathe. Heavily muscled, huge, and perched like a predator, her dark fantasy stood amongst the leaves. Silent. Waiting. Watching.

Except he was no dream.

Jac didn't wait for him to come down. She spun on her heels and bolted into the forest. She didn't stop to think. Every fiber told her to get as far away from the man as possible. Jac sprinted across the ground, leaping over fallen branches, ducking under limbs, and around giant ferns. Twigs snapped and branches creaked as the warrior pursued her. Her heart pounded in her chest as she pushed herself to run faster.

Jac heard a rush of wind and turned in time to see the dark hunter swinging from a vine, coming straight toward her. She dipped and rolled, evading his grasp. Jac heard what sounded like laughter tickle over her spine, but she didn't stop. She whipped around trees, lashed out against the lush plants, rushing as if the devil himself loomed behind.

Because for all she knew…he was.

* * * * *

Jac arrived at the river after a few hours, grateful for her years of conditioning. She was about to run up shore when the black haired man stepped from the jungle, blocking her path, a wicked grin slashed across his fiercely handsome face.

"Shit!" Jac screamed as she spun and dove into the water. She swam, her muscles straining against the current. She heard a splash and knew without looking he was behind her.

Chasing, shadowing, hunting.

Jac stroked harder, using every bit of experience at her disposal. The man pursuing her was strong and would easily overtake her in the water if she didn't use her intelligence. She let herself be carried with the current, diving under the water every chance she got. Jac took a second to glance back. The man was still behind her, but further away. Her plan was working.

Jac clamored to solid ground, clawing her way onto the shore through the mud. The afternoon sun faded fast. She didn't stop to empty her shoes or wring out her clothes, instead she sprinted. The vegetation thickened to the point where Jac was pretty sure she could find a good hiding place. She pushed on until she caught sight of a tiny break in the leaves and then dove for it, pulling her trembling legs beneath her.

The ground poked hard against her soaked body. Jac took a deep breath and held it. Damp and musky, the air pressed in, swamping her senses. The jungle was silent, as if it waited, listening. Jac let her breath out slowly, silently, and took another. Her ears strained to hear even the slightest noise, anything out of place.

She had started to relax, when she heard the sound of air swooshing above her.

The dark hunter was here.

Jac bit her lip to keep from panicking. She could just make out his muscled form through the thick leaves. Jac watched his arms flex and his thick legs strain as he climbed the vine to rest on a limb above her hideout. It took everything she had to keep from groaning, as she licked her suddenly dry lips.

He wore a tanned hide loincloth and nothing across his wide bare chest. He hovered above her hiding place for what felt like an eternity, sunlight dappling his features. His blue-black hair hung straight to his trim waist in a blanket of ebony. Eyes the color of rare jade scoured the area meticulously. His expression was fierce, possessive—hungry.

Something inside of Jac sprang to life. Her nipples beaded painfully against the thin material of her t-shirt. She squeezed her legs together to stop the sudden ache.

She may not know him, but her body certainly did. Jac fought the urge to spring from the bushes and throw herself, legs spread, onto the ground. This man was dangerous, anyone looking at him could see that. Hell, for all she knew he was one of Rumsinger's lackeys. She had enough problems dealing with the Professor. Jac certainly didn't need Tarzan thrown into the mix, no matter how intriguing she found him to be.

But no matter how much she tried to deny it, there was something about the man that thrilled Jac. She'd never been chased before—she'd always been the pursuer. The thought of this powerful man hunting her...actually turned her on.

I must be losing my mind.

Jac knew she wasn't, but it made her feel better to think it for a moment. She stayed hidden until the man moved on. Jac wasn't sure how long she'd be able to avoid him, but for Rachel's sake she'd have to try.

Ares sensed the woman was still in the area. Her presence coated the branches, scented the plants, but he failed to detect her exact location. He'd kept her safe from predators while she traversed the waters and this was how she chose to repay him. He ran a frustrated hand through his hair. Never in all his years as a hunter had anyone been able to avoid capture while he pursued. Adrenaline rushed through his veins and his cock bucked beneath his loincloth as he scoured the ground. A smile played at the corners of his mouth. His prey had found a very good hiding place.

He continued forward, until he was sure that all trace of her had ended. Today she'd gotten away, but tomorrow... Ares started back toward the river, his movements unhindered by the growing darkness. The sun would be setting soon. His muscles grew tired, weary from the chase.

Ares picked some fruit from the trees, then found a wide branch to spend the night upon. He'd resume his search in the morning. He sent out another burst of energy, to ensure his mate's safety against the night predators. It would be daylight soon enough.

* * * * *

Jac found a hollowed out tree as the last rays of sunlight sunk below the horizon. Luckily mangoes and bananas were plentiful in the rainforest and she wouldn't have to worry about starving. She settled in and ate her meal. She'd spend the night here and start out before dawn, hopefully avoiding the sexy beast following her.

Exhausted, Jac fell asleep. The dream kept repeating itself, over and over—she fell from the branch, except this time twigs poked her shoulder and Tarzan didn't catch her before she hit the ground.

The sensation continued, until the pain in her body was undeniable. Jac groped blindly at her arm and came into direct contact with a stick. She opened one eye. Donald Rumsinger, along with several armed guides, stood in front of her with twig in hand. The professor poked her again and Jac came fully awake. Her hand immediately went to her pistol. A flashlight followed her movements.

"Tsk...tsk." The smile he bestowed upon her was sickening. His thick lips split revealing yellow teeth. His ruddy complexion seemed flushed, almost anxious. But what disturbed Jac the most was the stare coming from his buggy brown eyes. There was no warmth, only hatred, and lust. Jac's stomach rolled. She rose, stretching to her full height. The professor had to tilt his head up to look her in the face.

"Ms. Ward, it's nice to see you again." His eyes wandered to her nipples, visible through her sweat soaked, blood-stained t-shirt.

Jac glared at him and he took a step back. "Spare me the pleasantries, Rumsinger. Where's Rachel?"

The professor paled, but didn't answer. Jac's eyes narrowed, as she fought rising anger. He was hiding something and she intended to find out what.

"I don't think you're in the position to ask a lot of questions." He pointed to the guns aimed at her.

Jac's voice lowered to deadly. "I'm going to ask you again, where is Rachel?"

"As you've seen today, the jungle is a very dangerous place, Ms. Ward. Anything can happen." His eyes wandered up her legs, pausing at her crotch.

Jac laughed, bringing his attention back to her face. "I didn't think I was your type, professor." She tried to calm her stampeding heart. If Rumsinger touched her…Jac's skin crawled and she shuddered. She refused to think about the professor's meaty hands upon her body.

"When one gets desperate enough, slumming it doesn't seem like such a bad thing." He shrugged his shoulders and licked his lips.

Jac blanked her face, as her mind immediately went to thoughts of the Tarzan-like male who had been chasing her earlier. Too bad he hadn't caught her. Not one to linger upon regrets, Jac shot a sideways glance at the armed men. There were too many to fight at one time. She could probably take a few out, but by then one of them would be able to squeeze off a shot.

She planted her hands on her hips. "So what happens now, Rumsinger?"

"For now, you'll come with us. The men have been yearning for a little female entertainment, although I'm sure you're not what they had in mind." He paused. "You'll have to do."

Jac looked from the professor to the men. Desire filled their eyes as they took in her long legs and small breasts. One guide stepped forward and ran the barrel of his rifle over her nipples. They marbled, growing erect. Jac cursed her responsiveness under her breath. Several of the men started talking excitedly and pointing at her breasts. A younger man caught her eye and rubbed his hand over his crotch.

Jac crossed her arms over her chest and glared at them all. The guide snatched her pistols from the holsters, before unsheathing her knife. He held the silver blade up, admiring the weapon for a few moments before slipping it into his pants. She hoped it sliced his dick off.

It would be a cold day in hell before she'd allow a bunch of yokels to fuck her. Even if Jac had to kill every last one of them with her bare hands, so be it. Her daddy hadn't been a SEAL for nothing…and he'd taught her well.

* * * * *

They marched through the jungle for the next hour or so. Jac's muscles screamed at her to stop. In the past two days she'd covered enough ground to qualify for two marathons. When Jac thought she couldn't go another step, they entered a small clearing, where tents had been set up.

Thank goodness.

"Take her over there and tie her up." The professor pointed to a tree at the far end of the encampment away from the tents. "We'll decide what to do with her tomorrow."

A guide placed the barrel of his rifle between her shoulder blades and shoved. Jac stumbled, kicking up dirt beneath her boots, but she didn't fall. The man started to do it again and Jac spun around catching the rifle with her hands. His eyes grew wide with surprise.

"If you do that again," she grit out. "You will regret it...I promise."

The guide pulled the gun from her hands and grinned, but he didn't touch her again. They reached the tree the professor had indicated. The man pushed her to the ground and proceeded to tie her with a nylon rope against the trunk. By the time he finished, Jac could barely feel her hands, as numbness set in.

Feeling brave now that Jac was defenseless, the man leaned forward and cupped her breasts, playing with her nipples through her shirt with his rough thumb. Jac's areolas hardened as he rolled them between his fingers, pinching and pulling them at the same time. The guide's eyes glazed and he licked his full lips. His dark brown hair was worn in a short crop above his ears. Jac glanced at the front of his trousers. His cock began to stir behind his zipper. Her eyes darted to the rest of the men scattered around the camp. No one seemed to notice them.

Jac swallowed hard, shoving her fear to the back of her mind.

She had to put an end to this before things got really ugly. It didn't help that her body, so attuned to sexual advances, refused to cooperate. Jac felt herself getting wet, despite her revulsion. Damn. She wasn't even attracted to this guy. The guide rubbed his hand down the front of his pants as he continued to caress her, his breathing growing ragged. His movements increased, he released the clasp on his clothes and his small cock sprung free. He immediately began jacking off in earnest, all the while playing with her aching nipples.

Jac squirmed, trying to get away from the guide's rebarbative touch. He didn't attempt to shove his cock in her mouth, thank goodness. Perhaps he was perceptive enough to realize she'd bite it off and spit it at his feet if he tried.

The muscles in the man's face tensed and she watched in fascinated horror as he prepared to come. A groan ripped from the man's throat and thick semen shot out of his prick. Jac moved her head at the last second, avoiding his spray. His putrid come dripped down the bark beside her. Jac curled her lip in disgust. The guide smiled again, giving her nipples one last pinch, then shoved his cock back into his pants and walked away.

She watched the man's retreat until he disappeared into one of the tents, then scanned the compound to ensure no one watched before testing her bonds. The rope bit into her wrists, shooting pain up her arms. She winced, but didn't cry out.

She studied the layout of the camp. The tents were arranged in a half circle, opening into a center fire, like at her base camp. Acrid smoke billowed in the air, as the men piled logs on the greedy flames. It looked as if the group had been camping here for a few days. The area was well worn and had enough wood stacked up to last for weeks if need be. For some reason the Professor had established a new base, instead of moving deeper into the jungle. Despite Rumsinger's earlier warning, it looked as if she'd be here for a while.

Jac blew out an unsteady breath. Blood pounded in her ears. She wasn't crazy about what had occurred, but as long as the men didn't touch her anymore than that, she'd be fine. Jac jerked against the ropes, knowing it was only a matter of time before they got their nerve up to do more. She had to figure out a way to escape and quick. Once she did, every last one of these bastards would pay.

Chapter Four

Jac awoke a few hours before dawn. Her back ached from leaning against the rough bark of the tree and her butt was numb from sitting all night on the hard ground. She'd give anything to be able to stand up and stretch her legs.

Anything? The question entered her mind on a whisper.

Jac's head whipped from side to side, looking as far behind her as possible, but no one was there. Her brows furrowed. Was she hearing things that weren't there? She searched the quiet campsite. A posted guard stood at the far end of the compound, but other than that, nothing stirred. Jac shook her head and closed her eyes. *I'm losing it.*

What would you give me, in return for your freedom? The voice spoke again, except this time there was no mistaking the deep rumblings for her imagination.

Jac's eyes flew open. She scanned the tents again. The guard faced the opposite direction, so he hadn't been the one talking. In fact, he didn't seem to be paying any attention to her at all. And there didn't seem to be anyone standing behind her.

I'm losing it.

The sky had gone from black to gray as the first signs of light appeared on the treetops. Jac looked around, searching for any sign of movement or subtle disturbance. Hell anything to prove she wasn't going crazy.

You're getting warmer. The voice teased.

Her eyes narrowed. "Why don't you show yourself and stop playing this childish game of hide and seek?" she murmured.

A laugh rumbled through her like the heavy bass of a stereo that had been turned up too loud.

"I don't like games," she grit out. Jac felt warmth brush over her nipples, in a light pennaceous caress. She sucked in a breath to keep from moaning.

I think that depends on who you are playing with. Masculine confidence rang out in his tone as her nipples puckered under the sensual assault.

The *phantom* from base camp was here. Jac shivered as she recalled exactly what he'd been able to do from a distance.

"What's it going to take for you to get me out of here?" She hated asking, but right now the bodiless voice was her only hope.

I'm afraid the price I ask is steep.

Jac struggled against her ties. "Just tell me what it is before the camp starts to wake up."

Very well...I want your total surrender.

Jac stilled, surely she hadn't heard him correctly. "You're kidding, right?" She pulled against the ropes again, twisting from side to side, rotating her arms, until her wrists bled.

Silence answered her.

"I've never surrendered to a man in my life and I'm not about to start now." Jac jerked against her confines, until her actions drew the attention of the guard.

Cautiously he approached her, rifle in hand.

Very well. I'll leave you to your fate.

The arrogance in his voice set her teeth on edge. How dare he leave her here? Who did he think he was?

The guard drew closer, his eyes taking in her struggles. Sweat beaded on Jac's skin causing her shirt to cling to her like a glove. It didn't help that her nipples ached due to the phantom's teasing. The guard glanced around as if to ensure their privacy and started to unfasten his clothes. *Damn it, not again.* Jac growled in frustration.

"Okay you win. I'll give you anything you want, just get me out of here." Her gaze darted from side to side, searching for an escape.

Confused, the guard hesitated, then continued forward, placing his gun against the side of the tree.

"If you touch me, I'll kill you," she threatened, knowing there wasn't a thing she could do in her present state.

The man chuckled and then proceeded to unbuckle his pants. He pulled out his cock and inched forward. His eyes locked on her mouth. Jac was about to scream, when a blast of light temporarily blinded her. By the time she blinked away the spots, the guard lay dead at her feet, smoke rising from his body. Jac panicked, her lungs labored for breath, as she inhaled the sickening smell of burnt flesh.

Once again she scanned the trees, a slight movement catching her attention. It crept like a shadow, silent, deadly, blending with the fading darkness. Not a leaf rustled as the silhouette made its way from tree trunk to tree trunk. And then she saw him, in all his dark glory…the hunter who had been chasing her.

Relief washed over Jac leaving her mood buoyant.

Stealthily he made his way to her. His jade eyes glinted red against the dying firelight. The devil himself wouldn't strike as much fear in Jac as this man did. Cocksure, he worked his way around the encampment, until he stood directly behind her. His musky, wood enhanced scent surrounded her, drowning her in his presence. Heat radiated from his body, surging through her limbs until she could feel her hands again. *This guy must have the body temperature of a furnace.*

Jac heard the slice of a blade as he cut through the rope. She sagged forward, unable to hold up her weight. Jac tried to stumble to her feet, but her legs had fallen asleep. It felt like a thousand tiny needles stabbed through her at once, and she groaned aloud.

The men started to stir within the tents. Jac attempted to crawl into the jungle when a large hand reached out and grabbed her around the waist from behind. She felt herself being lifted and then her world tilted when the muscled demon tossed her over his shoulder as if she weighed no more than a hacky sack.

The man bolted, surging through the jungle at a dizzying speed. A shout came from behind them as one of the guides discovered the guard's body and cried out the alarm.

Pow! Ping! Pow! Shots rang out in an eruption of sound, as guns were fired into the rainforest. Loud cracks sent leaves splitting and bark flying from the trees, as the deadly missiles neared their target. Jac screamed, but the cry was muffled against the phantom's salty skin.

Jac heard the shuffling of feet and several more shouts as the men scrambled in pursuit. The hunter raced through the brush, juggling Jac as if her weight was of no consequence. His muscles bunched and shifted beneath her hands. Long legs split with each stride. His hair brushed her face, carrying his unique spicy scent with it. Jac's fingers longed to twine themselves into the soft as silk thick strands.

Instead, she held herself perfectly still, afraid the smallest movement would give her original captors the advantage they'd need to catch up.

Tarzan continued to run, his flight swift, his feet silent upon the ground. A fine sheen of sweat covered his tanned skin, giving him a healthy after sex glow. Jac tried, without success, to stop imagining their bodies intertwined as he drove into her hot, aching sheath.

His step faltered as the thought flitted through her mind.

The guide's voices began to fade, until Jac could no longer hear them. Hope swept through her. Maybe they'd actually been able to lose them.

They arrived at the river within an hour. The hunter put Jac down, his breath steady, not winded like she'd have expected.

"Do you think you can make it across?" His eyes strayed to the swift moving water behind her.

Indignant, Jac crossed her arms over her chest and arched a brow. "I out swam you, didn't I?"

His eyes locked onto hers and then turned molten. A wicked smile kicked up the corners of his hard sensuous mouth. Jac's heart skipped a beat at the promise written in his jade gaze. She tilted her head so she could see him better. Dark and menacing, sinfully seductive, the man was made for sex. Long legs led to a washboard stomach. A tribal tattoo wrapped around his trim waist, disappearing beneath the lip of his loincloth.

Jac forced her mind away from where the permanent paint led. His wide chest seemed made for resting her head after a long night of lovemaking. And his hair, the color of raven's feathers framed his warrior's face to perfection. The temptation to run her hands over his muscled length overwhelmed Jac.

"We'll discuss earlier events later." He stepped forward, crowding her personal space, dwarfing her.

The air's temperature seemed to rise exponentially with his nearness. Jac had never felt small and vulnerable in her life — til' now. She pulled at her collar to loosen it. Once again Jac reminded herself to breathe. She raised her hand to push him back. Big mistake. The second her fingers made contact with the muscled wall of his chest, all thoughts spilled from her head.

Jac's palm heated to inferno and her nipples grew erect beneath her t-shirt. She flexed her fingertips, but he was so solid...no give at all. Every erotic dream, fantasy, or thought she'd ever had flooded her mind. It took about two nanoseconds for her brain to quickly replace all her previous lovers with the man standing before her.

He was sex incarnate. And she'd promised him *total* surrender for helping her escape.

Jac's knees started to shake as she pushed away and waded into the water. She needed to put some distance between herself and this man. He did something no man had managed to do—scare her.

Instinctively, Jac knew this giant of a man would never physically harm her, but that fact didn't set her mind at ease. There was something about this demon in a loincloth that made Jac nervous—really nervous. It was as if he could reach into her very soul with those jade colored eyes and take away any thoughts of freedom she secretly harbored. And she'd give them to him willingly.

Jac dove into the water, swimming as though Satan himself were after her. She knew in her heart of hearts there would be no escaping the hunter this time, so she didn't even try. He easily kept pace with her, the water not even rippling as he sliced through it. They reached the far shore in record time. He helped her from the water, his grip firm on her arm. Jac tried to pull away from him, but he refused to release her.

From a distance she heard the chopping of plants and small trees, then the sound of voices drawing nearer. So much for losing Rumsinger. As they stepped into the jungle the professor and his men broke through the trees on the opposite shoreline. The giant hurried her deeper into the cover of the jungle, protectively placing his body between Jac and the professor.

Rumsinger's angry shouts reached Jac's ears. She had the overwhelming urge to turn back around and fight, but seeing as though one of the professor's men had confiscated her weapons, it would be suicide to try.

The hunter led Jac through the jungle, taking care to ensure their tracks were well hidden. They walked throughout the rest of the morning and into the late afternoon. He'd tossed her a banana when she mentioned they hadn't eaten. Jac kept up, refusing to let herself slow him down.

At dusk they reached a tiny clearing and her rescuer stopped. "We'll camp here tonight."

Jac shifted her weight from side to side to alleviate the strain in her legs, with the circulation gradually returning to normal, they'd been hurting for hours. "What about the professor?"

The man didn't answer. He simply walked up to her and picked her up. Jac yelped, her hands automatically flying to encircle his neck, for fear he'd drop her. With no effort, he gently laid her on the ground.

"What are you doing?" she struggled to sit up.

He pushed her back down, his palm resting on her breast. Suddenly the hand on her right leg began to glow. Jac felt her eyes widen. Heat spread over her body, through her limbs, and into her tired muscles. Within moments the pain disappeared and she felt refreshed. He slipped to her other leg and repeated the process.

"Who are you?" She continued to watch his hands. "Better yet, what are you?"

At that question his gaze met hers, Jac gulped despite herself. His hands prevented her from scooting away.

"I am Ares."

He moved his hands away from her body and she felt a shock, much like static electricity. Jac sat up, her gaze never wavering from his face. She debated what to do next, deciding civility would get her further than conflict.

"Interesting name…" She arched a brow, "I'm Jaclyn Ward," and held out her hand.

Ares's lips twitched as he looked from her hand back to her face. He enveloped her palm within his and shook it twice. "I know who you are."

Jac frowned. "How? Did you hear the professor mention my name?"

His jade gaze dropped to the front of her shirt. Jac felt an inkling of warmth and then an invisible stroke across her nipples.

The tactic had worked, as Ares had anticipated. She'd forgotten all about her previous question. He wasn't ready to share how he had come to know of her existence until after the taming was complete.

"It *was* you that day at base camp." It was a statement.

His gaze lazily flicked over her abdomen, dropping further still, leaving a trail of heat behind. Jac swallowed hard. For the first time in her life, she was in over her head.

"Are you thinking about backing out of our agreement?" He shifted, a slight movement that sent his muscles rippling beneath his tanned skin.

Jac's jaw clenched and her eyes narrowed. "I'd never go back on my word."

"Good." His eyes sparked and her channel flooded.

She sucked in a quick breath. "Don't you believe in foreplay?" Jac nervously rubbed her neck and scooted a fraction further away.

He growled. "I thought that's what I was doing." A sexy grin tugged at his mouth, softening his fierce features.

Ares stared long and hard at her body. Jac tensed, her eyes growing impossibly wider, as she felt him enter her. She could no longer remain upright. Pleasure swamped her. His smile widened and the unmistakable sensation of his tongue, swirling inside her sent Jac over the edge. Her body shuddered. She flushed as her blood rushed close to the surface of her skin. She couldn't seem to catch her breath.

"Damn you," she finally spit out and hit the ground with her fist.

He threw his head back and laughed. "Is that anyway to speak to your new mate?"

Jac stilled as his words registered in her ecstasy filled mind. Had he called her his mate? What exactly did he mean by that? She struggled to sit up again, her sated body refusing to cooperate. Jac pushed herself to her elbows, so that she could see him clearly.

"What are you talking about?"

Ares stopped laughing and looked at her. Pure possession etched his rugged features. "You know of which I speak."

Jac rolled her eyes. "No, I don't. You better fill me in."

"As you wish." Ares eyes flashed again as his gaze bulleted to her pussy. By the time Jac realized his intent, it was too late to stop him. She felt the familiar pressure building inside about a second before her body convulsed with another orgasm.

When she'd finally recovered, it took all Jac had not to knock that arrogant expression right off Ares's face. He knew what she'd meant. He played with her, like a cat fiddling with a mouse right before the feline eats its prey. Jac squeezed her legs together as she pictured the dark warrior's head buried between her thighs. Her imagination went on to show his six and a half inch tongue slipping inside her pussy. She groaned. This train of thought got her nowhere. She needed answers and she wanted them now.

Before she could utter a word, Ares rose and walked a few feet away, gathering wood to build a fire. With a pile neatly stacked, he crouched down, placing his hands above the logs. Jac watched as his palms started to glow. In a flash the kindling burst into flames, providing them with protection from the encroaching darkness.

He glanced at her and she raised an eyebrow in question. "That's a neat trick, what else can you do?"

The expression on his face turned from mild amusement to out and out feral. Jac crossed her arms over her chest.

"Don't even think about it," she warned.

He gave her a knowing smile and turned back to the fire.

She didn't want to know, but she had to ask again. "What did you mean earlier when you said you were my mate?"

Ares dropped more wood on the fire as if he hadn't heard her question. When he finished he returned to her side and sat. He stared, his gaze distant, as if pondering her words. Finally he spoke. "If I choose to answer, you will not like it."

"Try me." Jac shifted, the ground suddenly growing extremely uncomfortable beneath her.

Ares released a breath. "You will sleep by my side, bear my young, and welcome me with open arms and legs for as long as we draw breath on this planet."

Jac's mouth dropped open, she couldn't help but gape. After the *bear my young* part Ares might as well have been *Charlie Brown's* teacher, because all she heard was waa, wa, wawa, wa. The trembling started with her hands and continued to rise until Jac's body vibrated like a top. She was pretty sure steam came out her ears.

Of all the antiquated, Neanderthal, bullshit ideas she'd ever heard, this one took the cake.

Jac jumped to her feet. There was no way she would to put up with this crap from him or any other guy. She didn't care how gorgeous he was. Her vision blurred, as the jungle took on a red haze. Jac clenched her hands into painful fists. She'd thank him and be on her way, obviously he was delusional.

"I appreciate you coming to my rescue, Conan," she said through gritted teeth.

"My name is Ares." He shifted, but didn't attempt to stop her.

"Whatever." She shrugged, the tiny motion making her tense muscles feel as if they would snap in two. "You've got the wrong girl for the job, so I'll be on my way."

Jac pivoted and strode into the jungle. She'd made it about ten yards when she slammed into something solid. She looked up and jade eyes flashed, capturing hers. The heat from his body flowed over her, melting her intentions, dissolving all thought from her mind, leaving her with nothing but the physical reaction created by his nearness.

"I need you to step aside," Jac whispered.

No. Came into her mind, but his lips didn't move.

"I don't want to hurt you."

His eyes flashed with what looked like amusement, but he didn't move.

Jac shrugged. "You leave me no choice." She raised her hands as if to strike, at the last second she swept her leg out, knocking his out from under him. Two giant hands snaked out, grasping her at the last second, and then they were both falling.

Ares's back hit the ground a second before Jac landed on top of him. A whoosh of air came rushing from his lungs. Her eyes widened when she felt the thick erection beneath his loincloth. He rolled her beneath him, as she started to rise. Soft ferns mashed under her back. Jac could feel the delicate leaves tickle the skin of her arms, stroking like tiny fingers.

She began to struggle, pushing against his heavy bulk, partly out of fear of Ares—but mostly she was afraid of her own reaction. Her skin heated as her body registered his weight. Jac fought like a wildcat. He held her down with little to no effort on his part, until she wore herself out and ceased to fight.

Her lungs heaved, with each breath her nipples scrapped against his muscled chest through her t-shirt. All sound stopped but the beating of their hearts. Jac glanced to his savage mouth and renewed heat flooded her system. Her tongue darted out. It was all the encouragement Ares needed. His mouth came down on hers, punishing, hungry, desperate. He licked her upper lip, following the outline of her mouth, then switched to nibbling the bottom one, until Jac moaned. He swooped inside her dark recesses, deepening the embrace. Like a half starved animal, he fed from her.

His tongue swirled, tasted, devoured her until Jac couldn't tell where he ended and she began. Her body came alive as every nerve ending fired at once. Jac's hips started moving of their own volition, grinding against his hard length, searching. She was aflame. Her movements seem to drive Ares harder. Soon his actions mirrored her own. He thrust against her, his hips pistoning. His hand closed over her breast and kneaded. Jac cried out, her pussy flooding with moisture.

She tugged at his loincloth like an animal in heat, scratching his skin, running her nails down his back. "I want you so bad," she heard herself say.

Ares growled and sat up, taking her with him. His eyes smoldered, tumultuous emotions swam in their green depths. He stood, pulling Jac to her feet, then strode back to the fire. They'd no more reached the area, when Ares untied his loincloth and the material dropped to the ground. Jac's heart skidded to a halt.

Good lord where does he think he is going to put that?

Jac's eyes practically bugged out of her head. She licked her lips and felt her clit twitch. He stepped forward and grabbed her t-shirt with both hands. With a quick flick of his wrist her shirt was off her body and floating to the ground. Jac's nipples stiffened under his intense gaze, engorging to the point of pain. His fingers immediately moved to her shorts, but fumbled with the clasp, his movements growing frantic, if Jac hadn't stopped him, Ares would have ripped them from her body.

They stood naked, staring at each other.

Ares's body trembled, his muscles flexed. "In all my years of existence, I've never seen such a beautiful sight as you have chosen to gift me with tonight."

Jac felt heat rush to her face. *Good god, I'm blushing.*

"You are most definitely made in the goddess's form."

Butterflies danced in Jac's belly at Ares's words. *I'm acting like such a…such a…girl.* Jac needed to bring back the control she was famous for, turn this situation around before she got so mixed up, she wouldn't be able to find her way out of these emotions without breadcrumbs. It would kill the mood, but the subject needed to be brought up before they went any further.

"I've got a condom in my pocket, let me get it." Jac dug through her pants pocket until she encountered latex. Glancing at Ares, her fingers trembled as she pulled the prophylactic out and opened the packet. Her eyes went to the condom to his penis and back. Dread filled her. There was no way in hell the rubber would fit over that monster instrument of his and this was the biggest one on the market. They wouldn't be able to have sex.

Damn it.

Damn it.

Damn it.

Jac's pussy creamed in protest. This isn't fair. She wanted to stomp, sulk, throw herself onto the ground and refuse to breathe until she got her way. But Jac knew that would be pointless. Her eyes locked with his.

"Houston, we have a problem," Jac said, hoping humor would lessen the blow.

Ares's brows furrowed. "I no not why you insist on calling me by every name but my own." He shook his head. "My name is Ares."

"I know what your name is Tarzan. I'm trying to tell you it's not going to happen."

"What?" Ares crossed his arms.

Jac put her hands on her hips, the condom tucked in her right palm. "Do I have to spell it out for you?"

He cocked his head to the side as if to say I'm listening, go ahead.

"The condom isn't going to fit your…'ah, um,' considerable assets." Jac nodded, indicating she referred to his staff.

Ares glanced down at his thick shaft and back at Jac. "What is a condom?"

Jac cracked up. She couldn't help it. She'd heard a lot of excuses why guys didn't want to wear a rubber, but asking what one was — well, a new one.

"Ignorance isn't going to work." She choked back a sarcastic laugh.

Ares pointed to Jac's right hand. "Are you referring to that strange substance in your hand?"

She nodded.

"What were you planning on doing with that?" Confusion shadowed his features.

Jac stopped laughing and took a serious look at him. He appeared genuinely confused. "You really don't know what this is for, do you?"

Ares shook his head, sending his ebony hair sliding over his broad shoulders. "No."

She cleared her throat. "You wear one of these over your penis to prevent disease, babies, you name it."

Ares looked horrified. "You want me to put that tiny thing over my staff."

"Yes."

"Absolutely not," Ares swept a hand through the air to indicate the conversation was over.

"No condom. No nookie." Jac glanced at the fire, the conversation beginning to get on her nerves. She wasn't about to give into temptation no matter how bad she wanted his cock. And she *really* wanted his cock.

Jac heard twigs snap. Her gaze shot up. Ares had taken a step closer. His eyes narrowed and a red flush colored his cheeks.

"I am not diseased," he ground out between clenched teeth. "My people are immune to the maladies of this planet." His gaze leveled on Jac, boring into her, willing her to believe.

Jac took a step back. "It's too bad I can't take your word for it, but in this day and age you can't be too careful." She would not concede on this point. "Who are *your people* by the way?"

Ares's face tensed as if considering whether to answer her question. "I agree with you about the perils of this time in which we live. The Earth is a very dangerous place, which is why we must soon leave."

Jac looked around her at the jungle surrounding them. "Leave?"

Ares waved a hand in the air as if to erase his last words. "'Tis unimportant."

"You obviously haven't gotten out lately." Jac's hands rested on her hips. "Disease is nothing to joke about."

"You think I jest?" He stepped closer. "Do you have any idea how old I am? What I am?"

Jac could feel heat rolling in waves from his body. She fought herself to keep from falling into it, drowning. He made resisting much harder than it had to be—than it had ever been before.

"I'd say you're about thirty-five." She looked at him, studying the lines around his eyes, the slight weathering of his skin. She was about to touch the second question he'd asked. *What in the hell did he mean by 'what I am'?*

It was Ares's turn to laugh. The muscles rippled in his six pack abs. Jac put her hands behind her back to keep from reaching out and stroking every ridge, every ripple.

Ares stopped laughing. He reached out and grabbed her upper arms, his thumbs rubbing her skin, sending shivers through her body.

"Try three thousand five hundred years old."

The trees behind Ares started to spin. Jac heard her blood rush, pounding in her ears, and then everything went black.

Chapter Five

Jac awoke with Ares leaning over her, fanning her face with a palm leaf. She blinked a couple of times until he came into clear focus. "What happened?" she croaked, her tongue feeling thick in her mouth. The last thing she could recall was talking about condoms and the ills of the world, then everything went black.

"You fainted." He smiled.

She tried to sit up, but Ares held her down. "I *never* faint."

Ares looked as if he tried hard not to laugh. Jac didn't think any of this was funny. For all she knew he'd put a whammy on her when she wasn't looking. Yeah, that had to be it. He'd been able to do a hell of a lot without actually touching her, so it stood to reason that was what occurred this time.

"I did not touch you." His eyes sparkled, dancing in amusement.

Jac clutched her head. "I wouldn't really know, now would I?"

"I've given you my word. 'Tis enough."

"You'll forgive me," she shoved his hand away and sat up, "if I don't quite believe you."

Ares shrugged. "'Tis no matter to me, believe what you must." He casually plucked at her nipple as he spoke, positioning his body between her legs at the same time. "You know I speak the truth. You have seen what I can do."

Jac had to fight to keep her eyes from closing, the sensations he created inside her body should be illegal. She leaned forward pressing her breast into his palm. He increased his movements, until Jac thought she'd go mad.

"I know no such…Please." Jac didn't even know what she asked for. The soft ground cushioned her head and body. Locusts buzzed, their scratchy sound filling the air with a strange kind of music.

Ares lowered himself until his head was between Jac's thighs. He threw her long legs over his broad shoulders, his gaze locking onto hers. Jac started to close her eyes.

"Look at me," he demanded.

Jac snapped to attention.

"I want you to see the man…the only man…who will ever give you pleasure from this day forth."

Jac's nostrils flared at his words and her eyes narrowed, but she refused to break contact. She watched as Ares stuck out his six and a half inch tongue and licked her from bottom to top. She groaned at the carnal sight. He did it again and again until Jac could no longer support the weight of her head. Ares nipped and sucked on her clit as if he'd never get enough of her, laving and lapping like a deranged serpent, his tongue an entity all its own.

Ares slipped her clit between his lips and hummed. Jac flew apart, shattering into a million pieces of light, falling off a precipice into the abyss. Her body strummed and pulsated. Her nipples stabbed skyward as they engorged with blood.

A heavy weight settled upon her body and Jac was only vaguely aware that Ares had risen above her. Jac's lids fluttered open. His elbows rested on either side of her face, his gaze intense and uncompromising. Jac could feel his massive cock dig into her belly, satin and velvet, hard and urgent. He stared at her until she'd finally floated back to reality and gathered her wits. His body pressed ever so slightly, letting her know without words, that he, in fact, dominated her. Jac's instant reaction was to tense and fight.

Ares lowered his head and kissed her tenderly, the pressure so light it felt like the scrape of butterfly wings over her sensitized lips. Jac's breath caught, surprised by his gentleness.

All fight left her body. She could taste her own essence in Ares's kiss. He lifted his hips and his shaft slipped down to her opening.

Ares pulled back until he could once again look in her face.

Her molten core yearned for him to fill her. Alarm bells rang in Jac's head. "We can't do this."

"We can and we must." The crown of his thick phallus slipped into her entry.

Jac fought the urge to buck her hips, drawing him deeper. The tip of his cock stretched her beyond limits. She bit her bottom lip, as her body flooded with moisture to ease his entry.

"See even your woman's center recognizes its mate." He slid an inch further inside.

"How can I trust you? I don't even know you," Jac reasoned, fighting panic and the demands of her body. She lost the battle.

She didn't have to add that she'd never trusted a man in her life, it was probably written across her face. Hell, she wasn't ready to have kids. At least she didn't think she was…Her sheath gripped him, urging him into her inner sanctum.

He licked her neck and nuzzled her ear. Jac shuddered.

You know all you need to know about me. I scare you because your body recognizes me as your other half.

Ares pushed deeper, then stopped. Only a couple inches inside her velvet walls and already he was overwhelmed. He fought the urge to rut in her like a wild bull. She fit him perfectly. The seer, Ariel had been correct. This woman was all he'd ever need. Jac would carry his sons and daughters in her womb and they would grow up to be warriors, just like their parents. Ares didn't bother to tell Jac he couldn't get her pregnant, because he wouldn't be fertile until after the joining ceremony.

You bring joy to my heart.

Her expression turned troubled. "How can you do that?"

He arched a brow. "Do what?"

"Talk to me in my head."

Ares smiled. *You learn a lot in three thousand years.*

Jac laughed despite herself. "You can't hear my thoughts can you?"

Ares's expression softened for a moment. He opened his mouth as if to speak, then as if changing his mind kissed her hard instead. *I fear I can wait no longer to claim you, my fierceness.*

Jac swallowed nervously.

Ares started chanting in a strange language. Heat emanated from his hands and spread throughout her body. Jac felt as if every cell in her began to regenerate, as if the mere act of touching her had turned back the hands of time. But that wasn't possible. After a few moments the heat subsided.

"It is done," he said, strain showing on his handsome face.

"What's done?"

"This," Ares surged forward embedding himself completely in Jac's tight sheath.

Jac screamed when she felt her hymen tear. Pain shot through her and she couldn't seem to catch her breath. It was impossible—no way in hell. She hadn't been a virgin since her eighteenth birthday party, but there was no mistaking the pain coming from deep inside her. Ares was so large she thought he might have split her in two, her breathing sounded as if she attended a Lamaze class. There had to be a logical explanation, but her mind refused to wrap itself around the idea.

"W—what did you do?" she sputtered out, straining to rise. Jac pushed against his chest.

Ares held himself perfectly still. "I know not what you speak of, my fierceness."

"V-virgin…I'm not a v-virgin…I mean, I wa-wasn't…when we started this."

"I healed you…*all of you.*"

Jac dropped her head back onto the ground. "Remind me to kill you later."

Ares grinned and then rotated his hips. Jac moaned. He repeated the action until the pain subsided and she was lost. His thrusts grew more frantic, animalistic, his need all consuming, feral. He drove into her wet channel. Her vaginal walls gripped him, pulling Ares back, refusing to let him leave.

His cock pounded into Jac, rocking her, turning her inside out until she balled up into a twisting mass of feelings, emotions — vague impressions.

His thrusts turned frenzied. He reached down and tilted Jac's hips, so that he could delve deeper still. The muscles in his neck corded. His hands heated, sending an energy burst into her clit.

Jac came so hard stars burst behind her eyelids.

Ares tossed his head back and grit his teeth as he joined her. His seed spilled from his body, filling her channel, his hips continuing to pump, long after his fluids had stopped. Her tunnel felt like fire, wrapping his cock in such volcanic warmth, that he thought he'd be permanently molded to her. All his instincts told him to fuck her again, until he'd driven from her mind every last thought of leaving him.

With a last shudder, Ares reluctantly slipped from Jac's molten core, then rolled over, pulling her on top of him. He ran a callused finger over her forehead, trying to rub away the frown forming on her pale face. Ares brushed his hand through her silky hair, their bodies drenched in sweat.

"You truly are the most beautiful woman I have ever seen. I am honored to have you as my mate."

Jac swallowed hard. She didn't trust herself to speak. The experience had been so wonderful that she didn't want to ruin it by telling him they weren't meant to be. She definitely wasn't the mate type, whatever that was. Jac didn't have the heart to break it to him.

A lump formed in her throat and she fisted her hands. *Damn it. I'm not the sappy, cry over a poignant commercial kind of gal. I don't even get emotionally involved. If this big oaf has mistaken sex for something more, then that's his problem, not mine.*

It was time she remembered the reason she'd come down to this hellhole in the first place. Jac was on a rescue mission, not a sexcapade. She needed to remember that—and fast. Rachel was counting on Jac to help her and she wasn't about to let her friend down, plus she owed the professor a big one. Jac wasn't one for vigilantism, but sometimes desperate times called for desperate measures.

Ares followed all Jac's thoughts as they raced from one end of the spectrum to the other. He didn't like eavesdropping in anyone's mind, but it was imperative for the taming that he knew what Jac thought. She would be the guide for his next move. He was glad she chose not to submit so easily, it gave him more time to coax her surrender. He felt a stab in the vicinity of his heart when she thought of her friend Rachel.

In all his years, Ares had never experienced guilt before, until now, and he didn't like it one bit. But he couldn't lead Jac to her friend or let her know of his full mental abilities until he was sure she was his. Then, and only then, would he take her to the village, where the joining ceremony could be performed.

Luckily his bloodline was different from most Atlanteans'. They were not only adept hunters, but spiritual advisors as well. Their power was so great that they earned a spot of honor among the Atlantean people. Ares didn't need to wait for the seer's blessings to physically claim his mate. He could bless the union himself. Ares had pitied his brother in arms, Eros. The King had to wait until after the ceremony before he was allowed to seek his release within the Queen. Eros had walked around before the ceremony for two days with tender balls. Ares had teased him unmercifully. His friend had told him to wait until he met his future mate, then they'd see who laughed.

Fortunately for Ares, his friend had been mistaken. There was nothing to this taming and surrendering process. When

Ares returned to the village he'd have to inform everyone how foolish they'd been in warning him. He smiled to himself and stroked Jac's short blonde hair, his heart swelling with unfamiliar emotion. Tomorrow the marking would begin, binding their warrior hearts for all eternity. If the taming continued half as well as tonight, then they'd be back in the village in no time.

Jac awoke several times in the night to find Ares's massive cock sliding in and out of her sheath. She'd come more times than she thought was humanly possible. All he had to do was look at her now and Jac's pussy wept. She couldn't seem to get enough of him, and he was insatiable. Fucking her at times with his tongue, then flipping her over onto her stomach and driving into her cunt from behind. They'd worn a clearing into the jungle floor from all the tousling. Jac didn't think she'd ever be able to look at another naked man with the same appreciation as she gave Ares.

Jac had her own living, breathing Tarzan, who fucked like a god. Just thinking about him made her clit pulse and throb. Pretty soon he wouldn't even need to use his energy beams on her, she'd come by simply looking at him. Jac clenched her inner muscles, in anticipation of squeezing his shaft. She could definitely get used to this man. The thought sobered Jac. This was sex, only sex and to prove it she'd take control, like she always did in her relationships. With the night beginning to fade to dawn, she made her move.

This time it was her turn to set the pace. She sat up, straddling his hips and positioned the head of his cock at her entrance. He had a lazy smile playing at his lips. Jac captured his gaze and then sunk down, taking him deep inside, until she'd swear she could feel him at the back of her throat. Then Jac began to ride, a slow gentle rocking at first, followed by a quick bouncing trot. Soon Jac's motions took on a full out gallop as she gyrated her hips around and around, rimming his cock base with her wet cunt. Her nails dug into the muscled flesh at his sides.

Jac felt full, stretched beyond imagination, aching. Her pussy gripped him, tempting him to spill his seed. The air around them filled with the aroma of sex and orchids from the nearby trees. The fire had died down to mere embers, but they continued to burst with inextinguishable flames.

Jac fucked Ares hard, grinding her clit against his abdomen at the same time. His chest rose and fell as he labored for each breath. His fingers grasped the round globes of her ass, lifting her up and pulling her down when Jac thought she could take no more.

She leaned over and sucked his flat disc-like nipple into her mouth, it beaded beneath her lips. Jac's tongue darted out, circling and lapping at his salty chest. Ares's fingers dug into her flesh and his nostril flared. He bit back a moan as his hips met her halfway, pumping longer and harder. A bellow ripped from his chest and then he exploded. Jac felt his hot seed squirt inside her, like a glorious fountain, jarring, pulsing, and spraying.

She collapsed on Ares's chest as his orgasm sent her over the edge into oblivion. The world spun around her. Colors grew vivid, sounds intense, smells keen, and tastes explosive. She quivered uncontrollably, her body on a collision course with the unknown. By the time she'd finally returned from her journey, Jac knew she was in deep shit.

For the first time in her life she wasn't so sure she'd be able to walk away unscathed in the end. Ares stroked his warm fingertips along her back, sending chill bumps over her skin. They lay, breathing as one. An unbroken infinity sign, heat to heat, body to body, soul touching soul.

Fuck.

Fuck.

Fuck me.

*As you wish…*the response rumbled in her head, as his voice dropped seductively lower.

* * * * *

Sunlight broke through the green canopy of the trees as Jac awoke to the sounds of monkeys clamoring. She sat up, her body sore from the sexual workout. Mangos, bananas, breadfruit, and berries rose like a pyramid, piled high next to the now extinct fire. Her eyes immediately sought out Ares. He was nowhere to be found. Jac took a shaky breath, debating whether to dress and bail on him. She knew it would be taking the coward's way out, if she didn't stay to face him, but right now she wasn't feeling too brave, at least when it came to her green-eyed Tarzan.

Jac threw on her clothes and hiking boots, then shoved a few pieces of fruit into her pockets for later. She bolted into the jungle. The heat and humidity had already started to climb to lethal heights, but she didn't stop. Jac ran, ducking under low hanging vines, leaping over primordial ferns. A few parrots dispersed, their angry squawks ear shattering. But Jac pushed on, her heart heavy in her chest.

Damn it. She didn't miss the big oaf at all.

The canopy of trees swayed gently, letting the dappled light shine down on the jungle floor. The breeze seemed to whisper Ares's name. Jac's eyes began to sting and her lungs burned. She wiped her face with the back of her hand, then glanced down at her fingers, which were now covered in wetness.

I am not crying…damn it.

* * * * *

Morning faded into afternoon, Jac had spent most of the time looking over her shoulder. She wasn't sure if she should be relieved or disappointed that Ares hadn't come after her. Maybe in the light of day it had dawned on him that what occurred last night was wonderful, but not something to build a lasting relationship on. Not that Jac knew what it took to do that — she'd had no firsthand experience to speak of.

Jac started around the palm tree, when she heard a twig snap. She froze, her heart slamming against her ribs. Had Ares caught up? Jac strained to hear, attempting to determine if what she'd heard was something or nothing more than her imagination. She pressed her body against the trunk of the liana infested tree and quieted her breathing. The sound came again, this time closer.

Jac grabbed the nearest liana and started to climb, her muscles strained as she hauled her weight up. She reached the top of a limb about fifteen feet above the rainforest floor. From her perch she could make out a man moving slowly toward her previous location. His eyes never wavered from the ground. He dressed in khaki pants and a matching shirt, with thick brown boots covering his feet. His skin was deeply tanned from over exposure to the sun. When he drew nearer, Jac recognized him and her eyes narrowed. He was the guide who had taken her pistols away the night she'd been captured.

Her gaze dropped. Holstered to his trim hips were Jac's weapons.

Anger sliced through Jac, then she smiled wickedly. *Paybacks are a bitch. And I'm the bitch to do it.* She crouched, ready to pounce when the opportunity presented itself. The man wandered closer and closer still, until he was almost directly beneath Jac's overhead position. He was about to take another step, when she sprung like a panther from the branch. The man's head shot up and his cocoa colored eyes widened a fraction of a second before Jac landed on him, knocking the man to the ground.

She didn't give the guide a minute to recover. Jac jumped to her feet. "Time to say goodnight," she hissed, kicking him in the face as hard as she could.

His lip split and his head snapped back, stunned. She reached down and unfastened the holster. Groggy, the man started to rise. Jac backhanded him. Her skin slapped against the bone in his face with a sickening whack. She shook out her fingers, making sure she hadn't broken anything. Her knuckles stung from the contact—punching hurt worse than she'd remembered. Jac pulled the pistols, along with the holster, from his body and fastened them on her hips.

She started to turn away when she spotted her knife sheathed at his side. Jac relieved the guide of her blade and slipped around the tree. She'd made it about twenty yards, when she spotted the guide's tracking partner. Her hand stung, but she couldn't resist getting a tiny bit even with her captors. She snaked around the brush, making her way from tree to tree. Jac took extra care not to step on any twigs or dead leaves. She wanted nothing to impede her attack.

Jac was within a foot of the second guide when she called out. "Hey, looking for me?"

He spun around, reaching for his rifle at the same time. Jac swept her leg out, knocking his knees to the side and sending him instantly to the ground. She followed the move with a series of frontal strikes, leaving the man incapacitated. Jac dusted off her hands and then bounded into the jungle.

Her work here was done.

She raced deeper through the dense canopy, her thoughts straying to her Navy SEAL father.

Dad would be proud, that I haven't forgotten everything he taught me. God rest his soul.

No man Jac had ever encountered lived up to the honor, strength, and pride her father had possessed when he was alive.

Ares's face floated into her mind. She quickly pushed it aside, choosing to ignore the obvious. She patted her guns. They were the only comfort she needed down here, at least until she was able to locate Rachel.

Where are you? She wondered.

Had the scouts been looking for her or something else? Jac knew she lacked a vital piece to this puzzle. Where had Ares come from? He didn't seem to be part of any tribe down here. His skin was different, his eyes, his…well everything about him was — different.

And where did he get those abilities? Jac had seen plenty of weird movies in her time, but those weren't special effects. They were real. Was that why the professor had come back down here? She'd assumed he'd fled to avoid possible prosecution, but that wasn't likely since Jac had been unable to convince anyone back in New York that a crime had actually occurred. Well, anyone but Brigit.

Brigit had decided the whole incident had been written in the stars, including Jac's impending journey to the jungle. Jac shook her head. She loved Brigit, but sometimes the girl was out and out kooky. Her thoughts returned to the professor and his motives.

Jac wasn't sure what they were, but she was damn sure going to find out.

Chapter Six

Ares's fury equaled the great disaster of Pompeii. By the time he'd returned to camp with more food and water, Jac had gone. Had he not proven that she needed him? Had he not convinced her that their bodies were meant to be joined? How could she leave him after all that he'd done for her? Anger surged through him, renewed by his visions of her. Was she laughing at his foolishness?

Ares crushed the fruit in his hand, sending sticky juice oozing over his palm and through his fingers. He sent an energy burst through his body, cleansing it instantly. When he found that little blonde sorceress he'd bind her and drive his cock into her until she was unable to reason.

He made sure to cover any trace of the fire and then proceeded deeper into the jungle. She'd hidden her trail well, but not well enough. After tracking Jac two times before, Ares had learned to look for the signs that she left behind...a crushed fern here, a snapped branch there, just enough clues. Little indications that he knew she was unaware of that alluded to her presence.

Ares had run some distance when he encountered two of the trackers from the red-devil's expedition. They appeared bloodied and bruised a sure indicator that his fierceness had been here earlier. He smiled, feeling his chest swell with pride. She truly was a warrior at heart. The guides Jac had fallen stumbled to their feet, shaking their heads as if to clear them. Ares watched them from the cover of the trees, and then sent out a stunning energy burst, knocking both men off their feet and out of commission for hours, if not days. They would not trouble her further.

The trail zigged and zagged, winding through lianas and vines, over ferns, through cats claw, and around ginger. His woman would pay when he caught up to her. Ares pictured her tied with the jade scarves he'd brought with him, her white skin glistening like a rare pearl under the moonlight as he lapped at her nether lips, bringing her to orgasm time after time. He could almost see her lithe muscles flex as she strained against the confines. Her slim hips bucking as he plunged his tongue into her wet chasm.

He growled. The rumbling sound rippled over his body going straight to his erect cock beneath his loincloth. Ares took a deep breath, scenting the air. Jac's musky perfume flooded his system, drowning him. His rod pushed against the confines of his clothing, demanding her return.

"Soon," he murmured.

* * * * *

Jac stopped to catch her breath. She'd been traveling for hours with no sign of Ares or anyone else for that matter. Jac couldn't believe that there were no trails anywhere. How in the world did anyone make their way through this place? Shouldn't she have spotted a sign that Rachel had been here before? There were always things left behind in the movies. Hell, right now, she'd be happy to have a sign anyone had been here before.

She scrubbed a hand over her face, her palm came back slicked with sweat. If the jungle floor got any hotter, Jac was convinced her blood would boil. The vegetation thickened and she proceeded forward at a slower pace. Her knife wasn't made for slashing at vines. Jac stepped forward, searching for a place to sit and rest when a giant of a man stepped around a tree twenty yards in front of her. Her skin prickled and her heart rate picked up to maddening. She took a step back silently, hoping he hadn't seen her. He wore a loincloth like Ares, but that was where the similarity ended.

Jac inched back once more, right into a snare trap. She shrieked as her feet were yanked out from under her, the knife flew from her hands, and the ground quickly slipped away. Jac twisted from her upside down position like a fish on a line, trying to keep her eyes on the approaching stranger. A smile quirked the corners of his lips as his gaze strayed from her feet to her breasts. Jac relaxed, bringing one hand to her side, until her palm rested on her gun.

He was as fair as Ares was dark and as strikingly handsome. His long blond hair hung to his trim waist like a Viking of old. His eyes were unusual, a rare shade of aqua that Jac had only seen in colored contacts. The man's gaze locked onto her face and he inhaled deeply as if he could pick up her scent from across the distance. Jac raised her arm and smelled her pit. It wasn't exactly roses, but she didn't stink *that* bad.

The giant smiled then, as if he'd read her thoughts. Was this guy from the same tribe as Ares? Not that she knew what that tribe was exactly. If so, why was he so fair? Surely he wasn't as old as Ares, he looked to be no more than twenty-eight.

God now Ares has me believing the three thousand five hundred year old crap.

The man raised his hand in what Jac took as a greeting, but she watched him closely, well as close as she could from her precarious position. She'd seen what Ares could do with his hands, not to mention the rest of his anatomy. The last thing she needed was to find another god-like man. She'd just gotten rid of the first Tarzan.

Her heart clenched at the thought of not seeing Ares again. She chose to ignore it.

Jac didn't think she could pull her gun before he could send one of those funny glowy things at her. His eyes were too intent, watchful, knowing. She felt like a gunslinger from the old west, weighing in who was the faster draw. In the end, Jac eased away from her weapon, deciding diplomacy was probably a better call here. The blond giant visibly relaxed.

"Hello there, big fella." Jac waved, trying to appear calm. "I could use a little help."

The man's smile widened and his eyes glowed. Jac pointed to the weapon.

"I can't cut the rope with my knife on the ground."

His gaze went to her blade and then to her snagged foot. He raised his hand once and his palm began to glow.

She wasn't ready for another one of those energy bursts. Her body clenched, then began to tingle. Her nipples peaked, tightening into marbles beneath her t-shirt. Jac's breathing deepened and her channel flooded in anticipation. She cursed beneath her breath. In a few short hours Ares had trained her body to respond. Damn it, she wasn't like fucking Pavlov's dog, but her body had different ideas as it readied itself for an orgasm. Jac clenched her legs together, fighting the overwhelming sensations.

The burst shot out. There was a loud pop. Birds squawked, taking to flight. The acrid smell of burning fiber assailed her nose. She glanced down, attempting to judge the distance, as the rope smoked and crackled. A second later it snapped. Jac found herself falling. She braced, readying for impact. Moments before striking the jungle floor she was snatched from the air into a pair of waiting arms. The giant had moved with lightning speed to catch her.

He held her cradled against his wide hairless chest. She inhaled. His body had the musky odor of sweat mixed with adrenaline, yet his breathing remained steady and deep. Jac's hand rested on his flat disc-like nipple. His skin felt warm, heated to the touch. His strong heartbeat thumped beneath her fingertips.

Jac pushed herself away, not liking the soothing comfort of his strength. He set her on her feet and took a step back. She ran a trembling hand through her hair, slicking it off her face.

"Thanks for the help."

She wiped her hands on the side of her shorts. It took Jac a moment before she could actually look him in the eye. When she finally did, Jac regretted it. This man looked amazing. His gaze locked to hers, holding her, caressing, challenging. Jac swallowed hard and put some distance between them. His brow cocked in that all too male, arrogant way, but he said nothing.

Jac brushed her clothes off. "I best be on my way." She attempted to smile at the man, but it came out as a grimace.

"Why are you here?"

His questioned surprised Jac. She'd assumed he could speak English like Ares, but even as the thought swept through her mind, Jac hadn't considered the strange response her body would have to his deep voice. *What was it about the men down here?* Jac gathered herself up to her full height. She tilted her head to look at the blond giant's eyes.

"And you are…" She held out her hand.

He glanced to her hand, then back to her face. "I'm Coridan Antares."

She dropped her hand to her side. "It's nice to meet you Coridan Antares." She nodded and pointed around them. "Have you been wandering around these parts for a while?"

He looked puzzled.

"Are you from here?" Jac restated.

"This is my home, if that 'tis what you ask." He nodded.

Jac thought about her friend and figured what the hell. It couldn't hurt to ask. "You wouldn't happen to know where I can find a friend of mine; she's about five foot two, dark wavy hair, answers to the name Rachel Evans?"

The man's brows furrowed. "You search for Queen Rachel?"

Jac's mouth dropped open. Surely she'd heard him wrong. Had he called Rachel, Queen? It only took her a moment to recover. She was so happy the stranger knew Rachel she didn't care what he called her, as long as he took her to Rachel this instant.

"Do you know where I can find her?"

The man nodded in the affirmative.

Jac's hands shook so badly she put them behind her back. "Can you tell me, or better yet, take me to her?"

"If that is your wish." The man stepped forward. He towered over Jac, like Ares.

She forced herself to hold her ground. The man's eyes wandered over Jac's legs, along her body, resting on her breasts, before returning to her face. His smile devastated her insides. He took another deep breath and the grin slipped from his face, like wet paint sliding down a wall.

"I see you have met Ares." It wasn't a question.

Jac shifted, her discomfort growing. She didn't like the way the man's eyes narrowed at the mention of Ares's name. He inhaled again. The next thought hit Jac in the gut. He could smell Ares on her. Jac didn't even want to consider that far too humiliating possibility. It had to be her imagination, anything else was unacceptable.

She considered the picture she must present, disheveled, flushed, lips swollen, like she'd been having mind-blowing sex all night. The guy didn't have to be a mind reader after all. Coridan scowled. Maybe Ares had been as much of a pain in the ass to this guy, as he'd been to her. Right now, Jac needed this man if she hoped to find Rachel.

So she did what Jac did best. She smiled and stepped closer into the man's personal space, her lashes lowered to half mast when she held out her hand again to introduce herself. "Forgive my rudeness. My name is Jaclyn Ward, but you can call me Jac."

His palm enveloped hers. "It 'tis my pleasure, Jac."

Coridan dropped to his knees and kissed her nipples through her shirt, before Jac realized what he was doing. His firm lips pressed against one, allowing the pressure to build, and then the other. He flicked his tongue over the latter and gently nipped, leaving a trace of moisture behind. The buds beaded instantly against his mouth's assail. All Jac could do was gape. Coridan smiled then rose to his feet.

"Why did you do that?"

He looked confused. "'Tis proper Atlantean greeting."

"Of course it is, sunshine. I don't even know why I asked." Jac made no attempt to hide her sarcasm.

His lips kicked up at the sides. "Let me take you to your friend." He grabbed Jac's hand as if she were a child, to lead her through the jungle.

She steadied her voice as they hiked along. "Has Ares ever met Rachel?"

Coridan nodded. "He prepared her the day of the mating ceremony."

"Prepared?" Jac yanked her hand from his and swallowed down her anger. "Forget it, I don't want to know." She needed the truth, but it wouldn't help her cause if she sounded like a jealous female. "Let me get this straight, Ares knows how to get back to the village, where Rachel is located?"

Coridan looked at Jac as if she were dense. "Of course."

That no good, son-of-a-bitch has been lying to me the whole time.

Jac recalled the conversation she'd had with Ares. No not lying, *deceiving*, this was just as bad in her book. Jac clenched her fists so tight she could almost feel her skin tear. A red haze clouded her vision. If she ever saw Ares again, she'd kick is tight ass all the way to Brooklyn.

Jac stared at Coridan's corded back for the next several hours afraid to speak for fear her anger would come raging out. He was so much like Ares, yet so different. While Ares was gruff and rough around the edges, with the most amazing pair of jade colored eyes, Coridan seemed amiable, as if he gone out of his way to be pleasant. He held branches so that she could pass. He retrieved water for her when she indicated she thirsted. Picked her up when she slipped, unable to make it over a five foot high log.

Damn but all his chivalry was getting on her nerves.

"So how do you know Ares?" She choked on his name.

Coridan shot her a glance over his shoulder, but kept walking. "He is part of my tribe."

Jac gritted her teeth. She'd figured as much. She couldn't believe she was about to ask this. "Are you part of the Atlanteans?"

He nodded again.

Jac shook her head. It was such a pity. Coridan and Ares were so handsome, yet so utterly insane. "Is he a friend of yours?"

She caught a slight smile at the question. "I wouldn't say that."

Jac's brow rose. "An enemy?"

"It is difficult for me to describe our relationship." Coridan laughed. "I guess the best word I could use would be challenged."

Jac joined in with Coridan's laughter. She could definitely see Ares and Coridan having a 'challenged' relationship. In the short time she'd been around Ares, she'd found him quite challenging. Her heart thudded at the thought of Ares. *I do not miss him.*

She latched onto Coridan's words. "That's a kind way of saying he's a pain in the ass."

Coridan shot her an amused look. "So why did you join with him?"

Jac stopped dead, almost tripping, a liana snapping beneath her boot heel. She could feel heat rising in her face. The muggy perfumed air refused to give her a breath. How much did she want to tell this man? How much should she tell him? It really wasn't any of his business what she and Ares had shared.

Coridan turned back and approached her. "Forgive me." He bowed his head. "I have upset you and that was not my intention."

"It's all right." She shifted uncomfortably. "No harm done."

"I noticed his scent on you and assumed you had chosen to become his mate." His jaw locked.

Jac shook her head. "Well think again, bucko. I may have *joined* with him, but I'm not anyone's mate." She poked Coridan in the chest. "Got it?"

He nodded and rubbed the spot she'd touched, but Coridan looked way too pleased for Jac's peace of mind. She didn't know what he was thinking, but he could stop it right now.

"I'm looking for my friend." Jac didn't know why she felt the need to explain herself. Normally, she didn't get defensive. She continued walking, Coridan met her stride. "As soon as I find her, we'll get the hell out of here, and out of everyone's hair." Jac glanced to the man beside her.

For a second Coridan's face shifted to a hard unreadable mask, but he said nothing.

Her gut clenched. Something wasn't right here. He wasn't telling her everything. "Rachel's okay, isn't she?" Jac put her hand out to stop him.

Coridan stilled. "The Queen is well. Her babe develops quickly. In another week it will have strength enough to be able to operate the transport from within her womb." His eyes flashed again, but this time in what looked like anticipation.

"Did you say b-baby?" Jac sputtered. She couldn't seem to catch her breath. The sound of the creatures in the jungle faded until all she heard was her heart as it stampeded in her ears.

"Are you—?"

"I'll be fine," Jac cut him off and waved him away. She simply needed a second to let everything sink in. Then she'd be able to formulate a plan. Yeah, that's what she needed, a new plan. Rachel was pregnant. Jac swayed and then shot Coridan a quick look, her gaze narrowing to slivers of ice. "Who's the father?"

Please don't say Ares. The thought swept through her mind before she could stop it. Her stomach threatened to rebel.

"'Tis not Ares."

Ares was an obvious guess on Coridan's part considering their earlier conversation. Jac let out the breath she wasn't aware she held. Relief surged through her veins. "W-who's the father?"

"Our King, Eros."

Jac weighed his words. "No wonder you call her Queen."

That made sense in a surreal kind of Alice in Wonderland sort of world. Rachel had conceived with a King. Her unborn child would soon be able to operate a transport. Transport? What in the hell is a transport if an unborn baby can operate it? Jac's head began to pound harder. They were all insane. None of this Star Trek shit made sense. She needed to stick to the facts. The truth never let her down. It held no real surprises. If Jac could do that, then everything would be all right.

It had to be.

Rachel couldn't be happy down here with these delusional people, who believed they were Atlanteans' and several thousand years old. "No way," Jac said aloud.

If Rachel was pregnant and happy, then Jac had come all this way for nothing. The next thought almost knocked her legs out from under her. *What if I'm pregnant?* Jac swallowed hard and refused to consider that possibility. It was unthinkable.

She tossed her hair back and lifted her chin in challenge. Conflict was safe, familiar, and she needed the tension desperately. "So do you think you're over three thousand years old, too?"

Coridan threw his head back and laughed. "I see Ares is showing his age." He shook his head, sending blond hair over his broad shoulders. "I am not *that* old."

"I didn't think so." Jac bit her bottom lip.

"Ares has always boasted of his accomplishments." Coridan's lips pulled tight over his teeth.

Jac watched him. Envy, jealousy, and something else swam in his blue depths. There was definitely no love lost between the two men. He vented and she had the sudden urge to do the same.

"He's the most arrogant man I've ever met," she added.

Coridan stopped and turned to Jac, his blue gaze serious as he scanned her face. "You could always teach him a lesson," he said hesitantly.

She didn't like the look in Coridan's eyes, but Jac figured she'd hear him out. After all, Ares could stand to be brought down a peg or two. "What kind?"

Coridan swallowed and he licked his full lips. "'Tis your right to not accept his proposed mating, if a challenge is set forth."

Jac snorted, throwing her arms in the air. "Who in their right mind would challenge Ares?"

His expression did not waver. "Me."

"Are you serious?" Jac placed her hands on her hips. "Why, what's in it for you?"

Coridan clenched and unclenched his hands. "I too, would like to see Ares bow to defeat, just once."

Jac ran her fingers through her short hair. "What exactly would have to happen?"

"I would challenge Ares for the right to mate with you."

Jac's gaped, a second before her anger returned. "You've got to be kidding me! Didn't I just tell you I wasn't interested in having a mate?" She shook her head and rolled her eyes. "Did you listen to a word I had to say?"

Coridan waited for her to finish, before speaking. "I heard your words. I would not take you to mate, unless you allowed it." His eyes wandered to her breasts, then lower. He didn't even try to hide his hunger. "I could make it mutually beneficial for the both of us."

Jac's eyes narrowed and she fought the urge to cross her arms over her chest. She wasn't about to give him the satisfaction of seeing her squirm. Any other time if a man looking like Coridan had propositioned her, she would have jumped at the chance to be with him. But now, after all that had happened between her and Ares, it wasn't appealing. It didn't *feel* right.

Damn it. She had to snap out of this. *Get over it, Jac.* She owed no loyalty to anyone but Rachel. Coridan stood before her, offering an opportunity to change her circumstances and Jac wasn't going to be a fool and pass it by. She steadied her voice. "Beneficial, how?"

Coridan held his hands out as if showing he had nothing to hide. "I would get to see Ares defeated and you could return to your people in the end, if that is what you truly wanted."

"That's all? You wouldn't want a little extra?" Jac arched a brow. It sounded too good to be true, there had to be a catch.

He cleared his throat. "I do not deny that I find you pleasing and would love to sink my rod into your channel."

Coridan glanced down and Jac followed his gaze. She could see his hard-on from beneath his loincloth. *Great.* These damn men were too virile for their own good. Her gaze shot back to his face.

"What about Rachel?"

Coridan blew out a heavy breath. "Queen Rachel would have to make her own decision on whether to remain with Eros or return with you."

Jac gulped. She was afraid he would say that. Her heart hurt thinking about leaving Rachel behind. If Eros looked anything like Ares and Coridan then Jac was in big trouble. To stay or go wouldn't be a tough decision if Rachel carried Eros's baby.

Being forever practical, Jac weighed the odds. She had better stick with Coridan for the time being, he was biddable and could be controlled. Ares on the other hand was dangerous, a wildcard who popped up out of nowhere, completely unpredictable. And let's not forget, savagely sexy, completely dominant, and way too tempting.

She took a deep breath. Yep, it was better to go with Coridan's plan. She'd at least see Rachel again and get in a little payback on Ares for his high handed ways. Her heart sank. It was best not to think about her jade-eyed Tarzan. He was probably tracking her right now and by the time he caught up, Ares would be pissed. She shuddered and her clit ached when she considered what kind of punishment he would come up with.

* * * * *

Ares picked up Jac's scent along with an all too familiar one. The shock caused him to slow. He clamped his teeth together to the point of pain and sniffed the air once again. Rage bubbled beneath the surface as he registered Coridan's male musk. He'd made no mistake. Coridan had found Jac and they headed toward the village. The muscles in Ares's body tightened. He was convinced that they'd snap.

Ares came upon the remnant of the snare. Had Coridan stumbled upon Jac or had he trapped her? What was he doing so far away from the village?

Ares scanned the area, searching for any signs that they might have joined. His heart slammed so hard in his chest, it was nigh unto bursting. How could Jac betray him like that? Had he not shown her of his feelings? Pain ripped through Ares, knocking the breath from his lungs. If he could get his hands on Coridan right now, he'd kill him. There was no doubt in his mind.

He raised his hand and sent out an energy burst. A tree exploded thirty yards from where he stood. Monkeys screamed and leapt to nearby branches as bits of wood fell to the ground. Ares raised his fists to the sky and roared. Anguish from deep in his core, bellowed out, spewing to the heavens.

His mighty body shook and his vision blurred. He wiped a palm across his face. It came away with wetness. Ares stared at the moisture—entranced. Never in all the years of his existence had he ever shed a single tear. Jac did not deserve his tears, nor did she deserve his love. But even as the wayward thoughts trickled through his tormented mind, Ares knew he'd fight with his last breath to get her back. He could have no other.

Jac was his…only his, and she had held his heart from the moment he'd set eyes upon her.

Chapter Seven

At dusk, Jac and Coridan arrived at his village. The last of the sun's rays crept behind the cover of the trees leaving everything in gray shadow. Jac couldn't believe it. Blonde, Aryan looking people with curious aqua eyes watched them. The group gathered in the center of the encampment, around a huge fire. No one came forward in greeting—their expressions were of shock and surprise.

Jac held her head high and met all their gazes. She was about to stop Coridan when she heard a scream. All heads turned in the direction of the sound. A small brown haired woman pushed past the people until she stood in front of the group, facing Jac and Coridan.

"Jac! You're really here," she shouted and rushed forward, stopping short as if she couldn't believe her eyes.

Shock slammed into Jac. Her mouse of a friend, Rachel, had transformed into the goddess Jac always knew she could be. Her long brown hair hung loose, falling down her back like an enchanted fairy. She was bare from the waist up, with only two gold hoops accenting her nipples. Jac shook her head. Surely her eyes deceived her. Rachel wore a long sheer, aqua colored skirt low on her full hips. Unbidden tears sprang to Jac's eyes and she quickly brushed them away. Rachel reached her and threw her arms around Jac's neck.

"I've missed you so much," tears streamed down Rachel's face.

"You didn't think you'd get rid of me that easily, did you?"

"How's Brigit?"

"Fine, but really worried about you," Jac laughed, but the sound was pained. "Of course, not so worried that she'd skip

Conlunar, you know Brigit. All I have to say is she better water my poor plants while I'm gone."

Rachel giggled, pulling back from the hug, a smile beaming across her face. "You and your urban jungle." She shook her head. "I can't believe you're really here." Rachel bit her lip, her chocolate eyes sparkling with moisture in the fading light. "I didn't mean to worry you guys."

"Yeah, well…" Jac shrugged. "I hear you're going to be a momma?"

Rachel practically glowed. "You heard right. Can you believe it?"

Jac swallowed the lump in her throat and pasted a smile on her face. *No she couldn't believe it. But she'd pretend like she could.* "That's wonderful. I'm happy for you." And she truly was happy for Rachel. It was the whole situation she found a little hard to accept.

Rachel frowned. "Where's Ares?"

Jac opened her mouth to answer, when Ares stepped from the jungle like a sleek panther. His jade eyes flared with fire as he looked from Coridan back to her. *Yep, he was definitely pissed.*

"Speak of the devil," Jac whispered loud enough for Rachel to hear.

Rachel stared wide-eyed at Ares. "What happened?"

"My Queen," Ares approached and dropped to his knees before Rachel, quickly kissing her left and right nipple, then just as swiftly rose. A wave of jealousy rushed through Jac, one she instantly crushed.

Rachel's brows furrowed. "Jac are you going to tell me what's going on?"

Jac glanced at Ares, her eyes boring holes into him, and then answered her friend. "There's nothing to tell." She saw a tic begin in his jaw as he squared his shoulders to face her.

With speed that left her blinking, Ares reached out and grasped Jac's upper arms. "We need to speak." He started to pull her away from the crowd, when Coridan stepped forward.

"Unhand, Jac," Coridan bit out, a warning flashing in his aqua eyes.

Ares's body tensed and then went deathly still. His gaze swung around to face the warrior, his eyes narrowed, glaring. His lips thinned until his teeth bared. Jac felt the tremor in Ares's fingertips as he fought for control. He took a deep breath and pulled Jac behind him. One hand released her, while the other slid from her arm, shackling her wrist.

"You dare challenge me for my mate?" Ares's voice dropped low, menacing, deadly.

"You have not officially gone through the mating ceremony," Coridan spat. The muscles in his arms flexed and he fisted his hands as if fighting for control. "Ask Jac, who she chooses to lay with in the bed furs."

Have you joined with Coridan? the whispered question in her head smoldered with anger and...*hurt?*

"What? No!" Jac trembled beneath Ares's grip, rage bubbling over.

How dare they fight over her like a couple of stupid bulls in rut? His thumb stroked back and forth along her pulse, whether to soothe or inflame, she couldn't be sure. Jac's heart leapt, sending awareness racing through her body. He brushed her again. With all that had occurred, somehow she knew Ares tried to comfort her.

Unfortunately her reaction to that simple touch also conveyed how much she still wanted him.

"Damn you," Jac muttered under her breath. "Why can't you just let me go?"

Ares flinched. *You wish to go with Coridan?* He asked in her mind, turning to face her.

No, was Jac's first thought, but she wasn't about to tell Ares that. She thought about telling him yes, but that would be a lie, and considering his current mood it wasn't a good idea. "I don't want either of you," she ground out, trying to pull her hand from his.

Jac stared at her jade-eyed warrior waiting for a reaction to her words, anything that would indicate he'd heard her and understood. Instead, he appeared relaxed, almost relieved as he rubbed her hand once more. Jac tensed, surely he was smart enough to take her seriously. He arched a brow and then turned his attention back to his rival, while Jac struggled to escape from his grasp.

"I ask again, are you challenging me, Coridan Antares?"

Coridan stepped forward. Jac stared at the trees for a moment and counted to ten. They had about five seconds to knock this shit off or she would throttle them both. This wasn't at all like Coridan had described. It seemed more dangerous, possibly life threatening, instead of a comeuppance.

Rachel's eyes were the size of saucers when she stepped around Ares. She rubbed her hands along her arms. A huge blond man gracefully stepped from the crowd, strength, power, and authority rolled off him in waves.

Jac glanced from him to Rachel and back. Without a doubt, this had to be Eros. His face was such chiseled perfection that he could almost be called pretty, in a masculine sort of way. He looked from Ares to Coridan, then Jac. His gaze narrowed, censuring, but he said nothing for a moment.

A beautiful woman with long flowing hair moved to his side. She was a dead ringer for a Baywatch babe. She held up her hands to calm the murmuring crowd. "A challenge has been put forth for the privilege of mating with this woman." Her elegant hand swept to Jac.

Jac glared and stepped forward to refute the woman's words. Ares stopped her, his eyes as sharp as fiery jade, sending a warning as clear as if he'd actually spoken.

The woman's gaze locked onto Jac, freezing her in place. "Although it has been many, many years since a challenge has been called, the rules are clear. Warriors, you'll have a day or so to prepare. Tomorrow I will announce the tasks to be achieved. The first to complete the challenge wins." Her gaze swept Jac's length. "And while the competition is taking place, there shall be no self healing. If a warrior is found to have healed himself, he'll be immediately disqualified from the challenge."

"Who is that?" Jac asked Rachel under her breath.

"She's the tribe's seer. Her name is Ariel," Rachel whispered.

Jac watched the gorgeous woman make eye contact with Coridan and then Ares. She lingered on Ares a little longer than Jac cared for, taking in his wide chest and muscled legs, pausing at the front of his loincloth long enough to be considered inappropriate.

The woman's lips quirked at the corner, accenting her natural sensuality, and then her gaze once again met Jac's. She had seen that look from women before. The seer sized her up. Jac squared her shoulders and defiantly stared across the clearing at the woman. If the seer thought she would intimidate her, she had another think coming. Ariel laughed, caressing Ares once more with her gaze, and then walked to the nearest hut, slipping inside.

"What does the bitch think is so funny?" Jac turned to Rachel.

"You never know with Ariel. She's got a warped sense of humor." Rachel's eyes darted to the hut door and back, concern marring her features. "You really don't want to fuck with her."

Jac arched a brow at her last words. "If she knows what's good for her, she won't fuck with me."

Rachel shrugged and attempted to hide her smile by glancing away. "This ought to be interesting."

The crowd started to disperse. Ares released Jac after Coridan left, then turned to face her. "You will be sorry for all the trouble you are causing me, my fierceness." His molten jade eyes captured hers, burning, promising a payback she would not soon forget.

Jac fought the strange urge to flee. She wasn't a coward and she never backed down from a direct attempt at intimidation, but there was no mistaking the cold lump forming in her stomach. "I told you." She cleared her throat. "I'm no one's mate."

Ares's eyes flashed again. "We shall see." Then he stalked into the jungle, leaving Jac with Rachel.

The King approached. Rachel grabbed him and pulled him forward. "I'd like you to meet my husband Eros."

Jac's gut clenched. It was worse than she thought. Not only had Rachel gotten pregnant, she'd somehow managed to marry this man. Jac's mind raced, convinced the agreement wouldn't hold up in a court of law. You needed special permission when you married in another country and she was positive Rachel hadn't gotten the paperwork. So there was hope...but a baby would certainly complicate matters.

Her arms felt like lead, stiff, heavy, and unyielding. "It's nice to meet you. I'm Jac."

Eros seemed to be fighting a smile as Jac's mind surged from one subject to another. He dropped to his knees and greeted her in traditional Atlantean fashion. Jac gaped and shot a look at Rachel, waiting to see her friend's reaction to her husband's actions. Rachel shrugged and pulled a face. Jac shook her head. Rachel really had changed in the short time she'd been down here. Eros rose and held out his hand. Jac shook it quickly and released him.

These people were outrageously crazy, even for her. This was too much. Challenges, Atlanteans, seers, and mating. Jac had to get the hell out of here before her sanity scooted off with the rest of these loons. She grabbed Rachel.

"If you'll excuse us." Jac glanced at Eros. "I need to have a word with my friend."

Jac tugged Rachel along, heading for god only knows where. She needed some peace, some distance. She needed New York.

Rachel pulled her hand from Jac's. "I know just the place we can go." She walked to the fire and picked up a small burning log to use as a torch and guided Jac down a well worn trail, leading to a small stream. Flowers scented the air. A gentle wind tugged at their hair. The soft murmuring of the current as it washed over the rocks soothed Jac's nerves—a little. When they reached the banks, Rachel stopped and stuck the log in the mud so that it would remain upright.

"Are you going to tell me what in the hell is going on here?" Jac's voice cracked. "Is this a camp for escaped mental patients who just happen to be gorgeous?" She shook her head. "Because the crap I've been hearing can't possibly be true."

Rachel crossed her arms over her chest. "I'm not sure where to begin."

Jac began to pace. All the nervous energy from the altercation flooded her muscles until they practically jerked with spasms. She couldn't take much more of this.

Rachel stilled Jac's movements. "I need to sit down, do you mind?"

Jac glanced to Rachel's stomach. "Sorry." She closed her eyes for a second and took a deep breath. She sat next to Rachel on the soft grasses lining the shore. The air smelled fresh along the stream and felt a tad cooler, when the slight breeze didn't shift the smoke from the burning log in their direction. At this point, Jac welcomed anything that would add to comfort. "Why don't you start with that lovely message you left me on my answering machine. It terrified me and when I played it for Brigit, she threw up."

Rachel grimaced. "God, I really regret having left that message." She frowned. "I tried to call you back, but the phone doesn't work in here."

"Shocker." Jac's gaze narrowed. "Where is here exactly?"

"We're in the heart of the electromagnetic field." Rachel gestured around her. "You remember me telling you and Brigit about it?"

"I recall you said you wanted to explore it and bring back your discovery so that you could get your much deserved promotion." Jac arched a brow.

Rachel rolled her eyes. "Yeah, that was the plan in the beginning…"

Jac's chest squeezed, pushing out the air in her lungs as the tension coursed through her. "And now?"

Rachel's brown eyes met hers. They seemed to be searching for something in Jac's face. "Things have developed that I hadn't anticipated."

"Like?" Jac drew the word out.

Rachel smiled. "Like I'm married and I'm going to have a baby."

Jac's lips thinned. "Congratulations."

Shadows filled Rachel's eyes as she answered, "Thanks."

Jac ran a hand through her hair. "That doesn't explain what happened down here."

"The professor sacrificed me." Rachel's hands trembled and balled up into tight little fists. "If it wasn't for Eros, I'd be dead."

Anger burned through Jac quicker than a spark on dried brush. "The bastard tried to pull the same shit on me, except he's gotten braver. This time he's out to make his problems go away permanently."

Rachel gasped. Her eyes roamed over Jac, as though making sure she was okay.

"I'm fine, "Jac said waving the worry away. "I escaped, with a little help."

Relief etched Rachel's features. "Who helped?"

Jac didn't answer.

"Jaaac," she prompted, her mouth quirking at the corners. "Who?"

"That dark, muscled, jade-eyed jerk called Ares."

Rachel burst out laughing. "So you *do* like him."

Jac stood up, her hands planted firmly on her hips. "I didn't say that."

Rachel shook her head, sending curls falling over her shoulders. "You didn't have to. The sparks were flying off you two every time your eyes met."

"So the sex was good." She shrugged. "Sue me." Jac looked away not wanting to meet Rachel's knowing eyes.

Rachel reached up and clasped Jac's hand, drawing her gaze back, and then rose. "You forget I know you too well. If it was only sex, you wouldn't bat an eye. You'd immediately tell me all about your latest conquest, in detail." She smoothed her skirt. "You also wouldn't be so mad."

"These people are crazy. Don't you understand?" Jac pleaded with Rachel. "They think they're thousands of years old. It's a classic example of mass delusion." Jac looked at Rachel, letting the fear she felt inside show on her face. "I don't want you here when this turns out to be some suicidal cult."

Rachel's expression softened. "I know what I'm about to say to you is going to sound completely insane. I thought the same thing when Eros explained the tribe's situation to me, but every word is true."

"Oh, Rach, not you, too." Jac shook her head and backed away. "Did they give you something strange to drink? That's how it starts."

Rachel balked. "Jaclyn Ward, when have I ever done anything crazy, out there, otherwise insane?" Rachel's hand slapped down on her thigh.

"Other than going on this godforsaken expedition?" Jac clenched her teeth and thought about it for a second. "Never."

"That's right. Never. So what makes you think I've gone off the deep end now?"

Jac tilted her chin and stared down at her. "It could be some kind of fever?"

Rachel snorted and rolled her eyes. "If you were around Ares for any length of time, then I'm sure you've seen some strange things—"

"That I'm sure can be explained logically."

"Try." Rachel arched a brow in challenge.

Jac threw her arms up in the air. "I don't know what's real anymore."

Rachel stepped forward and hugged her. "An open mind is a good start," she whispered in Jac's ear. "Now tell me, what do you *really* think of Ares?" She pulled back, her chocolate colored eyes sparkling in the fading firelight.

Jac began to pace again. "I think he's a sex god," she paused. "Who also happens to be a royal pain in the ass."

Rachel giggled.

* * * * *

Ares's anger raged deep. In three thousand years there had never been a challenge set forth for a mate. Ariel had foretold Jac's arrival. There had been no mention of a challenge for the right to mate with her. He'd already joined with her. He slammed his fist against the table, knocking a cup from its surface. He feared not of others hearing him, since his hut lay several hundred yards from the village. He'd always preferred being away from the others, giving himself space, but now he felt eons from Jac.

His heart clenched at the thought of his blonde demon lying with Coridan, even though he knew she had not. She could have stepped forward expressing her acceptance of Ares's claim, yet she chose to remain silent behind him. Had he misjudged her emotions? Nay! He knew his fierceness better than she knew herself. Jac was torturing him, tormenting him to no end. She knew not that she played with fire. And if she did, she mustn't realize how dangerous it was or else she wouldn't dare.

Ares rose from his chair and walked to a small hidden compartment in his wall, his lithe muscles tensing, ready to spring at any second. He pulled out a container holding a thick green liquid. The odor of melons and chocolate filled the air. He grabbed a cup beside the liquid and filled it to the top. He started to return to the table when he sensed Eros's approach. He turned and picked up another glass, filling it also, then returned the container to its place.

Enter, my King.

A smile touched Eros's lips as he came through the hide covered door, his eyes sparkling in the light of Ares's fire pot. Ares handed one of the glasses to Eros then returned to his seat. Eros raised the glass in a toast and then took a drink. He joined Ares at the table taking the seat across from him. For a few minutes they drank in silence, each giving the other time to gather their thoughts.

I take it there was trouble on the journey here. Eros didn't try to hide his amusement.

Ares's gaze met Eros's, then returned to his glass. *Nothing I cannot handle.*

It appears as if this woman-taming is a little more difficult than you anticipated.

Ares shrugged. *I find no humor in the situation. It's simple. Jac is mine.*

Eros laughed aloud. Ares's gaze locked to his, green clashing with blue.

Eros stifled his humor. "Forgive me, my friend, but after the little support you gave me during my trials with our Queen, I decided a moment of return was called for." He smiled wide, clapping his hand on Ares's shoulder, and then released him.

Ares couldn't help but answer his smile. He nodded, conceding to Eros's point, allowing the moment to lighten his heart as he recalled the few nights Eros had to leave the Queen's side with his nether regions in great discomfort. Now that the loincloth was on the other man, it wasn't quite so funny. Ares took another drink, his face once again hardening into unforgiving lines.

"What am I to do about the challenge?"

The smile left Eros's face. "Coridan was a fool to put forth such a thing. He cannot possibly win." He paused. "Ariel will state the challenge tomorrow and you both will have a week to prepare. Our rules are clear. You must accept or lose Jac."

"I will not lose what is mine." Ares's body stiffened, coiled. "I have claimed her as was my right. I've performed the healing ceremony on her. She has lain beneath me, writhing, as I slid into her body, again and again."

Eros released his breath, shifting uneasily in his chair. "Does Coridan know this?"

Ares nodded. "He must, my scent was all over her, there could be no mistaking what had occurred. I made sure I left my mark upon her creamy skin."

Eros's jaw hardened. "The only way he could claim her then is if he won the challenge and she *chose* to join him." He rolled his shoulders. "Do you think Jac would do that?"

Ares's eyes sparked, anger and pain clouding his voice. "I think Jac would do anything to avoid the feelings that I stir within her." He took another drink, then slammed the glass down. "She fears emotions."

"Does she not know what that would do to your name? Your family line?" Eros set his cup on the table.

Ares ran a hand through his long black hair, shaking his head. "She knows not of our ways. She wants nothing more than to escape this place...and me," he added softly.

Eros rose, his face a mask, concealing the emotions so close to the surface. "She will have to learn our ways. Our Queen did and so shall Jac. There will be no escaping her fate." With that said, Eros walked to the door. "Be well, my friend," he tossed over his shoulder, then exited.

Ares picked up the cup and stared at the green liquid, swirling it around and around. His body ached for Jac, called out and cried for her. His cock was so hard beneath his loincloth that he was sure it would burst before he got to thrust inside her warm walls once more. He finished the contents of the glass, then returned to the compartment where he kept the bottle, pulling it out as he returned to the table. Without Jac's company, it would be a very long night.

Chapter Eight

Jac slept like shit in the little hut Rachel had shoved her in last night. Sunlight splashed through the window, illuminating all the dust mites floating in the air. Jac shoved her hair out of her face and rose off the soft bed of hides she'd been laying on. Naked, she stretched and then recalled the previous night. She'd done nothing but dream of Ares's muscled body over her, under her, surrounding her. He hadn't come to her during the night and in all honesty, it pissed her off. His threat of payback rang in her ears, haunting her thoughts, scattering her mind. Who did he think he was making demands…her father?

In a flash she was twenty-two again, standing in her parent's kitchen, her father sprawled on the floor, his hand clutching his chest. He wasn't breathing. She'd done CPR until the paramedics had arrived, but it wasn't enough to save the man she'd always considered invincible.

Her father's face blurred behind the tears she'd kept buried so deep inside. Jac swiped a hand across her cheeks, wiping away all evidence of weakness. Her father had been a decorated Navy SEAL. He'd taught her how to swim, fight, and survive in harsh environments. He would have had her drop and give him fifty if he could see her crying now.

'Soldiers don't cry' he'd said. Jac sniffed a couple of times and got dressed. At times Ares reminded her so much of her old man it was frightening. Hell, the two would probably have hit it off. But her father had been in the ground for ten years now. Heart attack wasn't the way a SEAL was supposed to die.

When she finished dressing, Jac pushed the hide away from the door and walked straight into Ares's massive chest. The shock was like hitting a concrete wall. His hands closed over her waist to keep her from falling back. Warmth seeped through his fingertips into her back, tickling her spine. Her awareness of him was sharp, razor-like, and way too uncomfortable first thing in the morning. Jac shook her head a bit dazed, and pulled away.

Her chin shot up. "What are you doing here?"

He released her and crossed his arms, his lips quirking up at the corners. "I've come to escort you to the gathering area. Ariel is about to announce the requirements for the challenge."

She shrugged. "It doesn't concern me."

His brow arched and he tilted his head until he held her eyes. Ares crowded her with his big frame, backing her into the hut, surrounding her, until escape from the small room became impossible. "It most certainly does concern you." He slashed his hand through the air. "It is because of you this is to occur. I will not have what is mine taken from me."

She held up her hands to stop him from getting any closer. Jac could barely think. "You sound like a spoiled child angry over not getting his way. Don't be such a cry baby about it."

Ares's gaze narrowed. "Warriors do not cry."

Jac sucked in a breath as if she'd been punched. The words were so familiar, yet different. She steadied the emotion, racing across her face. It was a coincidence. His words didn't mean a thing. Her heart squeezed in her chest, then thudded heavily.

She pointed to the door. "Get on with it then."

Ares stared at her for a moment, as if to say something, then gave a quick nod instead. He moved to her side and grabbed her hand, wrapping it around his thick forearm, like homecoming night when the school announced the names of the year's court. Ares led Jac out of the hut and down a wide branch to the basket Rachel had used last night to bring her here.

She stepped in before he could help her, trying to put as much distance between them in the confined space as possible. It didn't stop her awareness of him for a second. Jac could still feel the heat emanating off his body from across the basket, sexuality, power, and strength oozing from his pores.

Jac took a deep breath and held it. Ares glanced down at the front of her t-shirt and her nipples poked out from beneath the thin material, responding to his intent gaze. The air crackled with tension, as if the slightest spark would send them both up in flames.

She watched Ares from beneath lowered lashes. His body was a marvel to behold. Solid muscles rippled like a god as he moved. He had a cock to die for hidden under his loincloth. Unconsciously Jac licked her lips as she recalled his thick length slipping inside her. Her breasts ached and she felt moisture dampen her thong.

Ares tensed, his eyes following her tongue's motion. Her thoughts were driving him insane. He wanted nothing more than to lay her on the floor of the basket and bury himself in her velvet walls. Her body wanted him as much as his needed her. Maybe by winning this challenge, Jac would realize the depth of his emotions...but he doubted it. She was not swayed by acts of strength and cunning. Those things only brought out her fiery temper, the shield she so readily wore to protect her tender heart.

He had to figure out a way around her defenses. Ares had come up with many plans, but none seemed suited for his quest. It required more thought. The basket came to a halt on the jungle floor, jarring him back from his musings.

Sunlight dappled the ground through the leaves of the trees. Coridan stood loose limbed, already positioned to the side of the seer. Ariel's left side remained vacant, waiting for Ares. He stepped out of the basket, helping Jac before she could protest. Her eyes hardened, flashing blue ice, but she didn't push him away. He fought the urge to chuckle. They were so much alike.

They walked to the gathering group. Rachel and Eros stood off to the side to witness the proceedings. Ariel's attention seemed unduly occupied by Coridan, Ares noted, before taking his place by the seer. Jac's expression burned hot when Ariel placed her hand on Ares's wrist. He swallowed, concentrating on keeping the elation from his face. It would only harden Jac's resolve to avoid him.

His other half stood eight feet away, a scowl on her face, arms crossed over her chest, with one hip cocked out to the side, her stubborn chin held high, daring anyone to say anything to her.

Ariel released Ares and Coridan, stepping away in the process. "The challenge is as follows. The first warrior to gather a pound of gold and traverse the river, bring down a mighty anaconda, and remain standing after an energy battle will be considered victorious." She paused. "And remember, no healing."

At the mention of the river, Coridan's face drained of color. Jac wouldn't have noticed, if she hadn't have been watching so closely. The crowd's attention riveted on the seer.

Energy battle...Jac blinked, as Ariel's words sunk in. "What in the hell is an energy battle?" she didn't bother to hide the venom in her voice.

All eyes turned to Jac. She glared at the group, tired of this macho bullshit and more than a little scared for Ares's safety, not that she was about to admit that any time soon. She already had enough problems.

Ariel stepped forward, her lips curled at the ends. "An energy battle is when two warriors face each other and try to injure the other until one concedes."

Jac's heart slammed in her chest. "Does it end in death?"

The seer's smile widened. "It can, but that has not occurred for several thousand years, so 'tis unlikely." Ariel turned away and faced the men.

Her words did nothing to calm Jac's worry. If anything it made it worse. Jac fisted her hands at her side. She had to do something to stop this crap before someone got hurt.

Someone like Ares.

"Why can't they heal themselves?" she grit out.

Ariel's gaze narrowed. "To do so forfeits the competition."

"So if they're injured…"

"Then they'll have to deal with the pain."

The tension in Jac's shoulders spun into overload. One more thing and she'd snap, not that she had done a good job of holding it together. "This has gone far enough," Jac commanded in her attorney voice, with as much power as she could muster. "I want this competition stopped at once."

There was a collective gasp from the crowd. Jac didn't give two shits whose toes she treaded on. Her eyes found Rachel's, who looked as if she was about to faint. Jac swallowed hard and shored up her resolve.

Ariel slowly turned to face her once more, and a spark of warning flashed in her eyes. "The challenge cannot be stopped without one of the warriors losing."

"I'm tired of this crap." Jac ran a hand through her short hair. "Let me talk to Rachel, then I'll get myself together, and hike my happy ass right out of this jungle." She swept her arm around. "If you two idiots want to kill yourselves, be my guest." Her eyes pinned Ares and Coridan in their place.

You will not be leaving. The words were a whisper in Jac's mind, but there was no doubt who they'd come from. The seer's seductive voice was distinctive. At that moment, Jac was grateful these people couldn't read her thoughts, for had they been able to their ears would've burst into flame by now.

Ariel watched her intently, waiting.

"You can't hold me here against my will." Jac shook her head in denial, her gaze honing in on Ariel.

The seer arched a brow. *I can do many things…the least of which would be to keep you here. But I will not. Your conscience will be your guide in this matter. You have brought these two brave warriors to stand against one another for the right to be with you. If anything happens to either it will be your fault…no other's.* Ariel paused, her head tilting from side to side as if considering her next words. *You must see this to its completion, even if the ending is unsatisfactory.*

Jac hauled air into her lungs. The bitch tried to guilt her and damn it, it was working. She looked up at the sky, trying to settle her tumultuous emotions, before returning her gaze to Ariel. The seer glared back.

"Fine," with that said, Jac spun on her heels and stomped off toward the jungle.

"Until it's completion you will make your home in Ares's hut, as you've already seen fit to spread your thighs for him before," the seer called out after her, amusement tinting her voice.

Jaw clenched, Jac stumbled at Ariel's words, but kept walking. She bit back the urge to respond verbally, instead without looking back Jac raised her middle finger high in the air for all to see. Some things were universal. She was sure Ares had a smile planted on his arrogant, blatantly sexy face. Jac knew if she turned and saw it right now, she'd have to drop him like the bad habit he was becoming. She marched through the jungle for several hundred yards, anger slamming into her from all directions. She didn't want to be responsible for anyone's safety, much less Ares' and Coridan's.

Fuck Ariel.

Fuck her mental telepathy, X-files crap.

Fuck them all.

Ariel could shove it all up that perfect ass of hers.

Jac was tired of being manipulated. She didn't even want to think about the fact she'd been the queen of manipulation back in New York, because that was different. *It was*! How it was different, wasn't exactly clear at the moment, but it had to be. She'd never met anyone like this tribe's seer. Any other time, Jac would respect a woman with that much beauty, power, and control.

Just not now, and — not her.

The bitch got on her nerves, always laying her long fingers on Ares's arm, brushing against his chest, scoping out his cock beneath his loincloth, and undressing him with those freakish aqua eyes. Ariel was like a splinter working its way deeper and deeper under her skin. Well Jac knew what to do with splinters. If need be, she'd hack off her own damn finger.

Jac looked around to ensure her privacy. She could no longer see the clearing, only solid walls of green from the Jurassic growth. At any moment she expected to see a Tyrannosaurus Rex sticking its head through the trees. With her luck, the damn thing would look like Ariel. Jac approached a defenseless tree trunk and let loose. She kicked and jabbed, timing each strike, using precise movements, until her lungs labored to drag in a breath. Then she dropped and started doing pushups. Jac collapsed onto the jungle floor, careful not to crush the tender ferns dotting the ground.

Jac lay there for a few moments trying to catch her breath, then she sat up and started weeding the area around the roots of the plants. Whenever she got upset or confused, which wasn't often because she prided herself on her control, she'd tend her plants. But since they weren't here, she'd have to make do. And Brigit damn well better remember to water them.

By the time she'd finished, at least an hour had passed. Jac cleared the area around her of tangled growth. She rose and dusted off her hands on her shorts and started back to the compound. She'd stay, biding her time with Ares, until this stupid contest ended and then she was out of here—with or without Rachel.

She hated the fact playing house with Ares didn't disturb her more, but always a realist, Jac simply accepted it for what it was— great sex, nothing more and she'd keep telling herself that until she believed it.

Jac wound her way back through the growth. Lianas curled across her path, twisting like giant snakes up into the trees. The air warmed, almost suffocating her in its intensity, but it never seemed to disturb the animals. Birds still sang their cheery songs. Monkeys howled and cried, leaping from branch to branch, using their hands, feet, and tails. Jac caught flashes of green, red, and orange among the leaves.

When she arrived at the compound, the smell of baking bread filled the air, causing Jac's stomach to growl. A few half-naked women worked over a bench, rolling out dough. They glanced her way once or twice, but seemed to be trying hard not to stare.

She strolled over to them and the blonde women turned in unison to face her. Their aqua eyes were intense, curious— Stepford in Jac's opinion.

Slightly embarrassed by her wayward thoughts, Jac stammered. "Do you think I might be able to…I mean would you mind if I…can I have a piece of bread, please?"

The women giggled behind their hands. One walked to the end of the bench and ripped off part of a loaf and then held it out to Jac.

Jac stepped forward, taking the warm bread from the woman's hand. "Thanks a lot. I appreciate it."

Jac held up the bread in salute, her mouth watered in anticipation, then took a big bite. The soft sweet grain melted, causing an explosion of flavor, light, airy, and utterly delicious, honeyed enough to be able to skip the butter. Not that Jac would put any on it. She avoided fatty foods if at all possible.

She looked around the campsite, wondering where Rachel had wandered off to. The well worn area appeared large enough for the whole tribe to gather in. Flowers perfumed the air, along with ginger plants. A long banquet sized table had been shoved to the side. Maybe these people had communal meals or rocking parties, too bad she wouldn't be sticking around long enough to see one.

Jac shrugged, swallowing the bread and took a deep breath. She should probably go find Rachel and apologize for her outburst. As far as Jac was concerned, Rachel was the only one here that deserved an apology.

Her eyes scanned the area again. Everyone seemed to be missing, with the exception of the three women cooking. Maybe in the late morning everyone here took a siesta. If that was the case, then she didn't want to disturb her friend, especially considering her delicate condition. Jac groaned, heaven help Ares if she ended up in the same state as Rachel. A baby was the last thing she needed right now. Make that *ever*.

Yet somewhere inside her, Jac's heart held onto the smallest spark of hope that she carried Ares's baby. She'd die before she admitted it to anyone, but it was there, buried inside, next to the pain of her father's death. Jac took another bite of bread, but this time it tasted flavorless. She broke off pieces of it and tossed them at the edge of the jungle for the birds and monkeys.

She spun around to return to the hut Rachel had put her in when Ares walked into the clearing. His eyes smoldered, even from a distance. His muscles flexed and tensed as he approached. Black hair flowed down his back, glowing blue in the muted light, like a dark angel, a conqueror of old. His jade gaze held her, drew her like a moth to a flame. The slash of his sexy mouth reeked havoc on her senses. Jac imagined those firm lips teasing her nipples, searing her skin, sucking on her clit.

Jac's wayward thoughts brought Ares's cock to full attention, tightening to the point of pain beneath his loincloth. Her eyes trailed down the front of his chest like a sensuous caress, leaving him trembling with need. He licked his lips and allowed his hunger to show upon his face. She flushed. Although Ares doubted she recognized the sexual response. Her body betrayed her mind.

He'd given Jac the time she'd needed to process the challenge. Now he would lead her back to his hut, where the taming would continue. Ares looked forward to having her creamy skin below him, writhing, as he buried his staff in her waiting wetness. He could smell her arousal from here. And he burned from it. Relished it. Cherished every last second.

"I'll take you to your new home." His voice dared her to deny his words.

Jac opened her mouth, then clamped it shut. Ares smiled and clasped her hand in his, leading her down a tiny trail, not visible unless one knew where to search. He could feel the tension in her long fingertips; they throbbed beneath his touch, a delicate balance of anger and lust. He would make sure that lust won out this day.

As she followed along behind Ares, Jac was so mad and horny she could scream. Part of her wanted to throttle him, while the woman's side longed to fuck him senseless. She didn't know which one would win out in the end, but she had a pretty good idea if the wetness between her thighs was any indication. Jac blew out a frustrated breath. God, she needed his raging cock—bad. If he didn't fuck her soon, she'd go insane. All he had to do was look at her and her body melted. What was it about this caveman that turned her on so much?

Jac shook her head. She'd probably never know the answer. Ares snaked his way through the brush, winding this way and that until they arrived at a heavily wooded area. She looked around but didn't immediately see anything except for thick brush and trees. He released her hand and strode forward about ten feet, then the hut came into focus. It had been so well camouflaged that Jac hadn't seen anything but brush.

Dad would be proud. Where that thought came from Jac didn't know, but she banished it straight away, dismissing the sentimentality.

Ares stepped further, pulling the furs up, and stepped aside. He lowered his head and said nothing. Jac stared at him for a few moments. His actions seemed strange, out of character. But hell, she didn't understand these people anyhow, so she covered the small distance in a few strides and crossed the threshold.

He expelled a breath, his shoulders instantly relaxing. Goosebumps rose on Jac's arms. She tried to rub them away. It was as if the simple act of coming in meant something…something important. Her eyes adjusted to the dimness of the hut after several moments.

A small wooden table, only large enough for two or three at the most, sat off to the side, with a couple of chairs arranged around it. A big bowl of fruit and bread had been placed in the center of the table overflowing with abundance, along with a tiny firepot. A bed of furs lay in the opposite corner, piled high enough to reach Jac's thigh. Four wooden spikes had been driven into the ground framing the bed. They didn't look to be decorative. Jac frowned and continued to scan the room. A carved out barrel of sorts tucked into a corner, brimmed with clear liquid. Water, Jac surmised.

There was a solitary window, surrounded by vines, which allowed very little sunlight to enter. The small dwelling still managed to feel cool in the late afternoon air. How? Jac wasn't exactly sure. There seemed to be a lot of strange things in this tribe. They had powers and abilities far beyond anything she'd ever seen or imagined, talking in thought, reading minds, glowing yellow fireballs shooting from their hands. Common sense told Jac she should be scared shitless, but she wasn't. It was not in her nature to allow fear to dictate her actions.

Ares pressed forward, reminding her of his presence. Not that she'd really forgotten him for one second.

"Is this acceptable to you?" His low voice seduced, yet held a modicum of vulnerability.

Jac's gaze found his. "It's fine." She looked around once more, then met his eyes again. "I like it."

His jade orbs flashed in approval, causing Jac's heart to swell. She glanced away. She didn't want to feel these emotions. She hadn't asked for them. They made her feel…feel…*vulnerable.*

Damn.

Her troubled thoughts washed over Ares, drowning him in sensation. Jac may not realize it yet, but she weakened. In time she'd know that in weakness one finds their greatest strength. But he decided he had better not point out that message yet or he'd find himself back where he started. For now he'd bask in the fact she'd crossed his threshold, therefore accepting him as her mate.

His gaze shifted to her clothing. The shirt she wore clung to her breasts like a second skin, molding, embracing, caressing her nipples like he himself longed to do. She smelled of spice, her lust mingling with the natural woman's scent that was her own.

He shifted, trying to alleviate the pressure from his growing erection. He'd managed to rein in his need in the time it had taken them to reach his hut, but now it was back with a vengeance, and he wasn't quite sure he'd be able to stop it.

Not that he truly wanted to. Jac's lithe body called to him. He wanted to stroke her short blonde hair and feel its silk beneath his fingers. Bury his tongue in her wet channel. Nip and kiss her inner thighs until she cried out, begging him to fuck her. Ares took a deep breath, his large body trembling with the effort it took not to act upon his desires.

Ares lightly placed his hands on Jac's shoulders and turned her until she faced him. His eyes wandered over her pale face, taking in her striking blue eyes, dark like the depths of the sea, radiant like the sun. Her lips parted slightly in anticipation of what would occur next. He could read her thoughts, sense her need, and strum her tension until she exploded. The time had come to continue the lesson. He released her and stepped back, his eyes never leaving her delicate face.

"Take off your clothes." A growl formed in his throat.

Her eyes widened in surprise… Jac's jaw tightened, ready to fight. Green clashed with blue in a war without sound. His next words stopped her dead.

"Or I will."

Chapter Nine

"Excuse me?" Jac's brow arched and her lips thinned. Surely she'd misunderstood. There was no way in hell she would strip out of her clothes.

Ares stepped closer. "You would do well to obey me on this." He held his hand out and an energy burst, much like a streak of lightning, shot from his palm and ignited the kindling inside the firepot, illuminating the small hut in soft light.

Jac jumped, but held her ground. "I will not be bullied by you or any other man."

He brushed a wisp of hair away from her face, his fingers lingering against the pulse beating directly behind her ear. Jac's heart leapt beneath the subtle graze that sent her senses into overdrive. She felt heat spread from her stomach and radiate out, until she could hear the steady pulse of her blood thumping like a drum in her head. She took a deep breath, inhaling the musky odor that was all Ares, all masculine — all sex.

Her nipples stabbed against the material of her t-shirt, so sensitive that breathing became a chore. She could feel moisture gathering between her thighs as her pussy flooded in anticipation of his entry. Jac took a step back, fighting for control over her hormones. Why did he have to be sex incarnate? She licked her lips, trying to moisten her parched mouth. His eyes followed the movement like a predator waiting for the opportunity to pounce.

The air seemed to close in around them, pressing, cornering, trapping. Jac glanced at the bed of furs in the corner, then back to the door, attempting to judge her chances of making it to the opening. At some point Ares had pulled the fur covering back in place, blocking out all trace of light. She'd been so wrapped up in her thoughts, staring into space, she hadn't noticed. The thin flap would definitely impede her escape.

"Do not even think about it," his voice dropped an octave in warning.

Jac crossed her arms over her chest, the tiny movement torture as she rasped across her puckered areolas. "You can't keep me here against my will."

He gave her an unholy smile. A hard glint of determination, the likes of which she hadn't seen before, reflected in his jade eyes. Jac made a mad dash for the hut door. She'd made it three feet when a vice-like grip closed around her waist, lifting her from the ground. Jac shrieked.

"Put me down you son-of-a-bitch! I'm not staying here another minute." Jac's arms flailed and she kicked out her legs in an attempt to dislodge herself from his unyielding hold.

Ares carried her back toward the furs, his muscles not even straining to keep her secured. When he reached the bed he transferred the flailing Jac to one hand and tugged at the pouch on the side of his loincloth with the other. Several silk scarves a deep shade of jade fell onto the bed.

Jac's eyes bugged. "What are you planning to do with those?"

His smile widened.

"Don't even think about it." But even as she said the words, Jac's body tightened in anticipation.

She'd played bondage games before, but had never allowed her partner to tie her to the bed. The thought of being spread eagled at Ares's mercy and out of control caused Jac to fight like a wildcat. Before she knew what was happening Ares managed to slip one scarf around her wrist. When she tried to pull it off, he snagged her other arm. Jac pushed against his chest, suddenly Ares released her and she sailed through the air.

Jac landed flat on her back atop the fur bed. Before she could jump up, Ares scooped up the last two scarves, leapt onto the fur bed, and straddled her. He secured her wrists to a couple of the wood stakes surrounding the furs. The scarves looked flimsy, but even with Jac pulling with all her strength they didn't budge. She tried to kick him when he grabbed for her legs. It took him ten seconds to capture and secure her ankles.

In the end, Jac lay staked to the bed. Her legs were spread in a wide vee allowing plenty of access to her drenched pussy. Her clit ached and pulsed beneath the material of her shorts as residual adrenaline pumped through her body.

"Untie me you son-of-a-bitch."

Ares got off her and stood to the side, smiling down at her straining body. When she got loose from the ties, she'd kill him for sure. Jac tugged again before finally giving up. No use wasting her energy on the scarves—they weren't going anywhere.

As soon as her body stilled, Ares approached. He ran his hands along each scarf, testing her bonds. His fingers lingered on her shins, gently scraping his nails over her sensitive bare skin.

Jac shuddered. Her lungs labored from the fight, thrusting her nipples boldly through the material. His eyes lingered on the tight buds as if willing away her clothing, then suddenly he pulled his blade from its sheath. Jac froze. Her eyes locked on the knife.

"Don't even think about it," Jac warned from her secured position.

Ares paused for a moment and then brought the metal to her stomach and began to slice through her shirt and shorts.

"Bastard!"

Within seconds she'd been laid bare, except for her socks and boots. He pulled the shredded garments from beneath her and tossed them into the fire pot.

Jac's arms strained as she pulled against the stakes, her gaze locked on her burning clothes. When all that remained was burning embers she turned back. "Damn you, now what am I going to wear?"

"You will not need anything for the next few days." His eyes caressed her, zeroing in on the thin slice of curls between her legs. "After that, I will provide you with proper clothing."

"Proper clothing, eh?" Jac arched a brow, trying to ignore the growing wetness his gaze caused. "What the fuck does that mean? Ares, if you don't untie me this second, I'm going to kick your ass all the way back to New York City."

Ares laughed, the deep rumbling sound vibrated throughout the little hut, sending shivers of delight along Jac's spine. "I beg your forgiveness, my fierceness, but you aren't going anywhere until I'm finished."

"And when will that be?"

Never…whispered in Jac's mind.

Ares looked around his hut. All was prepared and ready. He just had to visit the seer for the last items. He may not be able to formally approach Jac with a mating ceremony until after he won the challenge, but he could prepare, tame, and seduce her. He must see Ariel.

"I must leave for a moment."

Jac frowned, glancing down at her naked body. "You're not going to leave me like this are you?"

Her blue eyes latched onto his and for the first time they held something Ares hadn't seen before, fear. He approached the bed and knelt at her side. He leaned over, brushing her hair away from her face. His lips were but a whisper away. Jac's mouth parted unconsciously, which was all the invitation Ares needed.

He swooped down, capturing her lips in a searing kiss. She opened for him and he swept inside, tasting, hungering, delving. Her mouth consisted of the sweetest liquid, her warmth surrounded, urging him on. Their tongues dueled, thrusting. His lips firmed and then he pulled away. He had to get to Ariel. It pained him being around Jac's nakedness and not being able to sink inside her.

Ares stood, pressing one last kiss to Jac's forehead. "I'll be back as soon as possible. I must see Ariel."

Jac felt the color drain from her face. If Ares had slapped her it would have been less painful than his last words. He left her staked to the bed naked, to go to the seer. Her stomach knotted and Jac swallowed hard trying to keep bile from rising in her throat. She bit down on the inside of her mouth to keep from begging him to stay. If Ares wanted that blonde bimbo, then far be it from her to stand in his way, but he better not think she would welcome him back with open arms when he returned.

* * * * *

Ares made his way through the jungle to Ariel's hut. Jac would be safe within his home, for only Eros and the seer knew of its exact location. He knew that information would not stave off Jac's wrath when he returned, but it eased his mind. Ares reached Ariel's dwelling within a few minutes and held up his palm requesting entrance. The flap covering her door swung back and the seer stepped forward.

"I've been anticipating your visit." She moved out of the way and swept her arm, welcoming him inside.

When the fur covering the door had been put back in place, Ares dropped to his knees in traditional Atlantean greeting, kissing each of Ariel's nipples. They beaded instantly in response. Ares rose, keeping his head bent in respect.

I've come for the tools.

Ah, I assumed as much. Ariel's voice was soft and teasing. *Are you prepared to finish taming this woman?*

Aye. He glanced up, meeting Ariel's gaze.

She arched a brow. *You know you may lose her in the end. I had not foreseen Coridan's interference.* For a moment Ariel's face held pain, then as if realizing, she smiled erasing the emotion from her face.

Ares flinched and his jaw tightened. *I will not let her go.*

But what if Coridan wins the challenge? Her voice cracked in his mind.

Ares was too angry to notice. He fisted his hands at his sides. *He will not.*

She shrugged, her expression growing serious. *But what if?*

"Then I will call on Jac to make her decision," he spoke aloud, his voice low, almost pained.

Your woman could choose to go with the warrior she finds less — threatening.

Aye…but she won't. He shook his head. *By then she will be so attuned to my touch that any other will repulse her.*

Ariel smiled. *You are very sure of yourself, Ares.*

I have to be. She is my mate.

With those words, Ariel walked across her hut and retrieved the items needed for Jac's preparation. *Would you like me to ease your discomfort?* She pointed to the raging hard on beneath Ares's loincloth.

He shook his head no. *I thank you, but my cock needs but one woman. And she is bound and waiting for me back at my hut.*

Be well, my hunter. Ariel laughed and handed Ares the marking tools. Her face held a trace of relief.

Ares bowed and left the dwelling. He rushed back through the jungle, carrying the marking utensils in his hands. He felt Jac's fury before he entered his hut. It radiated out like a living entity, waiting, stalking, ready to strike the second he walked through the door. Her thoughts were in turmoil, focusing on Ariel and then himself. She pictured them lying together, joining. She was *jealous*. A smile tugged at Ares' mouth, he hid it, and then stepped inside.

Jac wouldn't meet his gaze. Her eyes were focused on the ceiling and her body appeared relaxed in its naked splendor. Ares knew better. She bided her time, waiting for the right moment and then she would attack. He was sure of it. Tied or not, his fierce warrior woman was nothing if not predictable. She may claim to not care for him, but her mind and body told a different story. One Ares hoped to get her to recognize before the week ended.

Jac kept her eyes off Ares. She'd tried every which way to escape while he'd been off visiting that bitch of a seer, but the binding held fast. Her heart seized at the thought of what they'd been doing in Ariel's hut. Well if he thought he would be able to waltz right in here and climb between her legs now, he was insane. She didn't know how she'd stop him, but she'd come up with something.

"Jac," he murmured, "look at me."

"Fuck off." She shifted her head until she faced the opposite wall.

"I told you I would return quickly and I have."

Jac tried to shrug, but it was hard with her arms staked out and slightly above her. "I want you to untie me."

"I cannot. Are you going to behave like this for the rest of the night?" he probed. "I can think of many other ways, far more pleasurable to pass the evening."

"Didn't you hear me, I said fuck off."

"I'd rather be fucking you," his voice slid over her like melting butter, pure temptation to Jac.

Somehow, in the short time she'd known this man he'd attuned himself so closely with her body, mind, and soul that she had a difficulty distinguishing between the two of them. It wasn't fair. Why him? Why now? After all the years she'd spent footloose and fancy free in New York, why did she have to find the one man she could call her equal in the middle of a suck ass jungle? And of course her main competition would just happen to turn out to be a walking, talking blow up doll.

It had to be some kind of cosmic, fucking joke. That was the only logical explanation.

She could hear Ares moving around the hut. He'd set something down on the table and then he'd walked to the water container in the corner to drink. In her mind she could almost see the long columns of his throat work as he swallowed the cool liquid. His bicep would be curled as he tipped a cup to his firm, sensuous lips. As he inhaled to catch a breath between sips his stomach would contract, sending the washboard rippling beneath tanned skin. The flat discs of his nipples would be dark and pebble- like against the wall of his chest. She wondered if his legs would be slightly spread, the muscles splitting, even in his relaxed state.

Jac wet her lips with the tip of her tongue. Did a drop of moisture slip past his mouth and trail down the side of his strong, arrogant jaw, perhaps tangle in his midnight black hair? Or would it slide all the way over his shoulder, down his strong back, slinking beneath his loincloth to curve around his tight ass? Jac swallowed hard, trying to fight the visions swimming in her head. She was hot, needy, and damn it, she wanted Ares anyway she could get him.

She turned her head to find him staring at her from across the room, glass frozen in his hand. His loincloth tented from his massive erection and his eyes were pure fire. He put down the glass he'd been drinking from and stalked toward the furs. His gaze never wavered as he approached her side.

"You should guard your thoughts, my fierceness," he warned, his voice gravelly with desire.

"Why?"

He ran a finger along her side, causing her to flinch when it tickled.

"Because you may get what you so wish for."

Jac's breathing deepened. She couldn't help it. His words were like throwing gasoline on a blaze. Her clit throbbed. Her nipples quivered. And all she could think about was uncovering his massive cock and guiding it inside her waiting pussy. Her eyes darted to the front of his loincloth. The bulge behind it seemed to grow under her perusal. Jac's lids dropped and she licked her lips again.

"Are you going to just stand there or are you going to *join* me?" a loaded question she knew. This by no means changed her feelings about what had occurred between him and Ariel, but she was desperate.

Ares groaned and began untying the straps about his waist, freeing the loincloth from his trim hips. His cock ached to the point of pain. He could feel it buck beneath the confines, demanding release. He slipped the hide down his legs and stepped over the material. The plum-like head of his staff glistened with fresh pearl liquid. He grasped himself and began to make slow, steady strokes. Jac's eyes followed his movements as if in a trance. His shaft lengthened, standing fully erect under his grip.

"Is this what you want?" he growled.

She swallowed hard, her eyes glued to his cock.

He groaned. "You must tell me."

"I want—" She choked, cutting off her words.

He continued to stroke his thick length.

"You," she uttered, barely above a whisper.

Ares took a ragged breath. "'Tis all you needed to say."

He moved to the end of the bed and slipped to his knees. He quickly unlaced Jac's boots and slipped them from her feet, taking her socks with them. Once her feet were bare, Ares stretched forward and ran his fingers down her long legs, settling his hands upon her heels. He lifted one leg as far as the bonds would allow, and slipped her big toe inside his mouth. His tongue swirled, then he slowly pulled it from his mouth.

Jac's eyes widened in surprise. "What are you doing?" she asked, her voice breathless.

"Savoring every inch of what is mine," he rasped and then slipped her toe back into his mouth. He sucked on it in the same motion as when he drove inside her. In and out. In and out.

She gasped, shocked by the erotic tension strumming through her. She'd never considered toes particularly sexy until now. Jac couldn't seem to catch her breath as Ares increased his speed. An answering pull started at the juncture of her thighs and drove right to the center of her being. If he kept this up she would come. Reading her thoughts, he added pressure, dipping his tongue between her toes at the same time as he sucked. Jac felt the familiar tension build. Heat spread throughout her body. In one swift move Ares slipped her toe from his mouth and licked the underside of her foot from her heel over her arch, to the fleshy part beneath her toes.

Jac screamed, shattering the silence of the hut as the orgasm broke over her, sending her body spasming in sheer delight. Her pussy contracted. It felt as if her nerve endings had all been set on fire at the same time. Never in all her years, had she ever experienced anything like what he'd just done. The blood pounded so loud in her ears, she almost missed Ares's grumble of satisfaction.

"That was incredible." Jac panted, her head thrashing from side to side. "How did you do that?"

"It was so in my time, as 'tis today. The way to a woman's heart is through her feet." He smiled and wiped the side of his mouth, but he didn't stand, instead he began to massage the bottom of Jac's left foot.

She closed her eyes for a moment and groaned. She felt like a satisfied cat, right after a big meal. If she didn't watch it, she'd actually fall asleep and it wasn't even dark out yet. At least she thought it wasn't. Jac had lost all track of time, since Ares had brought her here. When he finished with one foot, he moved to the other and began again. His hands were gentle but firm as he worked all the kinks out of her worn out muscles. Jac relaxed under his soothing touch, giving into the sensation, enjoying the pampering.

Ares was a strange man, one second acting like a wild animal, ready to capture and seize, the next caring, almost loving in the way he tended to her needs. Seeing to her comfort and soothing her. Jac didn't want to think about how easy it would be to get used to this kind of treatment. His palm slid up to encircle her calf, kneading and calming her frayed nerves. She hadn't forgotten the fact that he'd kissed her and then left to join Ariel. Jac didn't even want to think about what they'd been doing in her hut.

"Shhh-quiet your mind and enjoy my touch."

It came out as a command, but Jac sensed an unspoken plea behind his words. She wanted to ask what Ariel meant to him, but couldn't bring herself to do it. The implication would be obvious, even to Ares, and Jac wasn't ready to make that kind of statement. His hand slipped further up her leg encompassing her thigh. All thoughts of the seer left her mind as his fingers teased, reaching out, yet not touching the place she longed for him to massage. Jac groaned in frustration. She glanced down, her eyes locking on his handsome face.

"I want only you," he groaned.

Ares pretended not to notice as her hips bucked, urging him to go higher. A smile played at the corners of his mouth. He teased her, drawing out the sensations until all sanity slipped from her mind. Well two could play this game. Jac began to sway her hips, rocking them seductively from side to side. Ares eyes left her face, locking onto her waxed pussy. She could feel her body's juices begin to flow and knew that by now she'd be glistening. Jac tilted her hips up slightly and opened her legs a little more, exposing her entrance.

The air left Ares' lungs as he labored to breathe. The hut smelled musky and thick, as if they'd been fucking for hours. He couldn't seem to wrench his gaze away from the tiny opening swaying before his eyes. Ares licked his lips. She was sheer torture in human form. And Jac knew exactly what she was doing to him.

He had to taste her, touch her, slide his cock inside of her. The temptation grew too great. Ares leaned forward and inhaled, her woman's scent surrounded him, shattering the last remnants of his hard won control. He rose up and knelt between her spread thighs, stroking his staff one time, and then positioned it at her moist entrance.

"I can't wait, sorceress. You have tantalized me for too long." With that he slid inside, her velvet walls gripping him, urging him forward until he nudged her womb, buried to the hilt. He swallowed, trying to maintain a modicum of control, but it was too late.

Ares closed his eyes against the sensation, satin and heat, fire and ice, she burned him from the inside out. He thrust forward and her breath caught. When he did it again, she met him halfway. Rocking her slender hips, Jac slid him impossibly deeper, her channel swallowing him. His eyes flew open, his system in overload. In that moment the beast broke free, released. Shedding his humanity like a second skin, he existed on the primal.

"This time will be raw, forgive me," he rasped.

Her eyes sparked, urging him on. "I like it rough."

Ares surged forward, diving again into her molten core, as if she'd given him permission to unleash a demon. He couldn't control his hunger, his need. Ares thrust, giving free rein to his desires, his hips pistoning into her, driving her to the edge of release, but refusing to let her slide over. His grunts were animalistic. He couldn't seem to get enough of her. She was his. Only his. And if joining with her again and again was what it took to convince her, then that is what he would do.

"Your channel was made for my cock alone."

He gripped the furs at the side of Jac's head and dug in. Ares ground into Jac's clit with each upward thrust, taking them higher and higher toward that elusive zenith. She burned like fire beneath him. Her nipples stroked his chest with every movement, searing, branding him. Their bodies drenched in sweat.

By the time Ares reached his point of release, Jac screamed out another orgasm. Her body bucked beneath his, taking him into the abyss with her. His seed shot out, spilling into her womb. Ares kept moving until he collapsed, managing to keep the bulk of his weight off of Jac. Their ragged breathing filled the silent room. The air suffocated, stifling from their lovemaking, but Ares refused to move. He longed to stay this way forever. He closed his eyes and inhaled, hoping to store this memory inside for all time.

Ares wanted nothing more than to plant his seed deep within her. Bring forth offspring. Spend the rest of his days *battling* with Jac for dominance in their relationship. But without the energy from the mating ceremony and Jac's acceptance of him as her true mate, there would be no children for him...ever. She held his future, his very life in the palm of her hands, and she didn't even know it—nor would she, if he had any control over the fates.

Chapter Ten

It had been three days since Jac had been brought to Ares's hut. After day two she'd promised him she wouldn't try to escape without clothes and convinced him to untie her. He'd loved her so thoroughly that Jac didn't think she had a solid bone left in her body. She'd grown accustomed to Ares's touch over the past few days and didn't think she'd be able to ever sleep with another man, which created a problem for when she returned to New York.

Jac lay face down naked on the bed of furs, waiting for Ares to return and report his progress in the challenge. He'd informed her there would be nothing to see, since each warrior had to go off into the jungle on their own. Today could make or break Ares's chances. Part of her hoped he got his ass kicked, while the other half worried about his safety. Her nerves had been so on edge that she'd tidied the hut earlier, not that it had been dirty, and rearranged the sparse furniture to a more workable layout.

So far, Ares seemed to be doing okay in the competition, but Coridan still led by the amount of gold he'd managed to find. She didn't want to think about what would happen if Coridan actually *won* the silly contest. Jac turned over, placing her hands behind her head. She'd been unclothed for three days now, and although she'd never had a problem with nudity, she found the whole experience rather liberating. She didn't have to worry about laundry, detergent, things wearing out, or dry cleaning bills.

Who was she trying to kid?

Jac glanced around the hut, its walls pressed in around her. She was going stir crazy in here. Jac needed to pound the pavement, look at some skyscrapers. She was not cut out to be Sheena, Queen of the Jungle. How long did he plan on keeping her isolated? Jac kicked her foot down onto the furs. This was bullshit. She hadn't been allowed to see any of the tribal members, including Rachel for days. Jac hadn't come all this way to find her friend and then not be allowed to talk to her. Who did Ares think he was bossing her around? When Ares returned she would demand he take her to Rachel.

Jac stretched, letting out a loud yawn, her fingers scrunched the furs beneath her. Her muscles felt well exercised, Ares saw to that. She couldn't help but smile at the lengths he'd gone to, to keep her in shape. It still didn't excuse the fact that he'd basically been keeping her prisoner here in his hut. She felt like Sybil, happy one minute, pissed the next. Jac's jaw set. Ares wouldn't know what hit him when he got home. She glanced down at the furs and calculated whether she could fashion clothes from one of them. After struggling with the hides for about an hour she gave up and lay back down.

Her mind wandered. Jac thought about the Professor and wondered what had become of him. She prayed the caimans had gotten him, but it was probably too much to hope for. The poor beasts would take one bite and spit him back out. Jac giggled as she pictured a caiman wearing Rumsinger's glasses. Her laugh turned to a frown. Since when did Jaclyn Ward giggle? Like *never*.

The flap covering the door of the hut was pushed aside. Jac bolted up, her hands automatically crossing over her breasts. Ares stood in the frame, staring at her, his eyes unreadable.

"How'd it go?" she asked, not sure why she asked or if she wanted to know the answer.

He stepped inside and dropped the flap. His gaze wandered around the room, observing the changes she'd made. "I like what you've done."

Jac bit her lip. "Are you going to tell me or not?"

Ares opened the pouch at his side and pulled out a snake skin over twenty feet long, still damp with blood. Then a spark of amusement lit his jade orbs. "'Tis a fine day indeed for a competition." He smiled.

"You won." Jac jumped off the bed, then realized that she was about to run into his arms and congratulate him. She stopped mid-stride and added with less enthusiasm. "How nice."

Ares frowned for a moment, then let it pass. "The challenge is not over, yet." He glanced down at the snakeskin. "Tomorrow we duel with energy bursts."

Jac's chest tightened, her heart thudding madly against her ribcage. She'd been dreading that day all week. The seer's warning of possible death occurring rang in her ears. She swallowed the lump forming in her throat. Jac didn't think she'd be able to handle it if she lost Ares, but she wasn't about to let him know that, best to keep those disturbing thoughts to herself.

"Can't we call this nonsense off?"

His eyes locked to hers and his jaw hardened. "Nay, not without admitting defeat."

She glanced at his chest, taking in his broad shoulders. She reached out, her fingers trailed lightly over his bronzed skin. "Would that be so bad?"

Ares grabbed her by the forearms, pulling her forward, forcing her gaze up to his face. "It would mean giving you up." He paused. "Is that what you wish?"

Jac tried to pull away, but he wouldn't release her.

"Answer me," his voice was cold, demanding — *fearful*.

She took a deep breath and released it. "No," she whispered.

He gave her a curt nod, the tension easing from his ruggedly handsome face. Ares released her and stepped back. "Good, because I will not give you up."

Jac hated to admit it, but something inside her swelled at his words. He wasn't going to give her up without a fight. Hell, according to Ares, he wouldn't give her up period. She didn't know how she felt about *that*. Jac decided to examine it later. For now he needed to get some food inside of him. He must have worked up an appetite if he'd been off battling Anacondas.

What am I thinking? I'm not fucking June Cleaver. He can get his own damn food.

They sat at the table eating pieces of camu camu and mango fruit, along with nut filled bread. For a few moments Jac said nothing, simply enjoyed the silence of his company. She'd never been around a man who didn't require conversation. Most of the men Jac had dated had been so intimidated by her strength, they felt the need to fill every gap of silence with words. They hadn't lasted long. No man ever lasted long in Jac's life. In fact, if she'd calculated right, in a few days Ares would break her personal long-term record for being with one man. Jac shook her head. This jungle affected her mind in funny ways, and she didn't like it one bit.

"Tell me about the snake." She prompted, wanting to listen to anything but her own thoughts.

Ares's eyes flared and for a moment he said nothing. Then a smile started at the corners of his firm lips. He put down the mango he'd been eating and swiped a hand across his mouth, dispersing the juice.

"I was making my way along the river bank, when I spotted him." He used his hands to show how he wound his way through the brush. "He perched on a thick branch above the water, waiting for prey to come and drink."

Jac ripped off a piece of bread, took a bite, and began to chew. Her eyes remained locked onto Ares as he reenacted the hunt.

"He didn't yet see me, nor sense my presence until I readied to pounce upon him." His jade orbs widened for emphasis. "I sprang from a branch nearby, knocking him from his perch and us both into the water."

The bread in Jac's mouth lodged in her throat as she imagined Ares in the river with the anaconda. A thin sheen of sweat broke out on her skin as she realized he could have died pulling a stunt like that. She couldn't bring herself to speak.

"At one point, he wrapped his mighty body around mine and attempted to squeeze. Fortunately, I released an energy burst before he bound my hands. Had he encircled my wrists first..." he shrugged again. "I would not be telling you this story."

Jac rose from the table and walked the short distance to the water barrel. She cupped her trembling hands and drank deeply, trying to wash away the fear threatening to overthrow her control. Ares had made the whole thing sound like some big adventure, when in fact he'd almost died.

Jac cupped her hands again and splashed some water over her face, slicking her hair back in the process. The cool water dripped down her back and over her buttocks, sending a delicious chill spiking through her. When she'd finally gathered herself together she turned to face Ares, her mind made up. He stared at her with a strange look in his eye, one she was unable to read.

She took the few steps needed to cover the distance, placed her hands on Ares's cheeks, and slowly lowered her mouth to his. The kiss started out tentative at first, testing, seeking, searching for something more. Jac deepened the embrace, swiping her tongue along his lower lip. He growled, then opened, inviting her in. Jac dipped, her mouth urgent. She sucked on his tongue, tasting the sweet mango he'd been eating only moments before. She groaned. Her hands wandered down his neck and over his shoulders, her fingernails biting into the thick skin on his back. She pressed forward, her nipples brushing his chest.

Jac couldn't seem to get close enough. His hands remained at his sides, letting her explore to her heart's content. She brushed her fingers across the flat discs of his nipples and felt him tense. Her palms dropped further to the ties at the side of his loincloth. Jac pulled at the laces, without breaking the kiss, until they slipped free. Then she stepped back, heaving in a lungful of air. Jac reached for his arms, pulling on his biceps, which was equivalent to trying to lift felled logs. He smiled at her and stood, his loincloth slid down his muscled thighs, like a slow striptease, onto the floor.

She leaned in close to his ear. "I want to fuck you."

Ares sucked in a surprised breath...then he growled.

"But first I'm going to tie you up."

Ares stilled, his eyes roaming over her face, then he acquiesced.

Jac led Ares to the bed of furs, running her hand over one of the scarves still tied to the stakes. She arched a brow and looked at him, taunting, teasing, daring him to let her tie him to the bed. He stared but for a moment, then lay upon the bed, arms and legs outstretched.

Jac blinked. She couldn't believe it. Ares was actually going to allow her to tie him to the furs. Just the thought of having this great big muscled man at her mercy titillated her. Ares was hers, all hers and she'd never let him go. *What am I saying?* Jac pressed her legs together to ease the sudden ache. Her nipples engorged, springing out like two shooter marbles from her chest.

She slipped one scarf around Ares's thick wrist and then waited to see if he would protest. He simply looked at her and grinned. Jac quickly secured the other bonds before she lost her nerve or he changed his mind. Her body practically thrummed with excitement. With his legs spread and his enormous cock standing at attention, Ares looked like a delicious pagan god. And she planned to convert and worship at that massive cock of his until he made a believer out of her.

Jac licked her lips. His eyes followed the movement. "I have you right where I want you," she purred, ignoring the flip her heart gave in her chest. Very carefully Jac climbed onto the bed and straddled Ares's flat stomach. His muscles jumped beneath her clit.

She rotated until her bottom rested on his chest and she faced his cock. Jac leaned forward until her lips were an inch above his pulsing head. She blew out a warm breath onto his shaft and it bucked, urging her on. Jac slipped the tip of Ares into her mouth, swirling her tongue around his round plum sized crown. She heard him groan and pull against the restraints, but she didn't stop. Jac firmed her lips and began to suck at the same time.

"You are killing me, my fierceness," he groaned out. Ares' legs strained as he tried to wrest free. Jac giggled, vibrating the length of his shaft with her lips.

She continued to work, her head bobbing while she sucked and swirled, allowing her teeth to gently scrape his sensitive skin. Jac wrapped one hand at the base of his shaft and began to pump, following her mouth's movements. She could feel Ares clench and strain beneath her. Jac moved her other hand over his groin, through the nest of curls at his base, until she cupped his heavy sac. His balls were like two skin covered goose eggs that she lovingly massaged. Jac didn't slow her actions, only continued to stroke and add a little pressure.

"Let me up," Ares warned, attempting to buck her off.

Jac clung tight and sped up. Ares's sac drew up and every muscle in his body seemed to tighten. She stroked a few more times and Ares bellowed. Come shot from his body and straight down her throat. Jac swallowed his essence until she'd drained him, then sat up, a satisfied smile planted on her face. She tossed a glance over her shoulder in time to see Ares's hands come free. Jac had about a second to shriek before Ares had her bent over again. This time he pulled her hips back toward his face, his fingers digging into the soft skin of her thighs.

"You have tortured me enough. 'Tis my turn to love you."

She swallowed hard at his choice of words, but only had a moment to dwell, before her clit slid over his hairless chest. She tried to rise, but he pinned her down with one hand. Before she realized what he was going to do, Ares had her above his face, entering her with his six and a half inch tongue. Jac's muscles

132

closed around him and she closed her eyes, moaning. She refused to think about the fact she'd never get tired of this man. She could return to New York tomorrow and never escape the memory of his touch, of his length pressed to hers. Jac spread her thighs a little wider, giving him full access to her body, her soul. He twisted his tongue like a corkscrew over and over, repeatedly hitting her G-spot.

Ares pulled out of Jac's pussy to tease her clit. He laved her, sucking the tiny bud into his mouth, worrying it with his teeth. Jac shuddered and pushed down, smothering his face with her sex. Ares growled and continued to feed. Her juices ran freely, dripping over his chin. He lapped them up, catching every drop. Just as she neared her peak, he released her clit. Jac groaned and hit him in the side. He laughed, then plunged back into her channel, drawing in and out, fucking her with his tongue.

She leaned over, her nails sunk into his sides, as her lips locked once more onto his hardening cock. It was his turn to growl. Like crazed animals they ate at each other, nipping, tonguing, and sucking. He couldn't get enough of her wild musk, her scent everywhere, surrounding, enveloping. Ares picked up speed as he felt Jac's walls begin to spasm. He swirled his tongue, then sent an energy burst into her greedy pussy. Jac let out a strangled scream, before once again latching onto his cock and pumping furiously. It took but a moment for Ares to follow her into the abyss.

* * * * *

Several hours later, they lay sprawled over the furs, too exhausted to move. They'd fucked each other two more times, before Jac cried uncle. She couldn't take another orgasm. She still quaked from the last three. Excess energy radiated over her body and out of her pores from Ares's energy burst. Her cunt pulsed. It had taken an hour for Jac to finally stop twitching. They'd fallen asleep for a while, but were now content to lay in each others arms. Jac ran her fingers over Ares's chest in lazy circles. She felt well and truly sated.

"Ares?"

"Hmm…"

She shifted until her chin rested on his chest. Her eyes found his and her breath caught. Jac didn't think she'd ever get over how beautiful his jade eyes were, mesmerizing, flawless, like the jewel they resembled. She wet her lips.

"I want to go into camp tonight." Jac tried to sound restrained. She figured if she could convince Ares he'd tamed her, she'd have a better chance of getting her way. If this tact didn't work, she'd try another.

His face tensed, but his gaze never wavered. "Why?"

Jac looked to the side, playing demur, before returning to his face. "I haven't seen Rachel or anyone else for that matter for three days."

Ares' muscles tightened, raw emotion played over his features. "Do you wish to see anyone else in particular?"

Jac started. For a second, she wasn't sure how to answer, then she realized he thought she wanted to see Coridan. A smile teased at the corners of her mouth, before turning into a full-blown grin.

"Are you jealous?"

He shifted Jac off his body. "I know not what you speak of."

She laughed. "You know exactly what I'm talking about." Jac nudged him with her elbow.

"If you want to see Rachel tonight, then you must be prepared."

Her brows furrowed. "Prepared, how?"

It was Ares' turn to smile, a spark of mischief lighting his eyes. Jac decided she didn't like his expression. It made her nervous—very nervous. The last time he looked anything like that she'd end up tied to the bed for two days. Anger rose anew, but she pushed it down. She needed to get out of this hut before she went even more stir crazy.

God only knew what he was up to now. Was he going to put a collar around her neck and make her walk through the compound naked, on a leash? She had a feeling it would be much worse. But she also knew one more thing, if she didn't go along with whatever he wanted she'd find herself back tied to the bed and stuck here for days until this challenge had been completed.

Jac shook her head. That was unacceptable.

"Okay," she released a breath. "Give it to me straight, what do I have to do in this preparation?"

His smile widened. "I must mark you before you can be presented to the tribe."

"Mark me?" She raised a brow. "What in the hell is that?"

Ares carefully moved over Jac and rose from the furs. He walked over to a small compartment in the wall that she hadn't noticed before and withdrew more items, adding them to the ones he'd brought from Ariel's hut. They looked like tools of some sort.

"What are you going to do with those, build a birdhouse for a cockatoo?" Jac tried to joke, but her heart raced in her chest as if she were running a marathon.

He shook his head slowly, then curled his finger, beckoning her to come.

Jac couldn't seem to move a muscle. Every fiber of her being operated on red alert and there was no standby. She glanced from Ares to the table where he'd laid out the items and then back.

"F-first tell me what you're going to do," she stalled, trying to give herself enough time to come up with a plan of escape. *For fuck sake Jac, keep your voice steady.*

"The sooner I put the markings to you, the sooner you'll get to see Rachel." His tone dropped and his brows furrowed. "And whoever else you seek."

Jac swallowed hard and forced herself to move. Her legs trembled, threatening to give out on her, as she slipped from the bed. She took a deep breath and her chin shot up, her gaze unwavering. Jac strode the few steps needed to reach Ares with as much strength and pride as she could muster. She felt as if someone forced her to walk to her own execution. Jac doubted Ares would do anything to harm her, but she didn't like the look of those tools. Knowing Ariel, they'd probably been forged to use as some demented form of gynecological torture.

She squared her shoulders and faced Ares. "Get on with it then."

Ares smiled, pride showing in his green depths. He picked up the first instrument, resembling a thick knitting needle and dipped it into a black liquid substance contained in a small bowl. He raised the tool, bringing it toward Jac's abdomen. Unconsciously, she jumped back.

"It will not hurt." He reached out with his free hand and drew her back. "You have my word."

"I can take the pain," she protested. "I wasn't ready."

Ares brow arched, but he said nothing. He raised the instrument once more to her stomach and began to draw strange symbols onto her skin.

"What do those mean?" Jac pointed, trying to watch his movements, but it was difficult to see around her small breasts.

He didn't look up, but continued to work as he spoke. "They tell a story of sorts. One of bravery and honor. Dominance and submission."

Jac shook her head and Ares steadied her. "Don't move, it is crucial I get these symbols right."

She crossed her arms over her chest and tried to breathe shallowly. Jac had a feeling Ares wasn't telling her the whole story behind the symbols. The design he created looked exactly like his own. She decided once they arrived at the village she'd seek out Rachel to find out if she knew anything. Surely someone in the tribe would be able to explain them to her.

He continued to paint, making bold strokes with the black dye. When he'd completed the area beneath her belly button,

Ares moved onto her lower back. By the time he finished, Jac looked as if she wore a thin intricately woven belt. She took a step away when he laid the needle like tool down.

"We are not finished, yet." Ares grabbed her around the waist, heat poured from his hands, radiating throughout her body. A few moments passed and then he released her.

She stilled. "You've already covered my waist in designs—did the heat thingy, what more needs to be done?"

He snorted and opened another pouch, containing a red liquid.

"You've got to be kidding. Tell me you're not going to fill all those symbols in with color?"

"I am not."

"Then what are you going to do with that?" Jac pointed to the red liquid.

Ares smiled and lifted what looked like a paintbrush and began dipping it into the dye.

"Ares, I asked you a question…"

His eyes flashed with pure devilry. "And I'm about to give you your answer."

Chapter Eleven

Ares raised the brush that was dripping with red liquid, to Jac's nipple. The scrape of the bristles caused her areola to pucker. She held her breath as he circled the turgid peak until it had been thoroughly saturated in dye. Jac glanced down—her tit looked engorged. He proceeded to paint the other, lingering on the tip long enough to evoke her passion. She felt her pussy flood, drenching her inner lips.

Jac groaned and tried to catch her breath. "Is all this necessary, when I'm going to be clothed?"

The carnal look Ares gave her told Jac without words there was no doubt he was up to something.

But Jac would be damned if she could figure out what. She let him finish, before asking again. "You've ripped up my clothes, so what am I supposed to wear in the meantime?"

Ares dipped a brush in a clear fluid, rinsing the dye away. His hand moved up and down, then side to side. He didn't turn or even give a glimmer of acknowledgement, acting instead as if he hadn't heard her at all.

She looked around the hut. Jac supposed with his help she could create some kind of toga out of one of the furs on the bed. She could always wrap a scarf around her waist to hold the thing in place, but of course that hadn't worked earlier.

Ares put the brush down and sealed the containers. He walked to the hidden compartment and placed them inside. Before he turned back to Jac, she saw him pull jade colored material from the inside and then close the door. He walked back to her, his hand encasing the item. When Ares stood before Jac he held out the cloth.

Jac looked at it and frowned. The color was beautiful, but seemed of little use to her. "What do you want me to do with that?"

"I wish you to wear it."

She stared at the scrap of material, then looked up at Ares. "On what, my head?"

He snorted, his eyes never leaving Jac's face. "'Tis a skirt."

Jac took it from his hands and examined it. "Where's the shirt?"

He grinned again.

The skin on the back of Jac's scalp prickled, tightening to the point of pain. Surely he joked. She ran her hand over the skirt and it appeared to change color in the low light of the fire pot.

"No, I mean it." She tilted her head. "Where's the rest of the outfit? You can't expect me to run around half naked like the other women here."

"'Tis all you need." Ares laughed. "'Tis all you'll ever need, in Atlantean society."

"Yeah, well therein lies the problem." She moved her hands to her slim hips. "I'm not part of this society. I'm a New Yorker. We don't wear anything out of season." Jac shook her head. "Hell, we don't wear much that isn't black, so…" She handed the skirt back to Ares. "This isn't going to work for me."

He took it, running his palms over the material. It instantly turned black and then handed it back to her.

"Fine. Now if you can produce a top, we'll be set."

"Nay." He shook his head. "'Tis disrespectful in the eyes of *our* society."

Jac's jaw set. "Screw your society. I'm not going anywhere without a shirt."

His eyes hardened. "Then you go nowhere."

By the tone of his voice, Jac could tell he wasn't bluffing. *Damn him.* She glanced down at the sheer black skirt in her hands. She didn't have anything against nudity, per se. Hell, she'd been to nudist beaches before, but this was different. These people were different. They didn't view toplessness as anything unusual, but with the challenge going on, the thought of being semi-nude left her feeling at a distinct disadvantage. What if she ran into Coridan? And how in the hell was she supposed to kick major ass in a skirt?

Just as quickly as the thought entered her mind, Jac began to formulate a plan. If Ares was set on her going topless, then she'd make sure he was as uncomfortable as her. Jac planted the sweetest smile on her face that she could muster, then slipped the skirt on. She sashayed across the floor, adding a little more swing than her hips naturally had. She turned in time to see Ares's expression change from stubbornness to hunger.

Oh yeah, this might be fun after all.

"Lead the way, I'll follow." She smiled again, looking forward to the torture to come.

Ares led Jac through the jungle, careful not to let her trip on the lianas. She looked particularly seductive with her nipples rouged and her tattoo marking her. She thought it to be temporary, but he knew better.

The gleam in her blue eyes held nothing but mischief. There was no way he could predict her next move, only anticipate it coming. Ares chose not to read her mind, even though he could easily do so. He wanted her to trust him and that wouldn't happen if he continued to violate her privacy. Ares blew out a steadying breath, then pushed the last fern aside, so she could step into the compound. Jac hesitated but a moment, then walked on, head held high.

Rachel and Eros sat at the head of the feasting table. The rest of the tribe was seated along the sides. The table was surrounded by lit torches, illuminating the evening meal. They raised their heads when Ares entered the area, but said nothing. Ares did not miss the surprise, lighting their eyes. He led Jac over to the banquet and seated her near Rachel.

"You look fantastic. Is Ares treating you all right?" Rachel leaned forward and asked.

"Thanks, you could have told me I was going to wind up naked, too." Rachel's face flushed under Jac's sarcasm. Jac bit back a curse, then apologized. "I'm sorry. I get cranky when I'm kept away from all the action in town, you know that."

Rachel giggled, then shook her head in understanding.

"What else don't I know?"

Rachel flushed and looked away.

Ares raised a brow at Jac's question, then looked to Eros.

Has Coridan dined tonight?

Nay my friend. Eros answered in the preferred Atlantean method.

Ares's jaw clenched, as his eyes scanned the peripheral of the village. There was no sign of Coridan, but that did not mean he would not arrive. For some reason it disturbed Ares to have the young warrior lay eyes upon Jac in her proper attire. He fisted his hands.

Eros clasped Ares's forearm. *Sit my friend and break bread with us. It does no good to worry about what is not.*

Ares gave Eros a curt nod and sat beside Jac. The material of her skirt brushed against his hard thigh, causing every muscle in his body to go on alert. Five large bowls of fruit had been placed along the center of the table, cups, carved from the huingo fruit, containing mango and banana juice had been poured, ready for consumption. Ares snatched a cup, quickly passing it to Jac, then took one for himself. She acknowledged him with a tilt of her head, but kept talking with Rachel. He ignored the need to capture her attention. He wasn't ready to share Jac yet, with the rest of the tribe.

The hair on Ares's nape stood on end, the only warning he got of Coridan's impending approach. The young warrior stepped from the jungle. His eyes sparked blue fire as they landed on Ares, then moved onto Jac. For a moment his corded body tensed, then Coridan strode forward to join the group, his gaze unwavering from Jac's lithe body.

Ares gripped the edge of the table, every instinct screaming at him to fell his opponent before Coridan had a chance to take his mate. Jac may not consider herself his mate yet, but in time she would come to accept him...Ares hoped. He watched as Coridan made his way around the table, positioning himself next to Rachel. Coridan dropped to his knees beside her chair and greeted her in traditional Atlantean fashion, pressing his lips to each of her nipples, before standing to take a seat.

From Coridan's position he had an unimpeded view of Jac's pert breasts. Her puckered nipples stood out daringly, since Ares had applied the red dye. Ares felt the wood beneath his fingertips begin to splinter. Coridan's gaze had not left Jac's creamy peaks since he'd joined them. Ares shoved a glass of banana juice toward Coridan, almost upending it in his lap. The young warrior caught the cup at the last second, a taunting smile plastered on his golden face.

Ares cursed under his breath and brought his hands down to his sides. His knuckles accidentally brushed Jac's leg, causing her to jump. He didn't miss her quick intake of breath or the way her pupils dilated in response. The past few days had gone better than he'd expected. They'd grown so attuned with each other's needs and wants that words were no longer needed.

Ares had memorized every inch of Jac's pale white skin, long legs, and tantalizing lips. With a scrape here and a nip there he could have her coming for him within a matter of minutes. Her responsiveness had been a gift from the great goddess. She'd seen fit to send him a warrior woman to stand proudly by his side. He could ask for nothing more.

Ares sought out Coridan's gaze. When he had the young warrior's attention Ares let his lip curl back into a sinister smile, a subtle warning letting Coridan know, that in no uncertain terms would he surrender what was rightfully his. And Jac was his, whether she believed it or not. Coridan acknowledged Ares with a slight jerk of his head, but he didn't look away, in fact he intensified his gaze, allowed it to harden, sending a direct challenge right back.

"Come Coridan, eat." Eros pointed to a seat further down the table.

"Thank you, my King." Coridan's words were clipped, as he reached for some fruit and began to eat. His aqua gaze strayed back to Jac again and again.

Jac glanced sideways. Ares's concentration centered on Coridan, his face hardened into a mask of undisguised fury. He was *jealous*. She shook her head and tucked that bit of information away for later use. His distraction would give her time to ask Rachel a few questions.

"Do you have any idea what these markings mean?" Jac whispered.

Rachel chewed on her lip. "I noticed them when you approached, but I've never seen tattooing in this tribe." She glanced from side to side, then leaned closer. "It's common in other peoples, but not Atlanteans as far as I've seen."

"I tried to smudge one of the symbols with my thumb, but it didn't budge."

Rachel looked worried.

"What is it? What aren't you telling me?"

"You promise not to get mad?"

Jac shook her head. "No."

Rachel took a breath and let it out. "Fair enough. I think the markings are permanent."

"What?" Jac's voice rose, drawing everyone's attention to her. "You've got to be shitting me."

Rachel's eyes bugged out of her head as she mouthed for Jac to shut up.

The meal continued in silence and eventually drew to a close, a fire crackled and blazed in the center of the compound. The stars were starting to poke their twinkling heads out from behind the canopy of trees. Locusts droned and rasped, lending song to the hushed jungle. The Atlanteans broke off into various groups, positioning themselves around the growing flame. They told stories and jokes, like children do when they're sitting around a campfire.

Jac took in the simplicity of the sight. Something inside her swelled and threatened to burst. She didn't like Hallmark moments or anything else that brought out sentimentality, but for a few minutes she gave herself permission to just sit back and enjoy the company. Feast her senses on the night.

Rachel had been of little help when it came to explaining the markings Ares had put on Jac's body. With tattooing not being a common sight in the tribe, that explained why so many curious eyes sought her out.

"I'm the freak in the freak show," Jac murmured to herself and laughed.

She tried to ignore the stares, but it was rather like attempting to ignore a buzzing mosquito in the dead of night. No matter what you did, you still heard him. Ares had made his way over to Eros's side. Their heads were together like co-conspirators, planning their next caper. Coridan sat alone, off to the side, away from the group, staring in her direction. She really couldn't tell if he looked at her or watched the flames. Jac glanced over her shoulder to make sure Ares remained engrossed, then made her way to the other side of the fire.

As she approached, Coridan rose to his knees and grabbed her hips. His fingers were light upon her skin, yet his grip was unbreakable. His eyes glanced to the tattoo around her waist, then grew dark for a moment, before returning to their natural fire. Jac knew what he was about to do, but couldn't keep her body from flinching under his touch. Coridan's lips were firm as they latched onto her left nipple. From what Jac could gather, there only should have been kissing, but what Coridan did, went far beyond that. He swirled his tongue around her areola, bringing it to point. His white teeth flashed into a devilish smile the second before he nipped her.

Jac bit back a groan, but her stomach rolled as if his touch were repulsive.

With an unhurried slowness he moved to her other nipple. He waited for a hairsbreadth, before dropping upon her pink bud. Jac's body responded eagerly. His lips enclosed, sucking in the protruding nubbin, teasing, tasting, and longing for more. She fought the urge to push him away. The voices around them died out. Jac glanced around in time to see everyone staring at them. She felt heat rise in her face. Her eyes immediately sought Ares. Muscles tense, hands fisted, his jaw set, he glared at her, fire shooting from his jade eyes, singeing her to her toes.

Jac gulped, but met his gaze straight on. She gave him a bright smile, then allowed Coridan to pull her to the ground, until she sat beside him. She watched as Eros placed a hand on Ares's shoulder preventing him from joining her and Coridan. Jac let out an uneasy breath, then turned to face Coridan. Chest tight, heart racing, she proceeded with her plan. She had to let Ares know he didn't own her. She belonged to no man. In the end it would make it easier to walk away...at least she hoped.

"So," Jac tilted her head and glanced up into Coridan's aqua eyes. "How goes the challenge?"

His lips thinned, but he managed a smile before answering. "As you know, I won the gold test. Unfortunately, Ares took the lead for the anaconda. But I'm sure I can best him tomorrow," he added with enthusiasm.

"I'm sure you will." She patted his hand.

Jac didn't know how she felt about his boast. One side of her would love to see Ares brought down a peg or two, but the other, well the other was beginning to get used to those flashing green eyes and that great big muscled body of his lying beneath her after hours of lovemaking.

There was that word again...*love.* Jac had never believed it possible before, because she'd never experienced anything close to that emotion with the men she'd dated. Yet she found it popping up again and again surrounding thoughts of Ares like bees to honey.

Of their own volition, her eyes sought out Ares. He stood across the compound like a proud warrior. His body looked more relaxed, as if Eros had done something to calm him down. Jac exhaled, releasing the pent up tension that had been building up inside. Once again she turned her attention to Coridan. He appeared wounded, betrayed. *Had she been that obvious?* Jac decided whatever brought on the mood swing, she had to do something to sooth his ruffled feathers until she could get some information out of him.

She cursed the need to seek Ares with her gaze. In a few days dark warrior had managed to burrow under her skin to the point where her change in behavior became apparent, even to strangers. She really needed to knock this shit off right now. She decided to start by practicing on the man in front of her.

"Maybe you could help me…" Jac batted her eyes, something she'd never bothered with in New York, but found effective nonetheless.

Coridan smiled and leaned in. "What is it you wish to know?"

It was Jac's turn to smile. Men were so easy. She shook her head.

"Would you happen to know what these funny markings mean?" Jac pointed down at the tattoo Ares had applied earlier.

Coridan's gaze dropped to her waist and instantly hardened again. His jaw worked from side to side as if he fought to control his anger and his nostrils flared. He took a deep breath and let it out slowly, then shot a quick glance to Ares. Jac followed his gaze and saw what looked like a gleam of satisfaction on Ares's face. She shrugged it off as a play of the firelight. She'd seen enough pissing contests in her day to recognize one when she saw it. Jac chose to ignore the testosterone.

"Do you know what they mean or not?" Jac implored, her voice harder than she'd intended.

Coridan looked back to her and gave a short nod.

"Are you going to tell me or do I have to guess?" her sarcasm was unmistakable.

"'Tis a claiming chain."

"What?"

He ran his finger along the symbols as if by doing so would erase them. Coridan's lips pursed. "'Tis what a warrior from Ares's people uses to identify their mate after she's been tamed."

Jac's eyes widened, but she said nothing. The fire beside her was nothing compared to the one beginning to build inside her gut.

"'Tis what Ares uses to warn other warriors away from his claim. It states that your channel is his alone. And should he find any man trying to enter his domain, he reserves the right to kill him."

She swallowed hard, torn between outrage and excitement. Jac went with what was familiar. "If you'll excuse me, I need to speak with Ares. You won't have to worry about the warning, because I'm going to kill him." She rose before Coridan could even move and started around the fire to where Ares had been standing earlier.

Eros stood with Rachel, nuzzling her neck and rubbing her pregnant belly. Jac cursed. Where in the hell had Ares gone? She scanned the crowd, searching for the one dark-haired man in a sea of light. She found him standing next to the tree line, talking with Ariel.

Jac's gut clenched as the seer stepped closer, placing her slender hand upon Ares's chest. She stroked across his skin, clasping his bicep. He flexed beneath her fingertips. Jac's hands balled up into fists. She would throttle that blow up doll if she didn't back off. Rage seethed inside her, pushing out with an intensity that damn near blinded her.

Jac realized the ludicrousness of her thoughts and feelings, but didn't care. He'd painted the damn belt of symbols on her, not the bimbo, and it was high time he remembered. The seer's laughter floated on the air as she tossed her head back sending waves of blonde falling over her slender shoulder onto her rounded bottom. She leaned in closer until her ample breasts brushed against Ares's arm.

That was it!

"Do you see this fucking belt around my waist, lady?" Jac shouted, stopping all activity in the camp. Her fingers were pointed down at the tattoo for emphasis.

Ariel turned, her hand still clasping Ares, a sensuous smile pulling at her pouty full lips. Her eyes sparkled in the firelight, then she arched one sculpted brow.

"I see no claim upon this warrior," the seer said, pulling back from Ares enough to look him over from head to toe. "He has no mate."

The words stung, but Jac ignored them. She didn't want to think about the fact she had no actual claim on Ares. He was free to do what he wanted and be with whom he wanted. She didn't have the right to say a word. Hell, a minute ago she'd been thinking about leaving him. But this was different. He didn't need a blonde Barbie bitch from hell for a mate, even if Jac went back to New York City. Ares could do far better than Ariel. Jac's gaze scanned the camp, but none of the women fit her definition of what Ares needed in a mate.

She glared at Ariel once again. The seer waited for a response.

"You're right, he has no mate. So if you want him, you're welcome to him. Oh, and one more thing, fuck you!" Jac knew it wouldn't be the most mature thing to say, but it was how she felt. With that said, she turned on her heel and marched into the jungle.

Jac stumbled over lianas in the dark, unsure of the direction she traveled. She thought Ares's hut was somewhere around here, but after ten minutes of scrambling over logs and through bushes, she wasn't so sure anymore. Not that it mattered. Ariel's intentions had been clear, and Jac would have to be blind not to see them. Ariel wanted Ares. End of story. The seer had done everything short of fucking him in the clearing to let him know. She was probably screwing him now.

Jac stubbed her toe. "Shit!" She bounced a couple of times before continuing on.

Her whole plan had blown off course. Somehow a simple rescue mission had turned into the Poseidon Adventure and there wasn't a damn thing Jac could do to stop it. She was stuck here for another few days at least, until the challenge ended. Coridan was a good man and she had little doubt she'd have a problem controlling him, but when it came right down to it, Jac only had eyes for Ares. And it pissed her off to no end. *Why me?*

Men, they're all bastards, every last one of them. One minute they want you as their mate, the next they're whispering sweet nothings in a bimbo's ear. *Typical.*

Jac walked for twenty minutes more, slowly coming to the realization that she was lost. She should have arrived at the hut by now and with the growth and darkness, she doubted very much she'd be able to find her way back to the village. So she found a stump and sat down. There was no use going any further. Hopefully when dawn struck, she'd be able to spot a trail and make her way back. Jac didn't even want to think about the fact she was returning to Ares's hut willingly. *He'd pay for that too*, she vowed.

* * * * *

It had taken every fiber of Ares's being to keep from going after Jac. He'd started to do so, when Ariel stopped him.

She needs to sort out her emotions, she'd said. *Let her go. Give her time.* The seer had left him after imparting her words and joined Coridan by the fire. Ares had considered it unusual but his mind was elsewhere.

Time had passed and Ares felt no closer to relaxing. He wanted Jac in his arms. He'd only flirted with Ariel to show Jac how it felt to him when she'd sat with Coridan. Well, the plan had worked, better than he'd anticipated. In a few short minutes he'd probably destroyed everything he'd spent the last three days building.

Guilt and anger pushed vise-like against his chest. His warrior woman had pointed out the tattoo on her body to remind him of his claim, yet he did not answer her pained call. Instead, he allowed her to escape into the jungle.

Ares cursed beneath his breath. He had to find Jac, explain, apologize, and if need be, beg. He wasn't beyond doing so at this point. When he'd seen Coridan's mouth linger upon Jac's breasts he'd felt rage unlike anything he'd ever experienced, a beast reared its ugly head, demanding blood. His body had shook with such intensity, it had taken all of Eros's strength to hold him back, although he doubted anyone but the two of them realized it.

What had started out as a game between potential mates had turned into who could inflict the most pain. In the end, they'd both lost.

Chapter Twelve

Ares found Jac deep in the jungle curled up in a ball. He lifted her limp body from the ground and carried her back to his hut. It had taken him several hours to locate her amongst the dense shrubbery. For a moment his heart stopped when he'd come upon her still body. He'd feared the worst until she'd taken a deep breath. Only then did he allow his muscles to relax and his heart to continue to beat. It had been the longest fifteen seconds of his life.

He took his time, working his way over the trail, trying not to wake her during the journey.

Now, with Jac tucked safely beneath his furs, Ares waited for the first tentacles of dawn to reach across the sky. The energy burst challenge would be starting within an hour and he'd yet to rest a wink. Instead, he'd spent the hours watching Jac sleep, her pale face gleaming in the soft glow of the fire pot. She hadn't awoken, not even when he'd placed her on the bed, her lithe body limp from exhaustion.

It was his fault she'd spent the night unprotected in the jungle. Anything could have happened to her in those hours and he wouldn't have been close enough to help her in time. The thought of that sent shards of guilt lancing through his body, slicing deep enough to haunt him for a lifetime.

Releasing a heavy breath, Ares readied himself for the challenge, knowing his strength waned greatly from last night's events. He strapped on his blade, even though it would not be used during the combat. Giving Jac one last glance over his shoulder, Ares pushed the hide away from the door and slipped out. His senses were sluggish as he made his way to the village clearing. He'd traveled about a hundred yards when a subtle shift in the energy field caught his attention.

Ares stilled. He scanned the area around him, trying to determine the direction the disturbance came from. It was never exact, but he could get a fair idea of the general location. His body tightened, going into full alert as he realized the intruder was male. The man wasn't yet close, perhaps a day or two away, but drew nearer from the north. Ares's jaw clenched as the red-haired devil came into his mind. Was he the cause of the disturbance? He'd been unable to pursue the Professor since the taming ritual had started. Not content with Jac and Rachel, it seemed the danger had come looking for his people, too.

Ares was torn. If he did not hurry and reach the clearing he'd forfeit his chance to win Jac. But if he didn't pursue this new threat, there was a chance he would not be able to locate it again, by the time the energy battle ended.

Ares shook with fury at the thought of allowing the male to escape, but without Jac there would be no future for him. So with regret, he set aside his anger and pushed on, entering the clearing right before the seer raised her hands to give the victory to Coridan.

Ares broke through the trees. *I am here.* He announced to the gathering crowd. The entire village had turned out to see this part of the challenge. Part of Ares wished Jac was here, but thought it best that she wasn't. He couldn't afford the distraction. Coridan was younger and faster, but Ares had experience and patience on his side. As long as he kept the young warrior running, eventually he'd wear him out and finish him off with no one getting harmed in the process.

The men stood thirty feet apart, facing each other. With hands at their sides, they waited for Ariel to give the signal to begin. Ares flexed his fingers, preparing for the first strike. The seer announced the challenge and then signaled to begin. Ares had barely raised his hand before Coridan's energy burst struck him in the chest. Knocked from his feet, Ares flew through the air, wind whistling past his head, a second before he landed hard, flat on his back.

The hard ground was unyielding, as his lungs labored to get the air back that had been knocked away. Ares struggled to sit up. Rising up on one elbow, Ares caught the satisfied expression on Coridan's youthful face. The warrior was more of a threat than he'd anticipated. Ares scrambled to his knees and then stood. He brushed at the burning muscles in his chest as if the pain had been nothing, then positioned himself for the next round.

The signal dropped again and another burst rang out, this time catching Ares in the shoulder. His lips curled as his eyes met Coridan's face. *I see you've been practicing, young one.* He growled in his challenger's head.

The warrior's smile widened, then he shot back. *Jac will be mine, Ares. Soon I will sink between her welcoming thighs and plant my seed deep within her womb.* Coridan's eyes flared in warning. *And there is naught you can do to stop it.*

That is where you are wrong, young one. I will not willingly give up what is mine while there is breath left in my body.

The smile Coridan gave him was lethal.

* * * * *

Jac woke to an empty bed. Her head throbbed like a bass drum in a brass band. She couldn't remember how she got here. Jac swallowed, trying to get down whatever had died in her mouth the night before. She squinted, scanning the hut for Ares's presence even though she knew he wasn't there.

It had to be morning by now, but it was impossible to tell with only dim light illuminating the area. She pushed herself up, brushing the hair from her eyes, then threw her legs over the side of the bed and padded to the water bucket.

After splashing water on her face, Jac's head cleared. She strode over to the door and threw the hide back. The sun shone bright in the sky, dappling the floor of the jungle with gentle light. Creatures scurried and dashed, performing their normal daily dance. Jac yawned and scratched her stomach before stepping back inside to retrieve her black skirt. She glanced at her hiking boots. A part of Jac rebelled, the part that refused to be dictated to, the part that relished her freedom and would be controlled by no man. With firm resolve she slipped them on.

Not exactly a fashion statement, but down here, who cared. It would be weird strolling into the compound in broad daylight with only a skirt and shoes on, but she didn't have much choice in the matter.

When in Rome, flashed in her mind.

Jac proceeded toward the village, looking forward to seeing Ares getting dropped on his arrogant ass once or twice. She'd made it about a hundred and fifty yards or so when she heard shouts coming from the clearing up ahead. Her heart slammed against her ribs, knocking the breath from her lungs. Her mind scrambled as she tried to recall what the rules of the challenge were. Jac took off running, her booted feet squashing several ferns as she made a mad dash to reach the action.

She pushed through the brush as Coridan raised his hand and sent a bolt of energy sailing toward Ares's face. Ares twisted at the last second but the blast still clipped him on the cheek, jerking his head back, sending his ebony hair flying across his face.

Jac's hands flew to her mouth, smothering the shocked cry threatening to come out. She'd wanted to see her proud warrior a little embarrassed, but the thought of Ares actually being injured scared her more than she'd like to admit. This challenge was nothing like she'd imagined. Ares's body lay covered in bruises from his thighs to his head. It looked as if a crowd had ganged up on him and all taken a whack. Jac stood frozen at the edge of the trees afraid to continue watching and yet too terrified to turn away.

Ariel raised her hands and the battle began again. This time Ares caught Coridan unaware. He struck a fierce blow to the younger man's ribcage, knocking him to the ground. Ares glanced in Jac's direction, his eyes flicking from her skirt to her boots, and scowled, obviously not happy she was here. Well that was too damn bad. He'd have to get over it, because she wasn't going anywhere.

Coridan picked himself up off the dirt, holding his side, blood oozing from his split lip. He, too turned to look at Jac, but the seer dropped the signal before Coridan returned to position.

Ares fired two bolts at the young warrior, one landing on Coridan's rump and the other boxing his ear. He let out a yelp as a third shot hit him in the same spot on the ribcage. Bones cracked. A final lesser blow soared toward his lower abdomen. The young warrior moved at the last second and the shot caught him in the groin instead. Coridan fell to the ground rolling from side to side, attempting to soothe the injuries. Tribal members snickered, while a few laughed, before attempting to help him up.

Coridan pushed their hands away, fury blazing behind his aqua eyes. He struggled to his feet, his gaze not leaving Ares's face. "You will pay for this Ares. Mark my words."

Ares blinked, ignoring Coridan's heated words.

The seer walked to the center of the clearing and held up her hands. "The ruling is clear. I declare Ares the winner of the energy burst challenge."

Cheers rang out around them.

Jac took a step forward, then hesitated. The tension from the two men was so thick, almost oppressive. Coridan looked as if he'd meant every word he'd said. Jac's stomach flipped. She had a bad feeling about this whole situation.

The seer hushed the crowd. "There is one final trial to be overcome. When the warriors have completed the river challenge, then I will announce the winner. Until then, I suggest we get back to the tasks at hand. Warriors take your rest."

Rachel appeared at Jac's side, her eyes like saucers. The people of Atlantis gathered around Ares to congratulate him. Jac took that moment to speak with her friend.

"Why do they insist on going through with this stupid challenge?" She snarled under her breath. "Someone could have been killed today."

Rachel smirked and looked at Jac as if she had a hole in the middle of her forehead. "Have you and Ares been talking at all?"

Jac set her jaw, her blue eyes leveling on Rachel. "We talk. Not a lot, but we talk."

Rachel burst out laughing. "I'd suspected as much with Ares, he's more of an action kind of guy." She winked.

"He's a hard-headed, jackass kind of guy, who is too old to be playing childish games." Jac crossed her arms over her chest, suddenly aware of her nudity. "How did you get used to this get up?"

"I'm still working on it." Rachel pressed her lips together to keep from laughing again. "They're a little on the chauvinistic side, but they do grow on you, if you give them a chance."

Jac wasn't convinced. She loved Rachel, but obviously she'd been down here too long. "Are you going to come back with me when I go to New York?"

Rachel's features paled, then sadness filled her chocolate colored eyes. The air around them seemed to take a collective breath and stilled…waiting for her answer. Rachel glanced at the trees, then back at Jac, her voice quiet, when she started to speak.

"I've been helping these people translate some symbols that will allow them to return to their home planet."

Jac shook her head. "Oh, Rachel, come on, enough already. Tell you me you don't believe this Atlantean lost tribe crap."

Rachel's face looked pained, but she raised her chin in defiance. "I thought it would take me months, possibly years, to translate them, which was why I initially agreed to stay, but once I got started I found the code quite simple to crack." She paused. "And I fell in love."

"That much is obvious." Jac rolled her eyes.

Rachel looked around to make sure no one listened. "I will have the transport running within a couple of days."

Jac let out a ragged breath. "Then what, back to New York?"

"Then, hopefully the baby growing in my belly will be able to show me how to operate it."

"What?" Jac could feel the color draining from her face and then she started laughing. "That's a good one. You had me going until the baby part."

Rachel said nothing, color dotting her cheeks.

"You're kidding, right?" Jac grabbed Rachel's hands. "Tell me this is all some big cosmic joke, that you haven't lost your mind."

Rachel shook her head slowly from side to side.

Jac's heart sunk to her knees, taking all hope with it. She released Rachel. Oh my God, her friend really had lost it. She truly believed the mumbo jumbo she spouted. "You're planning on going with them, aren't you?" Jac found herself asking despite her disbelief.

Rachel bit her lip and glanced away again, as though unable to face her.

"I get it. I come all the way down here to this hell hole to rescue you, and you don't want to be rescued." A jagged laugh ripped from Jac's throat. She couldn't believe it, even though she'd suspected all along. "That's just great. What the hell am I going to tell Brigit?"

"Try to understand, Jac." Rachel grabbed Jac's hand back and twined it with her own. "I was hoping you'd change your mind and want to come too."

"And leave my friend behind," Jac yanked her hand from Rachel's grasp. "I'm not like you Rachel. I care whether or not I hurt my friends."

Rachel gasped.

Jac knew she wasn't playing fair, but right now she didn't care. Seeing Ares injured had scared the hell out of her, and now with Rachel standing in front of her, telling Jac she was leaving to go to another planet...well it was too much. Jac was happy with this planet, albeit it had its share of problems, but still... Their planet might not be any better. What if it was worse, assuming that it wasn't complete nonsense? Was Rachel willing to take that chance? Risk her life and the life of her baby on the outside chance things would be better?

From the look on her friend's face, Jac realized the answer was a definitive yes. She stared at Rachel for what felt like hours, yet no more than a few minutes passed. She'd changed so much in the few weeks she'd been missing that Jac hardly recognized her. And no matter how crazy Jac thought she'd become, deep down she admired Rachel for taking a stand, being strong in the face of such uncertainty.

Jac didn't know if she'd be able to follow Rachel into space, not that it was even possible. It was one thing to set out on a rescue mission into a jungle, where you could get back to New York in a matter of hours, but to leave the planet was a different ball of wax.

"I'd better let you get back to Eros." Jac hemmed. "I'm sure you have some kind of Queenly duties to perform after something like this." She pointed to the crowd surrounding Ares and Coridan.

Rachel gave Jac a sad smile and reached out to squeeze her hand. "I'll talk to you later tonight, at the feast."

"What feast?"

"The one honoring Ares on his win."

Jac's brows furrowed. "I thought the contest ended tomorrow."

Rachel's eyes flashed. "It does, but we honor the victor of the second challenge."

"Oh." Jac wondered who in the hell came up with these weird rules. Then she snorted. Probably the same damn people that convinced Rachel her baby could open the transport. *Where was that bitch, Ariel anyway?*

"See you later."

"Yeah, later," Jac parroted.

Rachel left in search of Eros. Jac watched until her friend's small frame disappeared, swallowed up by the crowd of Atlanteans. Sadness whelmed up, threatening to spill out. Jac pivoted and had taken one step into the jungle, when someone grabbed her arm. She didn't have to turn to recognize Ares. She could feel the heat from his fingertips. The gentle slide of his thumb, brushing against her sensitive skin, the intense energy that screamed *look at me* without having to say a word.

Jac turned, her eyes latching onto his slightly battered face. His green gaze remained sharp, hawk like, all seeing. She glanced down at her arm, where he held her and then back up. Ares slowly released her and smiled sinfully.

"Did you see the competition?" he asked, pride evident in his deep voice.

Jac shrugged. "Some."

He tilted his head down, nearing her ear. "And what did you think?"

"Do you really want to know?"

"Yes."

"Fine." Jac's hands flew to her hips. "I think you guys are nuts. You both could have been killed and for what, to spend time with me?"

Ares' nostrils flared and his eyes narrowed, to jagged jade shards.

"I told you before. I don't want to be anyone's mate. Certainly not the mate of a testosterone laden bonehead, not smart enough to concern himself with his own safety." She threw her arms up in the air, giving up. "And was it really necessary to shoot Coridan in the family jewels?"

Ares brow lifted and he seemed to be trying to suppress a grin.

"I don't think it's funny. You've humiliated the poor guy. They're going to be talking about this for years." Jac pointed to the crowd.

"Your concern for my welfare is touching, but I did nothing the rules did not allow. Besides I aimed higher."

"I didn't accuse you of cheating, only overkill."

Ares blinked, confusion marring his handsome face. "I know not what you speak of."

"You purposely embarrassed Coridan."

"He deserved it. Did you not see what he has done to me?" Ares pointed out his various bruises and cuts to Jac.

She winced when he turned, exposing a particularly nasty gash across his back. "Okay, maybe he deserved a little humbling, but you should have taken his age into consideration."

Ares stepped forward, crowding Jac with his muscled body. "He's not that much younger than me."

"That may be, but you're old enough to know better."

Jac ducked around and walked into the jungle leaving Ares staring after her. She knew he'd follow, because she headed back to his hut, at least that's where she hoped she was going. Hell, where else was there to go? The bruises on his body looked painful and would probably take weeks to heal. Jac didn't want to think about him being in pain. If she got off on that tangent she'd end up feeling sorry for him, helping, maybe even trying to nurse him back to health. Comforting wasn't her style, at least not when it came to men. Only Rachel and Brigit had ever been on the receiving end of Jac's caring and she'd made them swear never to tell a soul about it.

Jac glanced up at the sky through the leaf-covered canopy. Dark clouds were beginning to roll in and the wind had started to pick up. She took a deep breath, sweet smelling grass and the scent of distant rain assailed her. They were in for a storm, whether it would hit by this afternoon or later tonight she didn't know. The hair on Jac's arms rose as if she'd touched the electrical ball at the science center. She hurried on, wanting to be inside before the sky opened up and let loose its fury.

* * * * *

Ares watched Jac walk away. She'd gotten very good at doing so lately. He had to figure out a way to stop her from always running, but he wasn't sure exactly how to go about it. When she'd appeared at the edge of the woods, his heart had nearly stopped. He didn't want her anywhere near the energy challenge on the outside chance he'd suffer a fatal blow. It had taken all of his skill and concentration not to look at her after her arrival. He knew if he did, Coridan would take the competition and almost surely win Jac.

That was one thing Ares couldn't allow, not when he'd spent years mentoring the young warrior, teaching Coridan everything he needed to know to become a skilled hunter. The man standing before Ares today was not the same one who'd looked up to him, eager to learn. He was an altogether different creature, which Ares barely recognized.

For that reason alone Ares had ignored Jac as much as he'd been able, focusing solely on the young warrior, hoping he made a mistake. Luckily for him, Coridan had been as distracted by Jac's presence as Ares had been. Because of the strikes he'd gotten in earlier, Coridan had grown over confident, careless. When Ariel flagged the signal, it was the moment Ares had been waiting for. He didn't hesitate. He simply took aim and fired. And it pained him to admit, but Jac had been right about him trying to humble Coridan. The warrior had been goading him throughout the duel and wrong or right, Ares had, had enough.

He wasn't going to sit around and let him get away with being so disrespectful. So Ares had fired, catching Coridan in the ear and backside. He doubted the young buck would be able to sit for a week. The thought of that brought a smile to Ares's face. It wasn't mature, but it was how he felt. He glanced at the villagers, who had started to disburse. Coridan stood in the same spot, glaring at him. Ares knew in time the warrior would get over this public display, but from his stern expression he knew it would take a while…a very long while.

He signaled to Eros. *My friend I must speak to you.*

What troubles you at this victorious moment? Eros strode across the compound toward Ares.

Before I came to the challenge, I sensed a threat.

What kind of threat? Eros's eyes narrowed.

Ares shifted uncomfortably. *A human male has bypassed our safeguards and is making his way to the village.*

Eros's face hardened. *Do you sense him now?*

Ares stilled, sending his energy out into the jungle, but the strain from the battle had drained too much. *I can sense nothing at this time. I've used too much energy in defeating Coridan to be able to get an accurate reading.*

Eros nodded. *How close was he?*

I think he was at least one to two days travel away and closing fast. The readings were strange. He might have been moving away, but that would not make sense. Had it not been for the challenge I would have sought him out immediately and we would have our answers. Ares looked away, trying to hide the shame in his eyes.

Eros reached out and clasped him on the shoulder. *You have done what you needed to do to secure your mate. You could follow no other course of action.* He squeezed Ares and released him. *Nor would I ask you to do such a thing.*

Ares tried to smile. Eros was a good friend, a brother in arms, and the only man he'd ever called family since the fall of their civilization. But he could not alleviate the guilt Ares felt for choosing love over the safety of his people, especially when they were nearing the time of departure. Rachel had put together most of the transport, only a couple of pieces were missing. When they were in place, her unborn child would be able to activate it from inside her womb using the power of the

Atlantean people, allowing them to leave the confines of Earth forever.

Ares took a ragged breath and looked up into his friend's face. *I fear 'tis the red-devil come to haunt us again.*

We must be more vigilant in case he attempts to abduct one of our people. Eros glanced at the villagers. *We cannot afford to lose any more, for we know not what awaits us on Zaron.*

Ares nodded. *Once the challenge is complete I could lead a few men into the jungle to seek out this wily rodent.*

No. Eros glanced up at the darkening sky. *We will get our people out of here and leave him with nothing to find.*

I don't think he will be so easily dissuaded.

Eros arched a brow and cocked his head. *Have you forgotten about the mating ceremony? Do you no longer wish to go through the binding with Jac?*

Flinching, Ares' eyes widened. *What nonsense do you speak?* he choked out.

You talk of tracking off into the jungle, yet you do not mention the ceremony. He crossed his muscled arms over his wide chest.

Ares smiled and shook his head. *You know I think of naught else, but being joined to my fierce warrior woman.*

Then I suggest you work on conquering her and let the red-devil return to Hades where he belongs. Besides, I believe Jac is the more dangerous of the two. Eros waggled his eyebrows and laughed. *Be well my friend.*

Ares faded into the trees, following the thin trail leading to his hut. His feet fell silent upon the ground. The wind had picked up, whipping his long black hair about his face. He reached into the pouch at his side and pulled a strap to tie the mop back. The change in the weather had quieted the jungle beasts. It was as if every creature sought shelter.

His palms itched as he thought of running his hands over Jac's lithe body. Ares picked up speed despite the pain and exhaustion he felt, intent on making his thoughts a reality.

* * * * *

Two days journey away…

Manuel, the head tracker for Professor Rumsinger's expedition approached from the south, slogging through the rugged terrain. He'd been traveling for two days, pushing his body beyond its limits to give the professor the good news. He'd found the village. The professor would finally have his discovery and Manuel would get the riches the red-haired bastard had promised him. As for the villagers, he doubted they'd be alive come Saturday.

Chapter Thirteen

Ares was about seventy-five yards from the hut when he felt the first splatter of rain. The clouds had thickened so much it appeared as if night had swallowed the day. He moved around the now familiar trees, picking his way through the thick brush, every muscle in his body beginning to ache. Even if he was allowed, he doubted he had the energy left to send out a healing burst. He'd have to contend with the bruises and cuts for the night. Maybe the wounds would bring out the nurturer in Jac. He smiled. It was worth a try.

He'd made it twenty more feet when a burst of energy struck him from behind, knocking him to the ground. He'd barely been able to put his hands out to break his fall. He collapsed onto the thick ferns, his face resting against their cool leaves, as he struggled to gain his breath. He could smell the acrid odor of charred flesh and realized it came from his wound. Ares tried to push himself up from the ground, but couldn't seem to move, as if the blow had temporarily paralyzed his tired muscles.

I told you Ares, you would pay for the humiliation you caused me.

Ares didn't have to turn to know Coridan spoke. Pain and resentment burned in the younger man's voice, scalding his words, leaving the gaping wounds for all to hear.

What is it you want, young one? Ares tried to sound calm in Coridan's mind. He didn't want to agitate the warrior. *You are making a mistake. Have I not taught you like a father guides a son?*

You've taught me everything you know and now I'm going to use that knowledge to topple you. I need no other father, than the one who died those many years ago on Atlantis. And to prove it, I've come to show you that you can't get away with your arrogant behavior without repercussions.

Ares released a steady breath. *And just what are you planning to do?*

Coridan moved until he could peer down into Ares's face. *I plan on embarrassing you, like you embarrassed me. When the tribe sees you tied to a stake in the middle of the river, they'll realize just how far the mighty have fallen. It will take you centuries to live it down.* He laughed bitterly. *The great and mighty warrior, Ares, felled by an inexperienced young one. And to make it even better, your woman will be there to witness the fall. She told me how you needed to be taken down a peg or two. Well once she sees that I've done so, she'll be grateful, perhaps grateful enough to spread her thighs for a real warrior.*

Anger surged through Ares. Had Jac been part of Coridan's scheme? He didn't want to think it was so. The pain in his heart would be too great. She had always warned him that she would pay him back. Had this been what she'd been planning all along? Ares closed his eyes and struggled to rise, his feet refusing to cooperate. Coridan secured Ares's hands behind his back.

If you're wondering about your legs — don't bother. I've temporarily paralyzed your spinal cord. Coridan's voice hissed like an angry serpent in Ares's head. The young warrior heaved Ares onto his shoulder and slowly made his way through the jungle toward the river, leaving the hut fading in the gray afternoon light.

If you've healed yourself the contest is over. You've lost Jac.

Coridan laughed. *Jac and I care not for the contest, only your downfall.*

Bile rose in Ares's throat as he considered the implications. There would be no mating ceremony. He would have no offspring to continue his family line. Only the constant reminder of how his mate had betrayed him. Ares strained against his ties, unable to send an energy burst out with his hands bound, not that he had the energy to do so at this time. He was too exhausted from the challenge. Ares marveled that Coridan had managed to raise enough energy to not only heal himself, but incapacitate him also. He'd underestimated the young warrior once again and he was about to pay for his arrogance.

A half an hour later they arrived at the river. The rains had caused the current to grow swift, deadly. Coridan set Ares upon the muddy ground in a sitting position. The young warrior's expression grew troubled as he gazed at the water. Ares could see a stake had been set up in the center of the river, its ragged edge protruding out of the murky, swirling depths. A rope of vines had been strung from one bank to the other, setting up a safety net of sorts for the person trying to make his way through the current. Coridan glanced at Ares and pointed to the post.

That is where you will be in a matter of moments. Bound and humiliated, trussed like some great bird. When all is in place, I will call the tribe here, to witness your fall. They will hail me as a hero, perhaps even allow me to replace your position of honor amongst our people with my family's bloodline.

Are'-s jade eyes locked onto Coridan's excited face. *The village will not honor one who has shown that he is treacherous and cannot be trusted, even when he is showing the ignorance of his youth. You will become an outcast if you see this through. I suggest you untie me, before you do something that you will truly regret in the end.*

Coridan laughed. *Is that fear talking, Ares?*

Only truth.

For a second, doubt flashed across the young warrior's face. Just as quickly his expression hardened, all emotion pushed to the side.

Coridan threw Ares over his shoulder again and walked to the water's edge. One hand held Ares close, while the other gripped the thick lianas for support. He hesitated for a moment, before taking a step into the river, the current swirling violently around his shins. From Ares's upside down position, he saw debris of various sizes, ranging from twigs to animal carcasses float by.

Step after step, Coridan made his way deeper into the raging water. By the time he reached the post in the center, he struggled to hang on. Ares sensed the fear that registered for a moment in Coridan's confused mind, but the young warrior quickly pushed it aside and slid Ares off his shoulder and then slipped him onto the stake. The bindings on Ares's hands coupled with the swift current held his back firmly against the wood.

The water immediately came up to the top of Ares's chest. He would soon have to lift his head to keep the murky wash from coming into his mouth. His eyes sought Coridan once again. *'Tis not too late to undo the mistake you are about to make.*

Coridan looked at him one last time. *I'm afraid 'tis.* The warrior swung around and made his way back to the shore, his knuckles white as he gripped the vine. The liana beneath his hand strained as the muddy force of the river hit his chest, trying to sweep him away. By the time Coridan reached the bank, the color had drained from his face. He then turned one last time to look at Ares. *I will bring your mate here first, or should I say my mate, so she can witness your fall with me.*

With that he slipped into the jungle, leaving Ares to the fates.

Ares struggled to pull his hands free. The skies continued to dump bucketfuls of water. Coridan had done a good job of binding him. There was no breaking free. He glanced up at the gray clouds, and then at the rising current. The water already reached his collarbone. Within an hour or so it would surpass the stake and he'd drown.

He'd accept whatever the goddess willed. He let out a resolute breath as pieces of debris tore at his skin. Without Jac, maybe it would be for the best.

There was nothing left for him on this planet or off.

* * * * *

The rain started to fall in earnest, the spattering of drops tapped out a steady rhythm on the roof. Jac paced the small confines of the hut, wondering where in the hell Ares had gotten to. Her hiking boots made tiny crunching sounds with each step she took, while her long sheer skirt swooshed, scraping the ground. She glanced around the room as if searching for a clock on the wall. He should have been here by now.

Jac rubbed her hands along her arms, trying to ward off the sudden chill. Her stomach wrapped in knots and she couldn't seem to shake the feeling of unease snaking through her. She'd been so concerned over his safety earlier, that she'd practically bitten his head off. Surely he wasn't avoiding her. It wasn't Ares' style. He liked a good fight, like she did. It made life exciting or at the very least more interesting.

Jac pursed her lips and recalled the conversation she'd had with Rachel earlier. If all went well, her friend would be jettisoning, rocketing, or however in the hell they planned to travel into space, within a couple of days. Every movie Jac had ever seen raced through her mind, and when she got to *Alien* she shuddered. Heaven help them if acid for blood lizard monsters was what awaited them in space.

Jac ran her hands through her hair, shaking her fanciful thoughts. There were so many decisions to make. She couldn't just take off into outer space. *Could she*? Not that it was even possible.

No absolutely not. She had to get back to New York, her plants—Brigit. She didn't need to be traipsing across the galaxy with some muscle bound sex god. No matter how much he curled her toes. Not going to happen. No can do. It wasn't possible. *Was it?*

Jac paced for several minutes more, then decided to head off in search of her jade-eyed jackass. She walked to the door and through the hide back only to come face to face with Coridan. Jac gasped. Water ran down his handsome face in rivulets, plastering his long blond hair to his head. His golden muscles gleamed as the light from the fire pot illuminated his skin.

"What are you doing here?" Jac frowned and looked behind him. She thought maybe Ares would be here with him.

He smiled, flashing brilliant white teeth. "I've come to get you."

"For what?"

"I've done what we set out to do." His muscles flexed and excitement laced his voice. Coridan dropped to his knees and gave her a proper Atlantean greeting, kissing each nipple, but he didn't linger.

Jac forced herself to not move back. "I don't know what you're talking about."

"Come see." He grabbed Jac's hand and tugged.

She pulled away. "I don't think I better leave until Ares gets back."

The smile left his face for moment and his eyes seemed to dim. Then just as quickly Coridan recovered.

"What's going on?" Jac glared at him.

"I can't tell you." He shook his head, sending droplets to the earthen floor. "You'll have to see for yourself. 'Tis a surprise."

Jac stared at the young warrior for a few moments. She didn't want to be missing in action when Ares got back, but it was obvious Coridan wasn't going to tell her what happened, and she'd have to go see for herself. Jac slipped out of the hut, allowing Coridan to pull her along through the jungle. The air had cooled due to the continuing rain, yet still was oppressively muggy. She ran her free hand through her hair, slicking it back off of her face. The dark clouds had shadowed the jungle, until it no longer looked like day.

They stepped over felled branches and around trees. The sweet smell of rain laced the air, blending with the various strains of wild orchids growing in the area. Coridan marched on toward the river, dragging Jac behind, all the while mumbling about comeuppances, rivers, and pegs. Jac had no idea what he was talking about, yet the further they trekked into the forest, the deeper her sense of dread became.

Thirty minutes later they reached the banks of a muddy river. Jac stopped, halting Coridan in the process.

"Okay, we're here. Now tell me, what is going on?" Jac crossed her hands over her bare chest.

Coridan's eyes followed the movement, fastening on her nipple a second before she covered the rosy peak.

"I've done it," he said, his voice filled with excitement.

She shook her head. "Yeah, you've been saying that for a while, but I have no idea what you are talking about."

Coridan raised his hand and pointed to the water, before dropping his arm.

Jac glanced at the raging river and then back at his face, giving him a half smile in encouragement. "I still don't know what you mean."

He grinned and pointed again, this time leaving his hand up. Jac followed the line of sight, but didn't see anything out of the ordinary, other than debris, murky water, and a few stumps that had obviously lodged in the riverbed.

"I wanted you to be the first to see how the mighty has fallen."

Jac smiled back. "The first to see what? Coridan, honey, you're talking in riddles and to be honest with you, I've never been very good at them." She forced the edge from her voice.

Jac placed her hands on her hips and set her jaw. She grew tired of playing this guessing game. Soaked to the bone, she began to lose her patience. She needed to get back before Ares grew worried.

"He thought he could humiliate me and get away with it, but look at him. Who's the fool now?" Coridan smiled wide and nodded.

Jac felt the color drain from her face. Her eyes bulleted onto the water's churning surface, scanning. She picked out every piece of debris, identifying it, then moving onto the next. She stared at a post floating near the center. The wood appeared black on one side and started to tilt from the force of the current. Her gaze was about to move on when her eye caught a flash of movement. It had been so minor she might have missed it had she blinked. Jac focused on the log. The movement occurred again, like the last sparks of life from a fire before it fades to darkness.

Bile rose in her throat, the force of the situation hitting her square in the solar plexus. The black was Ares's hair and the movement she'd caught had been his attempt to catch a breath in the rising water. He was starting to drown. Jac couldn't seem to move. Air refused to enter her lungs. In that second, she was back in her parent's home, staring down at the body of her father. She'd tried to save him, but couldn't. She stood by helplessly, watching as her father's once vibrant life slipped away before her eyes.

The water continued to rise. The current roared with unchecked fury. Jac's muscles were locked in place, like the fear in her heart. She was going to lose him all over again, but this time it wasn't her father's lifeless body staring back at her, it was Ares's. The only other man she'd ever loved.

The realization socked her in the gut, almost knocking her to her knees. "What have you done?" she heard herself scream.

Coridan's expression showed extreme shock. "I did it for us." He struggled, trying to make her understand. "We needed to show Ares, he is not as great as he thinks he is."

"You're killing him." Jac grasped him, her nails sinking into Coridan's meaty arm. "Help me."

His eyes shot from her face to the speck that identified Ares head sticking out of the water. "I cannot swim."

"What?"

He shook his head and pulled away from her. The color had drained from his face. "I cannot swim. I took him out there using the vines."

Jac looked back at the water. She could see what appeared to be vines tied off on tree trunks, but they didn't seem to stretch across the water. "Where are they?"

"Gone. Washed away." Coridan turned, and raced off into the jungle as if the devil himself were hot on his heels.

Jac took a deep breath, trying to still her rising panic. Her heart slammed against her ribs. She stared at the water, unable to move. Ares head dipped below the surface before coming back up. She would have to watch him die, just like her father.

"Nooo!" Jac bolted upstream.

* * * * *

Ares saw the second Jac and Coridan entered the clearing near the riverbank. Coridan had been leading her by the hand, the warrior's triumphant smile clearly visible, even from Ares's precarious position. The water rose rapidly and within a few moments he would in all likelihood drown. His eyes locked on Jac's slender form, basking in her beauty one final time before leaving this Earth. His heart swelled as he recalled the moments he'd shared with his mate. At least he'd been lucky enough to find her before the goddess took him away. He only wished she'd cared enough to want to remain by his side.

He watched as Coridan pointed out his position. Jac looked and shrugged, smiling tentatively at the young warrior. Obviously she didn't care if the water swallowed him up. She glanced at the river's surface once again, then turned her attention back to Coridan. It was all Ares needed to see. He closed his eyes and gasped for breath. Water swirled around his head, tugging at his hair with ever building force, releasing the binding holding it. He pulled at the ties around his wrists, if anything the river had caused them to constrict.

Ares forced the pain away, letting go of the heartbreak, instead readying himself for the inevitable. The onslaught of debris scraped his skin raw. Soon there would be enough of his blood in the water to bring out the caiman. If the river didn't get him first, the caiman surely would. His mind centered, he forced away all thought. Then he heard Jac scream.

Over the roar of the water, it came like a whisper of hope. His eyes flew open and he sought her out. She stood like a shadow of her former self, white as a ghost, trembling with...*Fear*? He read her mind a second before she started to move. He knew in an instant she'd risk her life to save him. He couldn't allow that, though it pleased him greatly that she'd try.

Do not come out here, Jac. 'Tis too late. He sent the thought with as much force as he could muster. *You will not die trying to save me. You must stay on shore. Go back to your home. New York awaits you.*

Her thoughts scrambled in her mind. The past and present slammed into her, turning her upside down, inside out. Ares knew she heard him, because she hesitated. *I'm not going to lose you, too. I love you.* The thought slammed back in Ares's head. He knew Jac had no idea she'd sent it. His heart swelled, then pounded in his chest as he gasped for breath once more. He only had moments before the water took away the luxury of air. He would go to his death peaceably, knowing that she loved him.

So Ares sent out a final thought, hoping Jac received it before it was too late. *Please Jac, do this for me. Return to your home. Live your life. All I ask is that you remember the time we spent together.* He gulped, taking in a mouthful of water and began to choke. With a last gasp he finished his words. *I love you, too. Until we meet again.*

* * * * *

Jac felt the second Ares gave up. Tears were streaming down her cheeks as she glanced back and saw his head slip beneath the surface. She sprinted up the shore, tugging off her boots, and then slipped out of her skirt. Naked, Jac raced forward and dove into the swift moving water. All her training came back to her in a second. She had one shot at reaching him before the current swept her too far down stream to be effective.

Jac stroked hard, her muscles straining against the fierce pull. Her lungs screamed as she sucked in mouthfuls of water, but she didn't stop, she put her head down and swam harder. She broke the surface a few yards from where Ares had been. The top of the stake poked out of the water. With one final kick Jac dove, searching blindly in the mud and muck. Her hands latched onto limbs and rocks, releasing them instantly once she'd established their origin. Lungs burning, she refused to surface. Spots were forming behind her eyes and still she grasped.

Hope dwindling with every second, she lunged one last time and struck something hard, a log. Jac felt around it until she encountered flesh. She wrapped her arms as far around the object as she could and kicked to the surface with all her might. Jac's head broke the surface at the same time Ares bobbed up. His face was blue and he didn't appear to be breathing. Hot tears scalded her face as she tried to keep the log from rotating and flipping him face down in the water.

Jac worked her way along the stake, until she encountered his hands. He'd been bound. Her stomach rolled, threatening to empty its contents. In seconds she decided to leave him that way, because if he slipped from the log she'd never make it to shore toting his body weight. She continued forward struggling to reach his battered face. With one hand she clasped his nose, while the other pried his mouth open. Jac took a big gulp of air and forced it into Ares's lungs. The effort left her shaky.

Nothing.

The current carried them swiftly. She took another breath and exhaled into him, losing her grip for a moment, before pulling herself back up from the thrashing depths. His lashes lay like black crescents against his chiseled cheeks, so handsome, so strong...so much to live for. She wasn't going to let him die, too. Jac pushed breath after breath into Ares, without getting any response.

"Daddy, please help me!" Her cry rang out to the heavens, like a wounded animal, a tortured sound half woman, half child.

She kicked again forcing the log to stay upright, her muscles growing weary, balancing and fighting the endless drag. They were moving downstream at a frightening clip. "Daddy, please don't let him die." Her hands dug into Ares' muscled arms, as if by holding on tight, he'd be unable to leave her—wouldn't die.

She pulled herself up a fraction out of the water and then brought her fist down on Ares' wide chest. "Breathe, damn you." Jac punched him again and again, then took one final breath, forcing air into his lungs, refusing to let it escape. She pulled back and waited. Strength waning, Jac slipped beneath the water. A second later she surfaced choking, her fingertips still gripping the stake. "You can't die on me. I won't let you. You promised to be my mate." Pain and desperation ate at her. "Come back to me, damn it." She choked again. "I love you." She grabbed Ares by the hair, lifting his face to hers. "Do you hear me? I love you."

Water washed over them.

"If you live, I promise I'll stay." Jac cradled Ares' head in her hands. Her body trembled as she went into shock. She'd lost him, just like she'd lost her father. Both were so strong, so virile and full of life, and now they were gone. She clung to Ares, placing kisses across his face. Her heart squeezed in her chest, threatening to burst. With tears streaming down her face, Jac did the only thing she knew how to do.

She got mad.

All the hurt from the past ten years flooded her system, overloading her senses until blind fury took over. Like a shot of adrenaline, anger coursed through her veins. She dropped Ares' head back upon the log and began to strike his sternum, like a woman possessed. She kicked hard in the water trying to ease them sideways toward the shore, not stilling for a moment to lessen her blows. She knew there was no way they'd reach the bank without going with the current. Jac re-adjusted Aress' head, opening his airway. She balanced half off, half on the stake, as she filled her lungs over and over, emptying them into his massive chest.

Her head spun from dizziness and exhaustion when her feet finally touched bottom several miles downstream. She dragged the stake as far onto the shore as she could, continuing CPR. Jac didn't stop until she collapsed. She lay next to the log, her arm flopping against Ares' ribs. Her lungs labored. Her muscles cramped. But still she made some attempt to bring him back. Jac closed her eyes. It felt as if she'd been ripped in two. Her shoulders began to shake as unspent sobs racked her body. She unsheathed Ares' knife, slicing the blade through his bindings. His arms fell limp at his sides. Jac slipped the blade back into the sheath.

The water continued to thunder at their feet, its sound overpowering all others. Jac's hand flopped against his ribs, at the same time Ares' chest rose. Her body trembled so badly, Jac thought she'd imagined it. She opened her eyes and turned her head. Ares took a ragged breath and coughed, sending water spouting in the air. Jac froze, unable to move, fearing that her eyes were playing tricks on her.

She waited, holding her breath. His chest rose and fell. Laughter mixed with tears, as Jac began to cry in earnest. She looked up toward the heavens. "Thank you, Daddy."

Chapter Fourteen

Within an hour Jac and Ares were surrounded by members of the tribe. Eros and Rachel pushed through the crowd, their faces ashen with worry. Jac sat up. Coridan appeared at their side, his face twisted and full of pain.

"What is he doing here?" She glared at Coridan, fighting back the fury she felt being in his presence. "Where did you go when I needed you earlier?"

The young warrior flinched but did not leave, his face growing visibly paler as the true gravity of the situation sunk in. He'd almost murdered Ares.

"He's admitted all, even down to the fact that he couldn't swim and was unable to assist you earlier," Rachel said calmly. "He's here to help now."

The villagers raised their hands, palms facing down, and began to chant. Jac watched as a yellow glow spread throughout the group, building in intensity to correspond with their rising voices. Suddenly energy shot out, striking Ares in the chest. His body bowed up, rising from the log, before collapsing back down.

Jac tried to steady his movements. Her eyes sought Rachel's for reassurance. "They're not hurting him, are they?"

Tears pooled in Rachel's brown orbs as she shook her head. "They're healing him."

Jac fell back, her hand remaining on Ares' chest, too exhausted to move. She'd done it. She'd saved Ares. Jac had saved the only other man she'd ever loved. Moments later, Jac felt herself being lifted from the ground by Coridan and carried through the jungle. She snagged Ares' hand at the last second, refusing to release him into Eros's care. So side by side, the warriors walked. Ares slung over Eros's broad shoulder, while Jac lay cradled in Coridan's arms.

An hour or so later they arrived at Ares' hut. Eros deposited the jade-eyed warrior onto his bed of furs and Coridan placed Jac carefully beside him.

Jac peered at Eros. "He will be all right, won't he?"

Eros smiled and nodded. "Thanks to you, I still have my brother at arms."

Jac's gaze strayed to Ares's face. He seemed to be resting comfortably. She turned back to look at Coridan, not attempting to hide the contempt she felt for the man.

He stepped forward and lowered his head. "I have chosen to exile myself from my people in punishment for my deeds. I hope someday you will accept my apologies and be able to forgive me, Jac." With that he stepped back and left the hut.

Eros watched Coridan leave, then turned to Jac. "He came to us, full of fright, desperate for our assistance. We picked up his psychic cry before he made it to the village. He told us what he'd done and begged for our forgiveness. I granted it on one condition." Eros's face looked pained. "That he exiles himself from the village."

"I'm sorry," Jac said. It was a shame so many lives had almost been ruined because of what started out as lust for revenge.

Eros stared at Jac. "I think it best that you both get some rest. Tomorrow's ceremony will be a long, drawn out affair."

"Ceremony?" Jac's brows furrowed.

Eros smiled. "Ares has told me you have decided to stay."

"But how?" Jac's head jerked around.

A devilish smile curved Ares' lips.

"He couldn't of...no way... he was dead." Jac looked up to get confirmation from Eros, only to see the hide flap on the door fall. He was gone.

"I'll leave you two to work it out." Eros's departing words were followed by peals laughter.

Jac let the King's comment wash over her as she snuggled into Ares' side, too grateful to get upset.

* * * * *

Jac awoke the next morning, her head resting on Ares' chest. She could hear the steady thud of his heart as it beat against his ribcage. She smiled without opening her eyes, the sound, music to her ears. She encircled his waist and curled up tighter around him. Jac didn't think she'd ever be able to let him go.

"Ah, but you must release me, my love." His voice rumbled, snaking around her, settling deep within her stomach, before dropping lower.

Jac smiled again and shook her head in protest.

"Today is our mating ceremony. We must be prepared."

She sat up to look at him, bracing herself on her elbow, her sculpted brow slightly arched. "That reminds me...how in the hell did you know I said I'd stay?"

Ares grinned. "I may have left this realm, but I could still hear the words that were torn from your heart, for they spoke to mine."

Jac smiled back. She couldn't help herself. "I think that's a load of crap, but it's still nice to hear."

Ares laughed. The hardy sound rolled over her, embracing, lifting, and gathering her close.

"Just because I agreed to stay, don't think things are going to change." Her gaze leveled on his handsome face. The bruises had already started to fade and the cuts had scabbed over.

"I'm counting on that." Ares rubbed the rough pad of his thumb along her sensitive spine. "My fierceness." His eyes sparked fire as he glanced down at her nakedness, peeking out from beneath the furs.

"You've got to be kidding." Jac felt her nipples respond, tightening into tiny nubs.

Ares growled, his expression turning feral. "You deny a man who's been ripped from the jaws of death a little pleasure?"

Jac's clit ached and began to twitch. Even though it had only been a day, it felt as if it were a lifetime, since she'd last lain beneath his pressing weight. Her tongue darted out to wet her lips and was instantly captured by Ares' mouth in a searing kiss.

"Mine," he growled out against her lips and then he dipped deeper, swirling and sparring, tasting and tempting, seeking out her moisture like a man deprived.

His teeth nipped at her lower lip, teasing, drawing out her desire as only he could. His hands gripped the round globes of her ass, pulling her up and over until she was spread and lying on top of him. He kneaded her bottom as if it were dough, rolling and grinding her skin beneath his fingertips. Jac's sex dripped upon his staff, singeing him with her liquid heat.

Ares' muscles tightened in anticipation. He stroked over her outer lips, her channel moistened, readying her for his cock's arrival, all the while intensifying the embrace. Ares felt his shaft lengthen, growing thicker with each passing second. Jac reached down and grasped his throbbing member. Air hissed from his lungs. Ares pulled away from the kiss and clamped his jaw down. His fingers sought her entrance, then slipped inside.

Jac moaned.

He pulled her higher until he could push another digit in beside the first, then he began to finger fuck her. Jac's breath came in gasps, her vision clouded, as a haze of desire spread through her. Ares pushed deeper and she ground her hips against his hand. His thumb scraped her clit and Jac cried out. He continued to massage the hidden button, flicking his nail enough to intensify her pleasure. Jac sat up and began to ride his fingers.

Ares watched her creamy breasts bob up and down. The rosy peaks at the tips mesmerized him, capturing his full attention, as they engorged, stabbing out in search of his hungry mouth. He sat up, popping a bud into his mouth and began to suckle hard. His teeth nibbled and tugged, then he released one nipple and moved to the other. Jac's hips bore down, frenzied. She tried to increase the speed of the movements, but couldn't in her current position. So Ares released her breasts and sat back.

He slipped one moist finger from her cunt and slid it over her anus. The muscles in Jac's thighs clenched and her eyes widened in surprise, but she made no attempt to stop him. Ares circled the tight opening, moistening the edges, preparing it for his intrusion. Then slowly, very slowly he slid inside, matching the motions of his other fingers. Jac threw her head back and screamed, shattering against his hands in a violent orgasm. She collapsed forward onto his chest, her lungs laboring for breath.

Ares cock bucked beneath her, demanding entrance into her tight sheath. It had taken every fiber of his being not to drive his length into her awaiting body, but he knew he must hold off, saving his energy. He should wait until after the mating ceremony, when he'd be potent. He knew then nothing would be able to keep him from pounding into Jac's willing pussy.

Jac saw stars. She'd never allowed anyone to get near her ass during sex. She hadn't realized what she'd been missing—or maybe it was Ares' magical touch. Jac swallowed a couple of times, trying to slow her maddening heartbeat. Her body trembled and shook as the last of her orgasm rippled over her, shattering her nerve endings, igniting her desire, fueling her love. Ares' skin moistened beneath her mouth, with a quick flick of her tongue she tasted the salt from his sweat.

The air filled with the odor of musky sex. His skin heated to a raging inferno as she touched him. She tried to steady herself, regain her thoughts. She'd wanted Ares to fuck her so bad she hadn't been able to see straight. Yet, he hadn't. Why? When she could form coherent words again she'd ask.

They lay in silence for a few moments. Jac could feel Are' cock, hard as diamonds, beneath her belly. She started to rise up so she could take him inside of her, but he stopped her movements as if reading her thoughts once again.

His voice graveled when he spoke. "We cannot." Ares shook his head.

"Why not?" Jac couldn't help but sound petulant.

His jade gaze locked on her face. "The mating ceremony will take place in a few hours."

"So." Jac sat up. "You pleasured me. Why can't I take care of you?"

"'Tis different."

Jac frowned. "Don't give me that chauvinistic bullshit."

Ares' lips thinned, but his eyes sparkled with amusement. "Since we didn't get to spend the night apart, as is tradition, we must abide by this aspect if we hope for the ceremony to be a success."

"Successful?" Jac frowned. "I don't know if I understand, all we have to do is say, I do." Jac dropped onto her elbows and rested her chin in her hands.

"Is it not a tradition for the bride and groom to spend the night apart in your culture?" He tilted his head.

"Yes." She admitted grudgingly.

Are' face pinched with strain. "Given the circumstance, this is the best we can do."

Jac really didn't agree with his reasoning, but she figured it wasn't worth arguing about. Besides, her heart rate had sped up the second he mentioned bride and groom, and she couldn't seem to slow it back down. She pushed off of Ares and slid from the bed. Her finger trailed along his heavy length before stepping away.

"If you say so," she teased.

Ares' muscles tightened, straining beneath her fingertips.

"You better get going. You don't want to be late for the ceremony." She smiled and let her lashes drop to half-mast.

Ares took a ragged breath and pushed aside the furs. His body flexed and stretched as he got up from the bed, his enormous cock standing at attention. His gaze dropped to the floor. He picked up his loincloth, quickly slipping it on. He walked to the hidden panel and opened up, withdrawing a new black skirt. Ares handed it to Jac.

"Put this on," he said, then made his way to the door. He gripped the hide covering the entrance like a lifeline, before turning to face her one last time. His expression was grim.

"Later today, Eros will come to prepare you. I know I have not explained all, but please allow him to do this, my love. It is part of the ritual."

The pain on Ares' face showed clearly. Jac wasn't sure what he meant by *prepare* but was sure by the emphasis he'd placed on the word, she wasn't going to like it. At least Ares didn't seem to be any happier about the idea than she did, which was a small consolation. He gave her a half smile and then slipped through the door.

Jac paced the length of the hut, her imagination going overboard. She envisioned every possible scenario that could be included in a preparation and had come to one conclusion. She wasn't about to fuck Rachel's husband. No way. No how. So they'd have to come up with some other way to get her ready for the mating ceremony.

In fact, it kind of pissed her off that Rachel hadn't mentioned any of this when they'd gone down by the stream that first day of her arrival. Jac ran her hands through her hair. But then again, it wasn't like she'd actually given any indication she would stick around, so Rachel might have figured what's the point. Jac nodded, citing the likeliest scenario. By the time Eros got here there would be a rut running the length of Ares' hut from her pacing. Jac's nerves skidded across her skin, making her painfully aware of every creak, snap, and brush against the dwelling.

By the time Eros reached the door, Jac was going out of her mind. She glared at him, arms crossed over her chest. "I don't know what this is about, but if I have to have sex with you, you can forget about it, ritual or not." She sliced a hand through the air.

Eros's aqua eyes widened and the corner of his mouth curved in amusement, but he said nothing. He simply continued to stare at her, waiting for her to finish.

"Have you told Rachel what you're planning on doing?" She began to pace again. "I'm sure if you had, she wouldn't be very happy."

With the mention of Rachel, some of his amusement faded.

"You did tell her, didn't you?" Jac stopped to face him.

Eros looked decidedly uncomfortable. "The Queen is well aware of the duties I must perform concerning my station."

Jac laughed. "You didn't tell her."

"There is nothing to tell." He snorted, shrugging his broad shoulders.

"Chicken."

His eyes narrowed, bulleting on her face, but his expression wasn't as confident as his voice implied. "Let's get on with this."

Jac took a deep breath. "Fine."

"Take off your skirt."

Jac flinched, but her voice remained steady, determined. "Promise you're not going to fuck me?"

"'Tis a promise."

Jac swallowed hard, but did as he asked. It wasn't like he and the rest of the tribe hadn't already seen her naked the day before. She slid the sheer material over her hips and let it sink to the floor. Her eyes followed the skirt, as it settled around her ankles. She felt Eros's gaze burning over her exposed skin, focusing on the slim thatch of hair between her thighs.

Shoring up her strength, Jac met his gaze. His blue eyes held hers for a moment, then turned molten as he continued to peruse. The muscles in his chest tensed and she could make out the thick outline of his cock as it bulged behind the material of his loincloth. Jac's heart slammed against her ribs as Eros took a step forward, closing the distance between them. Just when she thought he would reach out and touch her, he stepped around her, walking to the table. He opened up the pouch at his side and pulled several small containers from inside.

Jac watched as he carefully laid the items out on the table. There were brushes and what appeared to be oils neatly lined up. He opened the container and began to slather his hands. Jac had a feeling she knew what he was about to do, but she still felt completely unprepared for the moment Eros placed his large hands upon her shoulders. Shivery tingles spread over her skin, radiating down to her toes. Her nipples kernelled and her pussy wept. He hadn't moved, yet heat spread over her, lapping at the farthest regions of her desire, fanning hidden flames. Jac pictured Ares.

Eros ran his hands over her shoulders and down her arms, leaving the delicate scent of vanilla behind. Fire seemed to shoot from his fingertips with razor like intensity. He moved to her back, rubbing, soothing, and stroking. Jac closed her eyes and tried to fight her body's natural response, but quickly lost the battle. His hands dipped lower, cupping her bottom, then drawing up to circle the tiny indents at the base of her spine. Jac bit her lip to keep from groaning.

She swayed as his hands continued their upward climb, looping around to brush the underside of her breasts. Jac could feel the heat coming off Eros as he stepped nearer to extend his reach, yet he didn't touch her with his body, which was just as well. The tension thrumming through him was tangible. She could almost taste it in the charged air. Jac imagined it was Ares' touch, as Eros's fingertips dipped toward her abdomen, circling the nerves surrounding her belly button until she gasped. He stroked lower, scraping the crisp strip of curls covering her woman's center.

Jac sucked in a breath and held it, willing his hand to go lower, yet at the same time not wanting him to touch her there. He slid down her legs, covering them in oil, then slowly made his way back up. Jac could hear Eros's strained breath as he massaged the inside of her thighs. Vanilla mixed with the musky scent of Jac's sex filled the air. The harder she fought the pull of his hands, the more turned on she became. To Jac's horror, her legs began to tremble.

His fingertips were hot as branding irons when he finally slid them along her warmth. Shudders rocked Jac, as he spread his fingers, opening her up to his intimate probing. Jac's channel flooded as one digit came close to slipping inside, then shied away. Her legs clamped shut, trapping his hand. Eros fell forward, his body gently colliding with Jac's back. His skin scalded her, his masculine scent surrounding, overwhelming, intoxicating. Suddenly Jac couldn't breathe. She relaxed her thighs, releasing his hand.

Jac felt Eros's thick cock buck beneath his loincloth, stretching the limits of its bindings. With his free hand Eros parted her nether lips and found her hidden nub. His thumb began making sensual circles around the nerve endings, urging her toward completion. In and out, he continued to work his magic. Eros's hips thrust of their own volition, matching the rhythm of his massaging fingers. Soon their movements were primal. Jac ground her sex against his hand, seeking release. She could hear Eros's desperate pant against her ear.

"Please, Jac," he thrust forward, his loinclothed shaft brushing her back. "Come for me."

Jac rode his fingers like a runaway horse, imagining Ares' large cock buried inside her. Eros slipped his fingers around her entrance and then reached up to pinch her nipple. All the while his thumb continued to work her clit. Jac's body flared. She writhed in his arms, drawing nearer and nearer to that elusive orgasm.

Eros released Jac long enough to spin her around in his arms. His mouth closed over a ripe bud, sucking the nipple between his teeth. He lifted Jac from her feet. She automatically wrapped her legs around him. Jac closed her eyes and pictured

Ares' starkly handsome face. Eros's fingers once again sought her hidden pearl.

He pulled away from her nipple then stuck out his six-inch tongue and flicked each peak, at the same time his thumb stroked her clit. Jac's body jerked back as she came, but Eros didn't release her. He continued his assault until Jac's screams of release filled the jungle. Then, and only then, did Eros quit rubbing her clit. He gave each peak one more quick brush with his tongue, then pulled his drenched fingers from between her legs.

Jac could still feel Eros's cock, straining for relief. In her euphoria, Jac actually considered offering to ease his discomfort. Then she opened her eyes, her senses coming back to her in an instant. Jac once again realized who she experienced intimacies with, and sobered quickly. She pushed away from Eros's chest. He slowly lowered her to her feet, making sure she could stand before releasing her and stepping back. For some reason, despite all they'd shared, Jac felt a little on the shy side. A feeling she decided she could definitely do without.

Eros dropped to his knees before Jac. "Thank you for doing me the honor of allowing me to prepare you for the mating ceremony." He kissed first one of Jac's nipples, then brushed his lips across the other. He rose to his feet and started gathering the items, placing them back into the pouch at his side. Eros turned to leave when Jac placed her hand upon his forearm stopping him.

Jac crossed one arm over her chest. "Did Rachel have to go through this sort of preparation?"

Eros's face hardened and his jaw clenched. He blew out a ragged breath. "Yes," he bit out.

Jac knew she wasn't going to like the answer, but she had to ask the question. "Who was given the task of preparing her?"

His eyes flared and then Eros seemed to calm. "The task was left to Ares. 'Tis long been an Atlantean tradition, yet it does not make it any easier on the mate." He gave her a half smile as if he finally understood what Ares had gone through.

Coridan's words from the day they met, rushed back to her. She hadn't known what preparation was at the time.

Jac shook her head. The full weight of the situation hit her and she was too shocked to actually speak. Her mind raced as she imagined her friend Rachel being stripped down and oiled up. That must have been quite an ordeal for her, knowing Rachel the way she did. Jac didn't want to think about the fact Ares had touched her friend the way Eros had touched her. No it was best to ignore that altogether or else she'd never make it through this ceremony without shredding someone. Jac glanced at Eros. Given the circumstances she and Rachel would have to call it even.

Eros picked up Jac's black skirt. He ran his hands over the length, changing the color to a beautiful jade green. "Put this on. I'll be waiting outside to escort you to the ceremony."

Jac clasped the cloth to her, the silky fibers brushing against her nipples. She watched as Eros slipped through the door, his broad back glistening with sweat. If this occurred before the ceremony, she couldn't imagine what would take place after.

Chapter Fifteen

Jac dressed quickly. Her nerves were skittering beneath her skin like thousands of tiny ants invading a picnic basket. She walked to the water barrel and wet her fingertips enough to slick her hair back from her face. Jac took one last steadying breath, then proceeded out the door.

Eros grasped her hand, placing it on his arm, and led her along the trail toward the village. The jade in Jac's skirt sparkled in the sunlight, and the air seemed particularly fragrant, as if all the flowers had bloomed for her big day.

Jac shook her head as she considered the magnitude of what she was about to do, but a promise was a promise. Besides, she really didn't want to go back on her word. When she'd almost lost Ares yesterday her scattered, self-centered life and the priorities in it had clarified, becoming crystal clear in a nanosecond.

She glanced around, luxuriating in the warm air and the mild day. She had gotten so used to the jungle that she didn't notice the animals chattering, even though truth be told they never really shut up. Jac thought about the preparation ritual she'd been through, unfortunately her mind jumped to the next logical conclusion.

"Does Ares go through a *preparation*?"

Eros glanced down at her and smiled. "Not like you're thinking."

She arched a brow. "What then?"

"Ariel chants over him."

"And?" Jac's gaze leveled.

"'Tis all. I swear." Eros put his hand on his heart.

Jac considered asking again, but before she got a chance, they reached the clearing. A crowd had gathered in the center of the compound, their eager voices murmuring in hushed tones. Jac and Eros left the cover of the trees a second before all eyes fell upon them. Ares stood next to the seer, draped in a jade loincloth, his tanned chest bared, showing his impressive muscles. His ebony hair had been plaited at the sides, with the back hanging free. It gleamed in the dappled sunlight, a striking shade of midnight blue.

Jac's breath caught as their eyes met and held for a second. Rachel stood off to the side, dabbing at her tear filled eyes with an aqua cloth. Jac immediately looked away from her friend. There was no way she would cry again. She'd done enough of that yesterday. Eros brought her forward until she stood beside Ares. Eros dropped to his knees and kissed her nipples, his aqua eyes glittering with amusement as he rose.

"Good luck," he whispered to Ares.

"I heard that." Jac shot him a censoring look that she hoped said I'll get you later. Eros strode to Rachel's side. He slid his arm around his wife's shoulders, lending her his strength, and gazed on in innocence.

Jac's attention returned to Ares. He grabbed her hand, giving it a quick squeeze. Ariel stood before them with her hands in the air. The crowd quieted.

"We are here to witness the joining ceremony of Ares and Jac." The words came out strong and clear as she spoke. "'Tis been a long time coming."

There were muffled giggles from the crowd behind them. Jac fought the urge to turn and glare. She knew the added comment had been aimed at her. She wasn't going to give them the satisfaction today. Jac kept her gaze forward, ignoring the fact she was so close to her rival for Ares' affections. As soon as the thought left her mind, in the peripheral Jac saw Ariel's lips twitch, as if she were fighting back a smile.

The seer bade them both to step forward and face her. She placed her hands on both their heads and began to chant. Jac heard a loud pop in her ears. Her palms immediately flew to her head, covering her ears. She waited for pain to appear, but there was none. The seer continued to speak about the love and bonds of the joining. Jac blinked, when she realized Ariel's lips no longer moved, yet she would swear she could hear every word. She glanced at Ares in confusion. He smiled and grabbed her hand again.

Do you hear me, Jac?

"Yes."

Good, then the ceremony is complete.

"Are you some kind of ventriloquist or something too?"

The seer laughed. *Not exactly.*

"Then how can I hear you?" Jac glanced around at the villagers, but no one seemed to think anything was amiss from the gleeful expressions on their faces.

'Tis the same way you were able to hear Ares, when he spoke to you. Your mind has been opened – expanded.

Everything they'd been saying was true, the planet, Atlantis—everything. Jac tried to smile, but the thought of anyone messing with her head without asking, really pissed her off. She felt heat surging in her face, as confusion vied with anger. Ares must have sensed her turbulent emotions, for he gave Jac a quick brush of his thumb along the back of her hand, as if to remind her of what was important here. The innocent move created a fire all its own within Jac.

She turned back to Ariel, her jaw set with impatience. "Aren't you going to say, kiss the bride or anything?"

Ariel's lips curled up in a smile. *If you wish…*

"I do."

You may now kiss the bride.

It's about time. Jac heard Ariel laughing in her head. She frowned. *Can you hear my thoughts?*

The laugh came again. *Of course I can hear you thoughts, we all can.*

Jac glared at Ares. *You've known what I've been thinking the whole time.* It wasn't a question.

My fierceness, 'twas for your own good, I meant no harm. I only sought your happiness.

She took a step forward. *It's a damn good thing I love you. But just so you know, this conversation isn't over by a long shot.* Jac opened her mouth to reiterate her stance.

We can fight about it later, my fierceness. Ares held his hands up in surrender. *I believe the seer said I may now kiss the bride.*

Without preamble, Ares pulled Jac into his arms, sliding one hand low on her waist and the other to the back of her neck. He felt the crush of Jac's breasts, the erotic scrape of her nipples, as she melded against his muscled chest. His lips were firm and insistent as they pressed against hers, coaxing her into opening for him. She did and he slipped inside, tasting, tempting, and luxuriating in the fact she was now his mate. He would not lose her to another. And best of all, his family name would live on. Ares pulled back and smiled. Jac's face held a soft glow to it, while her blue eyes shone bright in the afternoon sun.

He searched her face, taking in her expression, looking for any sign of regret. There were exactly two dark spots on her flawless skin and absolutely no second thoughts. Her ears were small and delicately curved, in contrast to her above average height. The clear hair on her arms was soft as silk against his rough hands. Ares glanced down at her perfect body, admiring her pert breasts. Long and lithe, muscled and fierce, smart and strong, she was the perfect mate for a warrior such as him. His chest swelled with pride.

Ares' smile grew impossibly wider as he imagined her flat belly expanding with their child. He had the overwhelming urge to drag her back to the hut, so they could start right away on a family. But he tamped down his enthusiasm when he considered the looks he'd receive from Ariel and King Eros. He'd have to wait a respectable amount of time, perhaps right after the healing feast, then slip away.

Jac's lips were still swollen from the kiss. His eyes fixed on her sensual mouth. *All right maybe not so respectable.*

"Your fate is sealed. Now go forth with your new mate," Ariel announced to the crowd, but her eyes were on Ares.

The crowd erupted into cheers and well wishes. Ares and Jac turned to face the onslaught. Rachel raced forward and gave Jac a bear hug, tears of happiness streaming down her face.

"I'm so glad you changed your mind," Rachel hiccupped out.

Jac felt her eyes growing misty. *Probably allergies,* she thought, because there was absolutely no way she was crying. She never cried — yesterday had been an exception to a very long standing rule in her life.

And, well, today was like any other, except she'd gotten married to a warrior from another planet. *The man she loved.* No reason to cry about that. Jac swiped at her eyes with the back of her hand, before pulling out of Rachel's firm grip.

"Stop that right now," Jac pointed to Rachel's watery eyes, attempting to scold.

Rachel laughed and hugged her again. Jac felt her own grip tightening on her friend's shoulders.

"Boy, wouldn't Brigit freak if she could see us now," Jac whispered against Rachel's hair, then she pulled back.

The women stared at each other, sudden sadness coming upon them.

Rachel sighed. "It's your wedding day. We shouldn't be thinking about sad things today."

Jac nodded, but her mind continued to wander over the miles, to Brigit. She'd be waiting for news of Jac's progress in finding Rachel. How could Jac leave her without explanation, head off to another planet and not let her know that she and Rachel were fine? Jac's heart squeezed, fresh tears filled Rachel's brown eyes. Jac didn't have to be telepathic to know they were thinking the same thing.

"What are we going to do?" Rachel asked.

Jac let out a worried breath. "I'm not sure, but we can't leave without a word. That wouldn't be right."

Rachel frowned. "I know, but we can't go back to New York. It would draw too much attention to this place. It's bad enough Rumsinger's slinking around down here, like the weasel he is."

Jac's expression hardened. "I should have shot that bastard when I had a chance."

Rachel nodded. "He'll get what's coming to him. I have no doubt in my mind, even if we have to come back to Earth to do it." She smiled, confidence radiating from her.

"Tomorrow I'm going to try to open the portal." Rachel's hands went to her mostly flat belly. "Well the baby and I are going to."

Excited whispers raced through the crowd.

Jac squeezed her friend's hand, and then glanced around at the Atlanteans' smiling faces. In the back of her mind, Jac still had doubts that the transport would work, but for now she'd at least show her support for Rachel. "I never thought I'd be going into space, always figured it was Brigit's job."

They both cracked up again, thinking about their friend's love of science fiction and her desire to experience space travel firsthand.

Rachel led Jac to where Ares stood chatting with Eros. She handed Jac into Ares' waiting arms and then snuggled against Eros's side.

"'Tis time to feast," Eros announced and led the procession over to the great table, which had already been laid out with fresh fruits, breads, and exotic orchids.

Ares and Jac sat side by side to Eros's right, while Rachel took a seat on the left. They were at the head of the table with

Ariel positioned at the opposite end. The Atlanteans' passed food to the newly mated couple first, then on to the rest of the guests at the table. Conversations varied from excitement over leaving, to what they were going to miss the most. Some even discussed the prospects of finding their true mates.

Jac still didn't quite understand the whole true mate business, but she recognized true love. In the end the decision had been simple, there was only one man for her—Ares. She continued to listen to the conversations with one ear, enjoying the fresh slices of mango on her plate. It seemed like no matter where you were from, problems in life were all the same. At some point or another, all people had to contend with moving, loss, and love. She smiled, reassured by the normalcy thrown into an otherwise abnormal situation.

Ares' hand rested protectively on her knee, as if he were trying to reassure himself that she was really there and not going anywhere. The air surrounding the table seemed to spark with a life of its own. It felt as if the temperature had risen by ten degrees within the last few minutes. Jac would have attributed the warmth to body heat, but they were outdoors, so it couldn't have made that much of a difference. If she'd had a shirt on, Jac would have tugged at the collar. She ran her hand over her neck in an attempt to soothe her prickling skin.

Jac's gaze darted along the table, searching to see if anyone else noted the change, but no one seemed to be paying attention. Rachel continued to pick at the bread and fruit on her plate. Every time she looked at Eros, a goofy expression crossed her face. Jac hoped she didn't look like that when she looked at Ares. If so, someone needed to shoot her now and put her out of her misery.

Ares laughed, sending her a sideways glance. "There will be no shooting today."

"Keep out of my mind. It's not a seven-eleven." Jac glared, but knew her bark sounded much worse than her bite right now.

He grinned at her, his jade eyes sparking. "I know not what you speak of, but I understand the meaning nonetheless." Ares gave her knee a squeeze under the table.

Jac stared at him and couldn't help but smile. He was so handsome. And right now the light in his eyes made him look like a mischievous little boy up to no good. She snorted and turned back to her food, amazed by the circumstance that brought her here and how strange a curve life had thrown at her.

The sun set a few hours later and everyone moved away from the table, gathering around a fire that had been built earlier in the center of the compound. The mood was buoyant as plans were made for tomorrow's journey. Ares stood behind Jac, cradling her against his chest, his arms about her waist. His chin rested atop her head, as if they'd been made for each other.

The bruises that had marred his body yesterday were all but faded. His peoples' ability to heal was impressive. Jac sank back into his warmth, relishing his returning strength. The river had been a close call, too close for Jac. She didn't want him putting himself in anywhere near that kind of danger again. Even though logically she knew it had been out of his control.

Are you happy? he whispered in her mind.

Jac thought for a moment and realized she actually was surprisingly ecstatic. *Very...and you?*

More than I thought possible, now that I have you in my life to stay.

Are you trying to sweet talk me?

He purred. *Maybe...*

Jac playfully jabbed him in the ribs with her elbow and laughed. *Well it's working.*

The dancing is about to start. Do you want to join in?

Jac smiled. She had other things on her mind and it didn't have anything to do with dancing. Ares rubbed his hardening cock against her backside.

If you're not careful…I may take you back to the hut right now.

Jac swayed her hips, suggestively. *Who's stopping you?*

Ares let out a growl and picked Jac up, tossing her over his shoulder, caveman style. Jac squealed, her hands coming down to pretend to beat on his back. With one arm, he clasped her, holding her in place, while the other playfully slapped her on the bottom. Jac choked with laughter, only Ares heard the moan she tried to conceal. His smile widened as he strode off into the jungle, leaving the others to pair up for the night. He had plans for his mate and they didn't include watching an orgy.

Ares strode down the trail toward his hut, his hands resting on Jac's long legs. He imagined the myriad of ways in which he would give her pleasure tonight. He'd take her slow and easy, hard and fast, and every way in between. His cock hardened to the point of pain as he thought about her long legs draped over his shoulders as he lapped her folds. He would hear her scream of release at least seven times before he'd let her seek rest. There would be nothing he would not give her, nothing he would not do. Tonight was for fantasies, his, hers, and theirs. And they'd start the second the flap covering the door dropped.

He picked up the pace, the sudden urgency too intense to ignore. Ares slid his fingers under the jade skirt covering Jac's sex. His hand found her bottom and he began to massage. He traced her crack, trailing one finger down its length. Ares felt Jac tense as she recalled exactly what he'd done to her earlier today. He followed the line all the way around until he encountered her already moist sex. Jac shuddered as he circled her entrance a couple of times then continued down her thighs.

Ares grinned. He liked teasing Jac. She would willingly play any game he put forth, adventurous enough to take said game and turn it into her own. Tonight they'd test each other's limits, discover boundaries to pass. His blood heated at the thought of her resting upon his face as he drove his tongue inside her awaiting channel, spearing her.

They reached the hut and Ares released Jac, setting her upon her feet. He stepped through the door holding up the hides so that she could enter. He turned a palm to the fire pot on the table and sent an energy burst out, the flames leapt to life. A soft glow illuminated the hut. Ares moved to the hidden compartment in the side wall, opened it and began removing the items he planned on using tonight. There were oils, similar to the ones Eros had prepared Jac with, brushes of various sizes, and a couple of scarves.

"What are you doing?" Her eyes narrowed, but her voice held a playful lilt.

Ares waggled his eyebrows at her. "Preparing..."

He juggled the items in his hands, careful not to drop any of them as he made his way to the table. He placed the items out, then began to examine the fruit. He picked out bananas and several camu camu, since they were similar in size to a plum and set them aside. Ares opened up a container of oil, poured some in his palm, and then began to rub his hands together. He didn't want to think about the fact that Eros had done the same thing when he'd come to prepare Jac for the mating ceremony.

Anger rose in Ares, at the thought of any man, including his friend, laying their hands upon his mate. The seer had come close to restraining him, to keep Ares from returning to his hut to stop the preparation. He'd gone mad as jealousy ate at his insides.

Ares took a deep breath, exhaling slowly. It was over and done. The ceremony had been completed, the healing performed. His eyes sought Jac. She stood near the door where he'd left her, watching him with hunger burning in her blue depths. The thought of stoking that fire had Ares hurrying with his task.

Ares approached Jac, his hands dripping with oil. Her eyes widened and her breathing hitched. He reached out and gently took her palm in his, twining his fingers through hers, locking her to him. Ares gave her a slight tug and she stepped forward.

I wish I could say that I promise not to bite, but it would be a lie, I'm afraid.

Nervous laughter bubbled from Jac. *You don't have to make that promise on my account. I love a good nip or two.* Jac licked her lips suggestively.

Instead of leading her to the bed, Ares walked Jac to one of the chairs situated around the table. The air was warmer there, near the fire pot, and he could easily reach the items he needed. Before allowing her to sit down, he slid the skirt over her hips, letting it drop to the floor. It made a slight rustle before settling on the ground. He held up her hand to help her step from the material, then guided her to the seat. Jac's breathing had deepened, causing her nipples to quiver. Ares focused on her face, trying to ignore the tempting morsels so near his heated mouth.

Once she'd sat down, he dropped to his knees. His hands came to rest on her thighs. Ares' eyes locked with Jac a second before he spread her wide, opening her for his perusal. When he had her positioned like he wanted, Ares sat back on his heels and stared. Jac's pussy was total perfection, pink and puffy, lightly furred, and held an odor of spicy musk that was enough to drive him insane. He licked his lips in anticipation. Mirroring him, Jac did the same.

Have I told you how beautiful I find you?

No, she whispered in his mind.

Ares stroked her a couple times, teasing the flesh with his callused fingers.

So soft…so sweet…so wet. And it's all for me.

"For you," she groaned. Jac closed her eyes and bit her lip. Before she opened them again, Ares picked up the camu camu fruit. The plum-like fruit although sweet to the taste, came loaded enough stimulants to keep a bull elephant awake for a month. Not that the fruit affected Ares that way. His people were immune to the plants indigenous to this planet.

Ares glided the fruit along Jac's nether lips, encouraging her to open further. Jac's eyes flew open and locked on his hand. Her gaze widened, as she realized what Ares used to tease her with. Two more passes and the camu camu lay covered in Jac's own juices. Ares circled her clit, then pressed down enough to send a jolt through her system. He slid the fruit down, until it rested at her entrance, then eyes locked on her face, he slipped half inside.

Jac's breathing grew ragged. She couldn't believe what Ares had done to her. It was like torture as he caressed her with the camu camu...delicious, erotic, sensuous, and oh so carnal torture. The fruit filled her entrance, stretching her wide, exposing her to Ares' seeking eyes. He pulled his fingers back, releasing the fruit. Jac went to remove it, but he stopped her with his gaze. His eyes flamed, as he leaned forward, drawing nearer and nearer to her fiery heat.

I want you, Jac. I dream of taking you, a thousand different ways.

Shivers of delight, shot through Jac as she waited for that first touch, taste. She didn't have to wait long. Ares tongue snaked out, circling the camu camu. Jac would have come straight off the chair had he not been there to stop her. He lapped at her folds, never touching the food, up one side and down the other, always bypassing her clit.

Your taste inflames me, tugs at my heart, shackles my soul.

Jac grabbed his hair, twining her fingers through the silky strands, trying to pull him closer, but he wouldn't budge. His words branded her, searing a permanent mark upon her core. He continued his slow assault, adding a nibble here and there. Jac thought she'd go out of her mind, when his tongue trailed along her thigh.

Ares please.

He lifted his head from her sex, arched a brow and smiled. His face dropped into her lap once again, except this time he bit into the fruit. Jac screamed with her first orgasm, even though he hadn't really touched her. The tension building within her had been too much.

Oh, god.

Ares dove in, frenzied. He ate the fruit like a man starved. When the camu camu was all gone, he continued to feast, as if the fruit had only been an appetizer and she was the main course. His lips and tongue fed upon her clit, drawing it out, stroking it, sucking it, and nibbling until Jac's body teetered on the verge of convulsing.

He plunged his tongue inside her core, lapping at the remnants of her first release. The muscle undulated, like waves on an ocean. He massaged her G-spot over and over, eventually drowning Jac in another release. His large palms covered her breasts. His fingers sought out her aching nipples, twisting and turning them, kneading and pulling. Jac felt as if she were on a sensual roller coaster ride, where each crest and dip blended with the last so quickly that her sated mind refused to keep count.

Your taste, your scent, you're driving me insane. I cannot get enough.

Ares plundered like a pirate of old. His mastery over her body frightened and excited Jac at the same time. He released one nipple, replacing his hand with a brush. The bristle stroked over Jac's sensitive skin, sending gooseflesh rising on her body. Jac shifted in the chair, trying to press closer. Ares tossed the brush down and sat back on his heels once again.

I could feast upon you forever.

His chin dripped with her juices and he had a smile planted firmly on his handsome face. He stood in one swift motion, pulling Jac up at the same time.

He swung her up into his arms, skin slapping skin. Jac hands flew to his neck reflexively. Ares strode to the furs and placed her upon them. He walked back to the table and picked up one of the scarves, leaving her sitting on the edge of the bed. He returned to Jac's side, his eyes flaring with desire. His cock pressed so hard against his loincloth that she could make out every ridge. Jac's eyes stayed locked on his impressive tool, imagining the moment when he'd slip inside her.

She licked her lips in anticipation. Ares placed the scarf over Jac's eyes.

Can you see?

Jac shook her head no.

Good. He secured the material at the back of her head.

Jac's hearing seemed to sharpen. She could hear the deep cadence of Ares' breathing, the rustle of the scarf as he tied it around her, and the gentle popping of the fire as each piece of wood caught and began to burn. Her other senses seemed to come alive as well. She could smell the citrusy odor of the oil he'd applied to her skin, the gentle brush of the furs beneath her bottom, and the scalding heat from Ares' nearness. The bed depressed beside her and she knew Ares had joined her. Jac tensed, listening.

The furs shifted a couple more times, then seemed to settle. Jac's body trembled, waiting to see what would come next. She felt Ares' hands as they slid around her narrow waist, then lifted her again. She fought the urge to tear at her blindfold. He lowered her onto his face, spearing her deep with his tongue. Jac groaned and threw her head back. Ares lifted her up and down until Jac caught the rhythm, then she pushed his hands away. Jac bounced gently upon Ares face, feeling the slide of his six and a half inch tongue inside her channel.

You drive me insane. I never thought I'd love a man like I love you.

Soft and slick, moist and firm, he continued probing her. Jac ground her hips, as she raced toward release. Her movements grew frantic and erratic. Ares thoughts plunged into her mind.

You taste of the most exquisite wine.

Your sex was made to be fucked by my tongue and cock alone.

I wish you could feel what I feel when I slip within your fiery depths.

Jac moaned, her fingers sinking into his thick black hair.

I want to feel you come in my mouth. Feel your inner walls grip my tongue as your orgasm slams into you, sending you over the edge, until there is no you, no me, only us.

Jac screamed as his words incited her. She fell to the side in the grips of an orgasm to end all orgasms. Her body quivered and quaked. One leg lay stretched across Ares' chest and the other drawn up near her spasming womb. With trembling fingers, she removed the blindfold and glanced at Ares. He lay on his back, sweat beading his brow. His lungs labored for breath. She shifted until she faced him, her eyes level with his straining cock. As soon as she could move, Jac sat up and began untying the bindings holding his loincloth in place.

Ares felt the first tentative brush of Jac's fingers as his loincloth fell open. His cock surged forth, free of its confines, the head had turned almost purple from the strain. He gritted his teeth as Jac trailed her hands along his thick length. He felt as if he'd split asunder if he couldn't enter her now.

I need you, Jac.

Ares closed his eyes and attempted to calm his breath. It seemed to be working, until Jac slipped his staff into her mouth.

Like this?

He released his breath with a hiss. His eyes flew open and bulleted to her. She had an utterly female, almost feline look of satisfaction pasted on her face. Ares glared at her, fighting the desire to thrust in her mouth.

Jac smiled around his cock, then flicked her tongue over his crown. *Do you like it when I suck you?*

The muscles in his abdomen tensed and he groaned. *You know I do.*

Her lips closed over him forming a firm seal and she began to suck. He thought his head would explode.

You taste so salty and delicious. I could swallow you up.

She watched him, her eyes locked on his face as she began to work her way up and down his staff. Jac's cheeks indented as she increased the pressure, then she wrapped her hands around his base. She had done the same to him earlier. This time Ares didn't think he'd be able to deter her. Not that he wanted to.

Closing her eyes, Jac's head bobbed as she sped up her movements. Ares felt his balls draw up. He could no longer stop his body's natural reaction, so he thrust, meeting Jac's downward swing. Her eyes opened in surprise for a moment, then closed again.

Ares' hips bucked against her mouth. Those luscious lips of her suctioned firmly around his throbbing cock. Jac's blonde bob fell forward brushing against his overly sensitive skin—that was all it took to send him over the edge. Ares gently gripped Jac's head, holding her in place as he thrust over and over, emptying his seed down her waiting throat. Jac swallowed every drop, never letting up, until the last drop had been drained from his eager body.

He released her and she sat up. A smile played at the corner of her mouth as she deliberately licked her lips. Ares groaned and dropped his head back.

I take it you liked that.

You know I did. Laughter filled his voice. *I believe you have drained my life force.*

Her eyes sparkled and she gave him a wry grin. *Does that mean you're not going to be able to fuck me?* she asked innocently, as if talking in the Atlantean manner was nothing new.

Ares' nostrils flared and his eyes narrowed. *For the record, there is nothing on this tiny planet that could keep me from sticking my cock inside your pussy right now.*

Jac glanced down, under her gaze she saw Ares' cock begin to rise from the dead. She looked back at his face, surprise clearly written on her expression. *You are a machine.*

He smiled. *Sheer determination. I have waited a lifetime for this moment.*

Jac laughed, then squealed when Ares reached out with lightning speed and pulled her up and under him. She could feel his hard staff dig into her belly. She got all hot and wet, thinking about what would come next. Ares inserted a knee between her thighs and nudged them apart. He kept most of his weight resting on his elbows, but allowed his lower body to pin her to the bed. Jac knew it was a sign of dominance. It was in the tension cording his muscles, the flash of challenge in his jade eyes, and in the spicy scent of his skin as it brushed across her body.

She started to protest and he growled in warning. This was one battle she would not win. He settled himself deeper, her hips cradling his massive cock and heavy balls. Ares slipped down, until the head of his cock lay positioned at her entrance.

You have no idea what this moment means to me, to claim you for all time. His breath shuddered in his chest.

Jac held his gaze. The intensity burning in Ares' eyes was like being swallowed by an inferno. She felt the tip of his head press into her opening, stretching, pushing, and filling her as no other could. He didn't hurry, but took his time, inch by exquisite inch, until he seated himself deep within her. Then he began to move, a slow rocking motion as he rotated his hips for deeper penetration. Jac's walls gripped him, as if never wanting to let him go. His thrusts deepened and angled down, catching her clit.

Jac's thighs began to tremble at the erotic torture he put her through. He drove into her channel over and over, his hips thrusting and bucking, stabbing and spearing, until Jac writhed beneath him, begging for release. He drove into her then, pistoning. His fingers sunk into the soft flesh at her hips, holding her into place as he plunged again and again into her wet heat.

Please Ares.

Strain marred Ares' handsome face as he continued to ride. Her velvet walls gripped him tight, pulling him deeper and deeper inside. *I'll never get enough of you.* His lips sought out the rosy buds that had been tormenting his chest. He latched onto her nipple and increased his speed. *You make me insatiable.* Laving and licking, sucking and kissing, he pulled again and again at her marbled peaks. Jac screamed and he covered her cry with his mouth, plunging his tongue inside her dark recesses, tasting her passion.

And then she came. Her pussy clenched around his shaft, pulsating like a thousand tiny mouths. Ares thrust once more following her over the precipice into the abyss below, his seed flowing freely. They lay locked together, stroking each other's arms, Ares secure in the knowledge that they'd just produced a life.

Do you sense the life beginning inside you?

Jac smiled and shook her head. She hadn't, but now that Ares told her, Jac was okay with it. More than that, she was thrilled. Never in a million years did she think she'd ever be happily married with children. Yet here, in Ares' arms, she found a peace that had eluded her all those years in New York. Jac was home. Are' fingers drifted lower, sliding over her flat belly protectively.

I love you.

I love you, too…my fierceness.

Jac knew that any child who came from their mating would be a force to reckon with on this planet or the next.

Epilogue

The day after Ares' and Jac's mating ceremony, the Atlanteans had gathered in a semi-circle around the now erect transport. Queen Rachel had arranged the last of the pieces, activating the system. All remained silent, as everyone concentrated on the unborn child Rachel carried in her womb. She stood with her bare belly facing the opening. Excitement thrummed in the air, as the crowd pressed closer to watch.

Jac stared half in awe and half in terror as Rachel's skin began to glow from the inside out. Beads of sweat dotted her friend's brow. Jac squeezed Ares' hand, the pressure increasing in small increments as her concern grew. A hush fell over the crowd, as the Atlanteans' held a collective breath, all hope riding on her friend's small shoulders.

Suddenly there was a loud crack and light shot out from Rachel's abdomen onto a spot on the transport. The crowd let out a collective gasp and stepped back, moving like a school of fish in the same direction. The stone symbols making up the transport began to rotate counterclockwise and rumble. The sound rose to deafening levels, scaring away all living creatures that could flee. Jac wondered if the animals were the smart ones, as everyone continued to hold their ground.

Rachel's hands flew protectively to her belly. The speed of the turning stones increased until the noise shifted into a steady drone. Faster and faster it whirled like an out of control top, turned sideways. The air in the center area of the transport began to shift, growing smoky, almost black in the bright sunlight, as if thickening into a solid.

All eyes remained glued on the twisting contraption. A bright light flashed from the transport. A cry of alarm rang out in the group, but everyone stayed, frozen in place, attempting to shield their eyes with their hands. Rachel's abdomen stopped glowing, but the transport continued whirling. Jac looked to Ares.

"'Tis time to go." He squeezed her hand in reassurance.

Jac's gut clenched.

Eros and Rachel stepped forward to the edge of the black void. Jac pulled free of Ares and rushed forward. She grabbed Rachel in a bear hug, tears stinging the back of her eyes.

"I don't want you to go."

"I know." Her eyes glistened with what could only be described as hope.

"Be careful, you hear?"

Rachel hugged her back, then pulled away. "Everything's going to be all right, Jac." She smiled. "I'll see you on the other side."

Jac nodded, glancing into the unknown before stepping back, fear beating at her chest like a drum. She watched as Eros and Rachel exchanged a loving look and then stepped through, disappearing instantly into the void. Two by two the others followed.

Ares had sent out a few scouts in search of Coridan, but they'd come back unsuccessful in their hunt. No matter the young warrior's past deeds, no one of Atlantean blood would be left behind, especially with the red-devil closing in. And Ares knew he drew nearer. He'd sensed him, along with at least a dozen others making their way toward the village. By the time the bastard got here, with any luck, the Atlanteans would be gone.

* * * * *

Professor Donald Rumsinger tramped through the brush, anticipation fueling his drive. He knew they were within a half click of the famous lost tribe. His pudgy hand moved to the holster at his side, rechecking the pistol secured there. He wasn't taking any chances after what he'd seen over the past few weeks. The men of this tribe were unusually large, virile looking subjects. He looked forward to studying and probing them thoroughly before reporting his findings to the world.

If he happened to encounter Dr. Rachel Evans again, he'd take care of her for good. Anger rolled through him as he thought about her and her friend Jaclyn Ward. The two women had made a fool of him more times than he'd care to remember and he wasn't one to take that lightly. They would pay. He'd make sure of it.

The professor called out to his lead guide, Manuel, "How much further?"

The brown skinned man squinted across the clearing they'd entered. "Twenty minutes at the most," he called back.

The knee-high grass was unusual in the jungle, but then again so were clearings. Donald Rumsinger stamped his feet to scare off any sleeping reptiles. Poisonous snakes loved to bake in the sun. The professor glanced at the sky and then down at his watch. It was almost two o'clock. They'd lose the light within three hours, as the sun sank below the tree line, leaving the jungle in deep shadow.

"Pick up the pace," Donald shouted to the small caravan of men. He didn't want there to be any chance for the tribe to slip away or hide before their arrival. The jog was hard on the professor. His body wasn't used to these kinds of physical activities. Donald gritted his teeth and wheezed out a breath, propelling his rotund body forward by the sheer excitement pouring through him. He was on the brink of becoming the most famous explorer of the century, perhaps of all time.

* * * * *

Ariel, Jac, and Ares stood in the empty clearing beside the transport, frowning. They'd been unable to locate Coridan and had run out of places to search. If the young warrior had left the jungle there was no telling where he'd gone. He had been shamed, outcast by his own people, for his foolishness. Ares looked to the two women standing beside him.

"We must go, the enemy is drawing nearer."

Ariel's eyes widened, in what looked to be fear. "We cannot leave Coridan behind for the red-devil to find."

Ares blew out a heavy breath, his heart troubled over the loss of a fellow Atlantean, no matter how misguided he'd been. His gaze sought out Jac's, her face instantly softening under his perusal. Ares tucked a strand of hair around her sensitive ear. She shivered.

"I shall stay here until I find him," Ares offered.

Jac's eyes widened to the size of saucers. "You're not staying here without me." "You must go. Danger draws near."

"What about you? That asshole Rumsinger could hurt you. Or worse. I'm not heading off to another planet without you." She shook her head and crossed her arms over her chest. Her jaw set firmly, leaving no room for argument.

Ares took a step forward, trying to appear threatening. "I will not have my mate putting herself in danger needlessly."

Jac tilted her head and glared at him. "I said I'm staying." Her hands moved to her hips.

"Do not make me pick you up and toss you to Zaron," he growled. "I do not think the first impression you make on the people should be on your bottom."

Jac's face flushed red. "You wouldn't dare," she hissed out.

"Try me."

"Enough!" The force of Ariel's one uttered word stopped their squabbling immediately.

They both turned in unison to look at her. Ariel's face held a calm façade that she probably didn't feel, but the bickering was getting them nowhere.

"I shall stay here and search for Coridan." She gazed at the trees, concern coloring her features, before glancing back.

Ares opened his mouth to protest, but Ariel held up a hand, stopping him before he could utter a syllable. "I realize I am not a warrior, but 'tis not as if I'm without means."

"I cannot allow you to make this sacrifice. You've guided our people for thousands of years. 'Tis your right to see our home planet, more so than any other." Ares spoke softly.

"I will see our Zaron…soon. But for now, you must leave this place. Make sure your mate is safe." She smiled at Jac, her eyes pleading. "Do this for me, Ares."

Ares sensed there was something the seer was not telling them. He once again went to speak, this time Jac laid her hand upon his arm, stopping him. "It's time to go. Ariel knows what she's doing." Jac smiled back at the seer.

Good luck, Ariel. I hope you find whatever it is you seek.

The seer grinned wider, an unspoken understanding passing between the two women, then Ariel bid them on their way.

Jac and Ares stepped toward the transport, their muscles trembling in anticipation. They looked over their shoulders once more at Ariel.

I'll be right behind you, after I have one more quick look around. Now go. The seer waved, then shoo'd them on.

Ares glanced down at Jac's face, her eyes met his, and he nodded, with that they stepped forward into their new life together.

Enjoy this excerpt from
Redemption
Atlantean's Quest
© *Copyright Jordan Summers 2003*

Ariel blew out a ragged breath. Relief curled in her belly like a satisfied cat wraps around your legs. Her people were now safely on Zaron—well almost all of her people. She'd find Coridan and get back here as soon as possible, then her duties to her people would be complete. Ariel paused, imagining what her new life would be like on the planet she'd never seen. Would Zaron be as beautiful as Earth? Would it possess the wonder this lush blue planet held for her? There was only one way to find out.

She closed her eyes for a moment as emotion overwhelmed her. The vision she'd had the night before of a warrior streamed through her consciousness like the currents of the wind, rustling the branches of a tree. Her stomach clenched. Surely, she had been mistaken. Her fate lay with her people, didn't it?

Yet she knew better than most, her visions could not be ignored. Psychic from birth, she trusted them with her life.

A white-throated toucan squawked with distress nearby, as if something approached its nest. Ariel looked in the direction of the cry, but saw nothing out of the norm. She brushed away the feeling of uneasiness that accompanied the loud caterwauling.

Ariel shifted one of the marked stones, effectively shutting down the device. She stared at the transport longingly for a few more moments, before reluctantly turning back to the village. She picked her way down the narrow trail, brushing past aromatic ginger flowers and purple orchids, soaking in their comforting fragrance, all the while cataloging the odor in her memory as things she would miss about this planet.

After a few moments, she reached the abandoned clearing. A light breeze caught at her blonde tresses, brushing the locks gently from her face and across her bare breasts.

It was quiet—too quiet.

The birds' songs no longer filled her ears with music and not being able to hear the chatter of her people caused excruciating mental pain. In that moment she realized that being left alone on this planet, no longer able to use her telepathic abilities to communicate, would drive her and any other Atlantean insane. Abandonment was tantamount to death.

She and her people had unknowingly sentenced Coridan to death. The thought had Ariel's lungs seizing, crushing inward with a pain rivaling the icy fear she felt, but refused to examine too closely.

Her skin prickled as a rustling noise came from inside her dwelling, drawing her thoughts back to present. At first it had sounded like a breeze, moving the flap, yet the air was not powerful enough to move the heavy hide. Tension filled her lungs, making it difficult to breathe. A cry from a primate shattered the silence. Ariel relaxed.

Monkeys may have already taken up residence in her hut, goodness knows she'd had a difficult time keeping the curious creatures out when she had lived there. The noise grew louder and something crashed to the ground in her hut. Ariel inched nearer. Perhaps Coridan had sensed the shift in energy that had taken place with the Atlantean exodus, and had returned.

She decided not to call out to him, some things were best done in person. Her heart swelled with anticipation—and fear. It was time to meet her destiny. She stepped forward and threw back the hide flap, a tentative smile painted on her face.

"How nice of you to join us, my dear," the red-haired man's voice purred menacingly.

Ariel felt the blood drain from her face, the normal warmth replaced with cold. She raised her hands to defend herself, but before she could fire off a single energy burst, two men stepped from the shadows, shackling her with their hands. Ariel struggled to no avail, the men easily keeping her subdued.

Her full breasts bobbed as she put all her strength into escape. The brown hands holding her arms tightened, threatening without words to snap bones if necessary. Sweat beaded her brow, and dripped lazily down her chest. Her gaze narrowed on the devil sitting behind her small table.

As if in a trance, his gaze followed the movement of the perspiration droplets as they caressed her pink nipples and rolled down her abdomen. Ariel ceased her struggles. She didn't want his eyes roaming any lower.

The professor's ruddy face split into a cold snake-like smile. She could see no teeth, but knew without a doubt he could and would bite if provoked. "You're not exactly who I was hoping for, but you'll do." His voice coiled around her.

"You must be Professor Donald Rumsinger." It wasn't a question.

About the author:

I'd like to say I'm the life of the party, a laugh-a-minute kind of gal, and outrageously cool, BUT that would be a slight fabrication.

I'm actually a thirty-something, ex-flight attendant with a penchant for huge bookstores and big dumb action movies. I prefer quiet dinners with friends over maddening crowds. Happily married to my very own Highlander, we split our time between two continents.

In my spare time...LOL...I'm kidding, I don't have any spare time. The hours of my day are spent writing, and when I'm not doing that I'm thinking about writing. I guess you could say I have a one track mind.

Jordan welcomes mail from readers. You can write to her c/o Ellora's Cave Publishing at 1056 Home Avenue, Akron OH 44310-3502.

Why an electronic book?

We live in the Information Age—an exciting time in the history of human civilization in which technology rules supreme and continues to progress in leaps and bounds every minute of every hour of every day. For a multitude of reasons, more and more avid literary fans are opting to purchase e-books instead of paperbacks. The question to those not yet initiated to the world of electronic reading is simply: *why?*

1. *Price.* An electronic title at Ellora's Cave Publishing and Cerridwen Press runs anywhere from 40-75% less than the cover price of the <u>exact same title</u> in paperback format. Why? Cold mathematics. It is less expensive to publish an e-book than it is to publish a paperback, so the savings are passed along to the consumer.

2. *Space.* Running out of room to house your paperback books? That is one worry you will never have with electronic novels. For a low one-time cost, you can purchase a handheld computer designed specifically for e-reading purposes. Many e-readers are larger than the average handheld, giving you plenty of screen room. Better yet, hundreds of titles can be stored within your new library—a single microchip. (Please note that Ellora's Cave and Cerridwen Press does not endorse any specific brands. You can check our website at www.ellorascave.com or

www.cerridwenpress.com   for   customer recommendations we make available to new consumers.)

3. *Mobility.* Because your new library now consists of only a microchip, your entire cache of books can be taken with you wherever you go.

4. *Personal preferences are accounted for.* Are the words you are currently reading too small? Too large? Too...**ANNOYING**? Paperback books cannot be modified according to personal preferences, but e-books can.

5. *Instant gratification.* Is it the middle of the night and all the bookstores are closed? Are you tired of waiting days—sometimes weeks—for online and offline bookstores to ship the novels you bought? Ellora's Cave Publishing sells instantaneous downloads 24 hours a day, 7 days a week, 365 days a year. Our e-book delivery system is 100% automated, meaning your order is filled as soon as you pay for it.

Those are a few of the top reasons why electronic novels are displacing paperbacks for many an avid reader. As always, Ellora's Cave and Cerridwen Press welcomes your questions and comments. We invite you to email us at service@ellorascave.com, service@cerridwenpress.com or write to us directly at: 1056 Home Ave. Akron OH 44310-3502.

Make each day more *EXCITING* With our

Ellora's Cavemen

Calendar

www.EllorasCave.com

THE
☥ ELLORA'S CAVE ☥
LIBRARY

Stay up to date with Ellora's Cave Titles in
Print with our Quarterly Catalog.

TO RECIEVE A CATALOG,
SEND AN EMAIL WITH YOUR NAME
AND MAILING ADDRESS TO:

CATALOG@ELLORASCAVE.COM
OR SEND A LETTER OR POSTCARD
WITH YOUR MAILING ADDRESS TO:

CATALOG REQUEST
c/o ELLORA'S CAVE PUBLISHING, INC.
1056 HOME AVENUE
AKRON, OHIO 44310-3502

ELLORA'S CAVEMEN

TALES FROM THE TEMPLE

Try an e-book for your immediate
reading pleasure or order these titles in print from

WWW.ELLORASCAVE.COM

ELLORA'S CAVE
THE BEST IN TODAY'S ROMANTICA™

Discover for yourself why readers can't get enough of the multiple award-winning publisher Ellora's Cave. Whether you prefer e-books or paperbacks, be sure to visit EC on the web at www.ellorascave.com for an erotic reading experience that will leave you breathless.

www.ellorascave.com